THE NOT QUITE PERFECT MURDERER

Also by Margaret Duffy from Severn House

TAINTED GROUND
COBWEB
BLOOD SUBSTITUTE
SOUVENIRS OF MURDER
CORPSE IN WAITING
RAT POISON
STEALTH
DARK SIDE
ASHES TO ASHES
DUST TO DUST
MURDERS.COM
STONE COLD, STONE DEAD
GILLARD'S STING

THE NOT QUITE PERFECT MURDERER

Margaret Duffy

First world edition published in Great Britain and the USA in 2021
by Severn House, an imprint of Canongate Books Ltd,
14 High Street, Edinburgh EH1 1TE.

Trade paperback edition first published in Great Britain and the USA in 2022
by Severn House, an imprint of Canongate Books Ltd.

severnhouse.com

British Library Cataloguing-in-Publication Data
A CIP catalogue record for this title is available from the British Library.

ISBN-13: 978-0-7278-5061-4 (cased)
ISBN-13: 978-1-78029-814-6 (trade paper)
ISBN-13: 978-1-4483-0552-0 (e-book)

All Severn House titles are printed on acid-free paper.

Typeset by Palimpsest Book Production Ltd.,
Falkirk, Stirlingshire, Scotland.
Printed and bound in Great Britain by
TJ Books, Padstow, Cornwall.

He liked to be called Spike, but his contemporaries at school saw no reason to do so, and if they addressed him at all, which wasn't very often, it was as Goggle on account of his rather expressionless, staring, large blue eyes. His mother, Karley, called him by the name she had given him: Damien. He hated it and didn't like to ask what his father had thought about it as that subject was taboo. He'd once questioned her about him and the fact that he seemed to be missing, and she'd flown into a temper and hit him. This hadn't been too much of a shock as she'd always hit him a lot anyway.

Spike, then. He liked that as he spiked up his hair with some gel stuff he'd bought in a chemist's but only when Karley was out – which was most of the time – as she'd hit him after he'd done that, too. At school, he was bottom of just about every subject but excelled at PE – strange really considering how odd his body was. For Damien was slightly disabled with long arms and big strong hands, and no matter how much help he had had in the past from physiotherapists – when his mother bothered herself with the appointments the doctor had made for him, that is – he still had a unique way of walking, with his head thrust forward. Being thin, probably on account of malnourishment as Karley couldn't be bothered to feed him properly, meant he had pointy elbows and knees, which didn't help his image either. Some medic or other had said he was 'double-jointed' and that made him feel even more of a freak.

Whatever the truth, it didn't stop eleven-year-old Damien from going up a climbing wall in the school gym like a gecko. He loved climbing, and when it was dark and he was supposed to be in bed, he escaped from the house through his bedroom window, shinned down a drainpipe almost entirely covered with old ivy and went off exploring the city. Quite often walking for some distance, he climbed trees. There were hundreds of them in the Regency squares and lining the roads, but the plane trees were his favourite. Up there, he was king looking down on everyone else and people never noticed him. Bath had many old stone houses and he discovered that it was quite easy to climb the walls of those as well: they often had cast-iron drain-pipes, which were strong and sometimes had his friend, the ivy, growing up them as well. This meant that he could look in the windows. He really enjoyed looking in windows. You never knew what you were going to see, and he was amazed at what people got up to. He abandoned modern brick-built or reproduction stone homes as they were more of a problem and were usually furnished with plastic pipes and gutters which, from his point of view, were useless, if not dangerous. He had had one alarming fall due to those but had luckily landed in a bush so had escaped with a few cuts and bruises. Karley hadn't noticed.

ONE

Just over a year later

Detective Chief Inspector James Carrick of Bath CID was a happy man. His present sunny and smiling disposition – rare for him as Scots are not normally extravagant with open signs of emotion unless very, very angry – was due to the fact that he had finally caught up with the man who had tried to kill him. There was an underlying suspicion that this afterglow wouldn't last long, but while it did, he had every intention of enjoying it. Yes, he kept telling himself, ex-DCI Derek Rogers of Dalesland Police, at one time stationed at Wemdale in the north of England, was in custody, the man who a couple of years previously had banged him up in an old factory boiler on a derelict industrial estate and left him to die. Carrick sometimes still had nightmares about it: the hours of trying to kick at the rusting hinges until he had fainted from the pain in his legs, of almost getting jammed as he had tried to turn round inside it in order to tackle the ill-fitting door – daylight cruelly visible round the edges – with his hands. Nothing had worked.

Rogers, together with DS Alan Terrington, had been in association with a criminal by the name of Frank Norris, otherwise known as Smiler, and they had collaborated to their mutual benefit. Everything had then gone wrong when an investigative journalist-cum-film producer, Martin Gilcrist, had made a short series of TV documentaries about police corruption, and in one of them had exposed what was going on in Wemdale. Shortly afterwards, his body had been found on the weir in the River Avon in Bath, not far from where he had lived. He had been murdered – battered to death – and that was when Carrick had become involved.

The fact that he still existed on the planet was due to a friend, Patrick Gillard. Gillard had not only tracked down where he had been incarcerated but fought off sundry lowlife who had been thicker on the ground than the average man would have been able to deal with. But Gillard wasn't average: a retired army officer, late of MI5 and the National Crime Agency, he was also frighteningly efficient at what Carrick could only describe as filthy fighting, learned in the back streets of God knows where. He had bettered the yobs in the pay of Smiler in a fashion that still gave Carrick, who could take care of himself handsomely if the situation arose, goosebumps when he thought about it. And, just a week previously, in connection with another case entirely, they had caught up with Rogers, and Carrick had arrested him for the three murders he had committed since the Wemdale episode.

But that was in the past and Carrick had to attend to the present. Right now, that entailed finishing his breakfast, two slices of toast and marmalade, as he gathered together various possessions to toss into his document case. Then he downed a mug of black coffee, brushed his teeth, looked in on his little daughter, Iona Flora, who was still sound asleep, waved goodbye to their live-in nanny, Marion, who was in the kitchen making tea, and left the old farmhouse that he and his wife, Joanna, had made their home. Joanna, a constable in Frome, was on duty and he wouldn't see her until he got home that night. He was using every quiet and unobtrusive means at his disposal to get her transferred to Bath.

Bath Police Station, where, as far as he was concerned, most of the action happened, was now situated at Redbridge House in Midland Road. This was on account of the building housing the original nick having been deemed too large and outdated. It had been sold to the university. As far as the general public was concerned, contact with the police could be made at a One Stop Shop situated not far from its predecessor in Manvers Street, a stone's throw from the railway station. Carrick wasn't sure that he liked the new arrangement, and there was no custody suite on site – that was now in Keynsham. One didn't have to be very clever to realize that where at one time everything had been more or less happily under one roof, now it was three.

When Carrick got to his office, he quickly discovered that there had been a break-in at a jeweller's in an arcade off Milsom

Street overnight, a gang wielding sledgehammers and crowbars having literally smashed their way into the shop. Lynn Outhwaite, recently promoted to DI, was overseeing the investigation, having got to work early and gone off to the crime scene to see things for herself. Carrick, seating himself behind his desk, quite envied her. He had at least a morning's work in front of him, writing reports and reading through the stack of official papers that he never seemed to be able to get to the bottom of. But as he worked, just now and then, like a little beam of sunlight, came the memory of the clip to the jaw he had given Rogers, who had been calling himself Kevin Freeman, when the man had hurled himself at him when arrested.

There was a knock at the door and Sergeant Derek Woods, who knew he didn't have to wait for permission to enter, put his head round it. 'Got a minute, sir?'

'Of course. Have a seat,' Carrick answered. He always had time for Woods and had not been looking forward to the time when the custody officer, as one of his roles had been at Manvers Street, retired. Woods was a walking encyclopaedia on the ungodly, their families, friends, associates and enemies in the city and its environs. He had reached retirement age, but a rare and miraculous bout of thinking had been done by those in authority and he had been asked if he wanted to stay on to undertake general duties. Absolutely: Woods loved his job and had a misery of a wife.

'How are you now?' the DCI enquired. The man had had a mild heart attack some months previously.

'Not too bad at all now, sir, thank you.'

'So, what's the problem?'

'It's not actually a problem, but I might have some information about that break-in last night,' said Woods in his soft Somerset burr, having seated himself. 'I intended to speak to DI Outhwaite but she's not here.'

'Information from one of your sources?'

Woods nodded soberly. He had 'sources' in all kinds of places, mostly pubs.

'I'd be very interested to hear it.'

'Word has it that the Baker gang, who I should imagine are prime suspects for the raid last night as it's exactly how they operate, have a backer – some kind of rich character who was described to me as being a big cheese but having a screw loose.'

Carrick leaned back in his seat, unable to prevent a smile at the description. 'How accurate d'you reckon that news is, Derek?'

Wood's lined face creased even more as he also smiled. 'That bit of gossip isn't exactly gold-plated, but there's something else that is. I have a chum who's stationed at West End Central in London. We joined this force together here and a couple of years later he asked for a transfer as he married a London girl who had a much higher-paid job than he did. She still does. Lovely girl, too.'

'Wise man,' the DCI commented. Woods must never be hurried.

'Rob – that's my chum – phoned me this morning. He's been working on similar cases down there as the one last night – he keeps abreast with what's happening here – and a few weeks back they succeeded in arresting a gang member who had been knocked down by the getaway car on one of these raids. They'd left him for dead. He did die, unexpectedly, shortly afterwards but not before he'd been identified as Les Baker, wanted by this force for burglary and assault. As you must know, sir, the whole lot were from Shepton Mallet originally and old man Baker – Freddie, I think he was referred to – and several brothers were in the stolen car trade until the law caught up with some of them. He died in prison after being attacked by another inmate, but most of the others are now on the loose again. It's a big family – at least ten of them, and that includes numerous cousins and hangers-on who hire themselves out to what they regard as the big time as bruisers, yobs for hire – call it what you will. It's all very vague but the latest is that they're back – here.'

'They might have moved back into home territory because it got too hot for them in the capital, then,' Carrick said. He hadn't known anything about the ancient history of the Baker gang; what Woods had told him had occurred quite a while before he himself had come to the West Country.

'That's possible, but the main point of what I'm telling you, sir, is that Rob's heard their big sponsor, who's also originally from this neck of the woods but has a base in London, is now back here as well, either in Bath or the surrounding areas.'

Carrick was beginning to wish that, with so many ears to the ground, Woods worked for CID. 'OK, thank you. Leave it with me. I'll inform Lynn and get on to the Met. They might have some more info that'll help us to track them down.'

Woods got to his feet. 'Thank you, sir.' He added, 'I'm glad you caught up with that bastard who tried to kill you up north.'

'Does everything get trumpeted around in this place?' Carrick asked.

'Probably,' said Woods as he went out.

At one time, before they were married, Joanna had been Carrick's sergeant and they had made a good team. Carrick had been married to Katherine at the time and she had been dying, with agonizing slowness, from a rare form of bone cancer. Towards the end, carers had come in several times a day to look after her. Then, one night after a particularly difficult raid on a house where armed criminals were known to be hiding, when Carrick and several members of his team had been slightly hurt, he had driven Joanna home. Everything had got completely out of hand and they had made love right there on her hall carpet. Their affair had continued.

The superintendent of the day, now retired, had received a tip-off from a reporter on the local newspaper, a criminal on the quiet, who had been making it his business to spy on Carrick. The super had hated women in the job and broken rules to remove Joanna from her post. She had been offered a dead-end position. Not the sort of woman to tolerate this kind of treatment, she had resigned from the police. Although he knew that a super wouldn't be allowed to do what he had now, Carrick still felt horribly guilty, and cowardly, for not having fought for her cause. At the time, he'd only recently been promoted to DI and had felt vulnerable – no excuse, he knew. Now, some years, a wedding and a baby daughter later, Joanna had rejoined the police.

'You'll have to get a shift on, James,' she said, dressed to go out, when Carrick got home a bit later than usual. 'We're meeting the Gillards in the Ring o' Bells for a meal in half an hour.'

Carrick kissed her cheek and went off to have a rapid shower. It was the first he'd heard of it, and right now it seemed as though he was surrounded by people who knew things that he didn't. Not only that: if there was one thing he hated, it was rolling up late to anything social. But at least the village of Hinton Littlemoor, where the Gillards lived, was only a few miles away.

It was gratifying to discover when they got there that they were the first, but Ingrid, Patrick's wife, arrived about five minutes later. She told them that Patrick had got home from work later than normal and she had left him in the shower. A dark-haired and attractive woman, once described by a Russian mobster as 'formidable and beautiful', she had worked with her husband first for MI5 in a department called D12 and then with the Serious Organised Crime Agency, now absorbed into the National Crime Agency. Both had then been involved with that organization until Patrick officially retired. Only in reality he hadn't. There were occasional contracts, even though he had taken what he called a 'day job' as a claims investigator for a national insurance company.

This fourth member of the group, tall and slim, turned up shortly afterwards, shed his coat and came and sat down. So was it raining or had he forgotten to dry his hair?

'It's lashing down,' he announced, solving the mystery and running his fingers through it, thus sprinkling his wife liberally with water. He picked up his pint of Jail Ale, a 'visiting' bitter beer that seemed to be a permanent fixture in the pub these days, thanked Carrick and had an appreciative taste. 'I hope we're not going to have a debriefing on what happened in Wemdale,' he said, all seriousness.

'You mean *another* debriefing, don't you?' Carrick said.

The fine grey eyes appraised him. 'I only said it because I knew you'd smile. God, that was a good ending, wasn't it?'

When they had ordered their food, Carrick told them what Sergeant Woods had said to him that morning.

Joanna said, 'When I was James's DS, I once arrested a Karley Baker for soliciting – in Bath, outside The Star in the London Road. I wonder if she's a relation.'

'Well, apparently there *are* hordes of them,' Carrick told her.

'She tried to get out of being arrested by saying she had a young child.'

Carrick changed the subject, saying to Gillard, 'You still on the straight and narrow?'

'If you mean am I working like crazy to prevent people from succeeding with false claims, the answer's yes.'

'They just take one look at him and fold,' Ingrid said after taking a sip of wine.

This was understandable as the grey eyes had in their repertoire a stare that could practically skewer people to the wall. On another occasion, he had told those present that he was now an official 'troubleshooter', but it hadn't resulted in any increase in his salary. Carrick didn't think this would concern him unduly as he knew Gillard was now in receipt of his army pension, which meant he had turned fifty. It went without saying that he was utterly wasted in this 'day job' he had now.

Ingrid said, 'I wonder if this local so-called sponsor already has, or had, a crime set-up of his own in London and fancies branching out nearer to home? Too much of a bore to keep getting the train perhaps.'

She wrote bestselling crime novels sprinkled with a little romance under her maiden name, Ingrid Langley. Joanna reckoned the romance was due to Patrick's influence. Ingrid had fallen in love with him when they had met at school. The couple had three children of their own: Justin, Victoria (known as Vicky) and Mark, which was amazing if you took into account the fact that he'd been seriously injured in an accident with a hand grenade while serving with Special Forces. They had adopted Matthew and Katie, his brother Lawrence's children, after Lawrence was killed. Their real mother – a 'basket case', according to Ingrid – was in and out of rehab most of the time and wanted nothing more to do with any of them.

All four had work to do the following day, so they left shortly after finishing their meal and hurried through the rain, the Carricks to their car, the Gillards across the village green to their home in the old rectory.

It should have been summer by now, but rain was still pelting down the following morning, and although wearing a waterproof, Carrick got quite wet walking from where he'd been forced to leave his car. There was very limited provision for police personnel to park near the nick, even for senior officers, and local residents had been complaining that they had been leaving their cars 'in the wrong places'. Carrick kept a tactful silence on the subject – don't upset the natives – even though their previous place of work had had a large car park.

DI Lynn Outhwaite, petite, extremely good at her job, was in his office, putting yet more paperwork in his in-tray. 'DC Gascoign's ill, guv,' she reported. This wasn't actually her job but she had wanted to speak to him.

He preferred her to call him that rather than 'sir'. 'Sir' was too formal for a woman of her ability and professional manner.

'What's wrong with him?' Carrick enquired, grimacing at the new additions to his workload.

'Not known yet, but it sounds quite serious. He's in hospital.'

'Please find out as soon as possible. We're understaffed as it is. Is there anything I need to know about events overnight?'

'Scenes-of-crime found a half-eaten chocolate bar on the floor of the jeweller's that was broken into the night before last and they hope there's DNA on it. Other than that, there's little to go on at the moment, and the staff are still trying to list exactly everything that was stolen. There's nothing else you really need to know about, but to keep you in the picture someone tried to steal a car parked on Wellsway but disappeared when the alarm went off. Also, there was criminal damage in Abbey Churchyard where a couple of drunks threw empty bottles against a shop door, breaking the glass. One member of a group of girls on a hen night, also drunk, tried to cool off in the river. She was hauled out by passers-by and taken off to casualty suffering from hypothermia and cuts to her arms and legs.'

'She was lucky. Cold water kills you pretty quickly when you've had too much alcohol. In my experience, it's usually young blokes and they usually drown.'

'Women have more fat on their bodies.'

He stared at her. 'Is that right?'

'Well, it is right, but whether it had any bearing on this occasion, I've no idea.'

'I'm not questioning your knowledge,' he was forced to say.
'Good,' Lynn said, and went.

Carrick sighed. Perhaps she'd had a long walk through the rain, too.

The morning crawled by. The rain continued to thump against the window, people came and went, and Carrick began to wish he hadn't been promoted. At least when he was DI he was able to go out more; everything was more hands-on. Right now, life was an anticlimax after his involvement with the case that had resulted in the arrest of Derek Rogers aka Kevin Freeman. Unconsciously perhaps, he shook his head. His involvement with Gillard in connection with that had begun with a murder in Glastonbury, not even on his patch. If Patrick was involved with a case the world went entrancingly haywire.

'And I don't want people to be murdered to make my life more interesting, do I?' he said out loud, hurling a fat chunk of stapled-together pages into a wire tray, the contents of which were destined for shredding.

No, he didn't.

Lynn put her head round the door, which he usually left ajar. 'I'm afraid it's very bad news about Gascoign, guv.'

'What's happened?'

She came in. 'He's dead. An aneurysm on the brain.'

Speechlessly, he waved her to a chair and, in a rare insight – for a man, that is – on the subject of relationships, finally said, 'You liked him, didn't you?'

Her face crumpled and she just got out, 'Yes,' before she began to cry helplessly.

This was terrible news. Everything else apart, Gerard Gascoign had not only been a personable and valued member of the team but had not brought with him the kind of attitude as had young Constable Morris who, although the DCI didn't know it, Patrick Gillard had once described as 'an uppity little sod'. Gascoign would have gone far in his career.

Carrick put a box of tissues within Lynn's reach and told her to stay put and he'd fetch her a cup of tea. He went out, his mind in a whirl, trying to compose what he was going to say to Gascoign's parents. He wouldn't just write a letter, which the chief constable would also do; he fully intended to go and see them. The only positive thing about it, a tiny crumb of comfort from the force's point of view, was that the man hadn't been killed by the carelessness of anyone in the force in the course of his duties.

Joanna was standing in the reception area, in uniform, and looked as though she had just walked through the door.

'For God's sake, ask for a transfer to CID and then to Bath now,' he said to her quietly as he went by. 'Right now. Your husband desperately needs you.'

'Whatever's happened?' she understandably asked.

'Please go to my office and comfort Lynn,' was all he said as he headed for the small room where they could make hot drinks, all the while feeling Joanna's gaze boring questioningly into his back. He discovered later that she had had to visit an address in the city and had just called in to say hello.

The following morning, a teenage boy's body was found on a building site near the river. Perhaps more correctly, it ought to be described as a potential building site, as although later additions to a Victorian warehouse had been demolished, work hadn't started on the main project, which was to turn the building into high-end apartments. Carrick went straight there – it was quite early, just after eight thirty. Even though the area had recently been fenced off, vandals had already broken it down, using, Carrick knew, a stolen JCB, which they had then driven around knocking things over before finally trying to torch it. They had failed, but it had been seriously damaged. The developers hadn't yet repaired the fence, but this now meant that police vehicles could gain access. Several were parked hard up by the perimeter to avoid any contamination of the crime scene.

Lynn Outhwaite was already organizing the response team, so he left her to get on with it and had a look at the body. Forcing himself to be dispassionate he wondered if this was merely the place where the body had been dumped and the boy had been killed or died in an accident elsewhere. Although the pathologist had not yet arrived to carry out a preliminary examination, the DCI could detect no outward signs of a shooting or stabbing, the only visible injuries severe contusions and bruising on the left side of the face.

'Who found him?' he asked Lynn when she came over.

'A sort of homeless man who's dossing down here in what was a downstairs office,' Lynn replied, putting up the hood of her anorak against the thin drizzle. 'The boarding over part of the window had been wrenched off, but he said he didn't do it.'

'A *sort of* homeless man?'

'I didn't speak to him, but Constable Tanner, who did, reckoned he could be Drug Squad and keeping an eye out for dealers who are reputed to hang out here.'

'Tanner's suggestion makes sense – why would a down-and-out report finding a body? Is he here now?' Carrick asked, his gaze on the pathetic figure at his feet.

She shook her head. 'No.'

'Would you rather be somewhere else?' he enquired quietly.

'I've plenty to do at the nick,' she answered. 'But thank you; I ought to be here for a while.'

'Any ID on the body?'

She should have already briefed him on all these details but, as he had just thought, was not only upset by this child's death but also Gascoign's, a little bird in the shape of Sergeant Woods having told Carrick that she and Gascoign had been dating.

'Oh, no, sorry, guv. As you can see, he's wearing what I would call a tracksuit. Nothing in the single pocket of the bottom half, but we can't turn him over to see if there's anything in a back one until the pathologist gives permission. Tanner said these kinds of garments for blokes are referred to as loungewear now and are really pyjamas. Apparently, young guys wander round in them at weekends.'

She didn't sound as though she approved, but Carrick quite liked the idea.

'But it's not the weekend, so I wonder if he should have been in bed, especially as there's nothing on his feet,' he mused. 'I take it no child answering this description has been reported missing.'

'Not so far.'

'But he only looks around twelve or thirteen, so must have people responsible for him somewhere – people who would surely be around when he was going to school.'

If Lynn thought this a little naive, she didn't say so.

'He's a strange-looking lad, though, isn't he?' Carrick said. 'His hands and wrists are almost the size of a strong adult man's.'

An enigma.

That evening, they were no nearer to finding out anything about the boy – a murder victim? – despite house-to-house enquiries. There weren't many people living in the immediate vicinity due to the whole area being in the process of redevelopment. The post-mortem wouldn't be carried out until the following day. No one answering the description had been reported missing. This meant that Carrick had no feelings of guilt at leaving work just before the usual time as he had a rugby match that evening. It was a police team, the Ferrets, and he had been playing with them for a few years, some of the original team members now describing themselves as 'seniors'. He didn't think of himself as a good player but could still run like blazes for short distances and his tackles had been described as 'awesome'. This had come in handy for apprehending male suspects who had been unwise enough to try to flee.

Towards the end of the second half, when things were getting a bit heated, the Ferrets just ahead on points, there was a ruck that was more like a multiple car crash, and Carrick, somewhere near the bottom of it, had his right leg broken.

TWO

The house on Brassknocker Hill in Monkton Combe, Bath, was situated close to the bottom of that steep road, the end nearest the city. Virtually hidden from view by mature trees and select flowering shrubs, it had originally been built by a rich industrialist who had made his money quarrying Bath stone, that rich cream building material that causes the city to glow almost gold on a sunny day. These days, the property was owned by Mortimer Mansell, whose character, had he known it, was not far removed from the original Regency owner of the place. In a word, grasping. But he wasn't interested in anyone who had lived in his home in the past – the present and future were all he cared about. And money.

Mansell knew that his shrubs were select because he had chosen them and organized their planting himself, and if any on offer at the nursery hadn't had the Royal Horticultural Society's Award of Garden Merit, he'd ignored them. This attitude to his surroundings was mirrored inside the house as well. He had what he regarded as a superior art collection. This was for his eyes only, and most of it was kept in a locked room on the second floor that he liked to refer to as 'the gallery'. The new kitchen on the first floor was top of the range – he didn't cook, just used the eye-level fitted microwave – and the bathroom and three en-suites had recently been completely refurbished even though he had created for himself a bedsit, his private 'retreat', on the second floor in what at one time had been servants' quarters. His pride and joy was a kingfisher-blue velvet sofa in one of the two reception rooms on the first floor – the furniture was all from an upmarket department store – but he rarely sat on it, preferring to keep it in pristine splendour. It toned in nicely with the blue carpet, and when he had visitors – not friends or relations because he didn't have any of those, just business associates – he put a throw over it.

In his view, most of these associates, shady dealers in various kinds of valuables, were little better than vermin, but they ate out of his hand, almost literally, as he entertained them lavishly, using staff from his outside catering company – an off-shoot of his restaurant business – and he needed his guests' services so there was mutual satisfaction. It was always arranged in advance that after an evening, or perhaps, extremely rarely, a weekend of hosting a group, he would have a firm of professional cleaners come in and restore the whole place to what he regarded as perfection. He was expecting them soon and would ask for extra vigilant vacuuming of the room that had been used the previous night, not his best living room with the blue sofa by any means – not for that lot, different people, employees who were worse than vermin. No, the *other* room. One irritation was that he had forgotten to roll up another pride and joy, the polar bearskin rug. It was a real one, and he told himself that if someone couldn't kill a vicious animal and have its skin to decorate his house, the world was a sorry place. His worse-than-vermin had trodden on it without even noticing.

The gathering afterwards, never mind the raid, had been a disaster, and he was still in a state of quivering nerves. When dressed, he had looked at himself in one of the long mirrors in his bedroom and gazed hard at his reflection to see if there was any visible shaking. To his horror, there was. His chin – chins, really – was quivering, as were his hands when he held them out. Mansell didn't like still having what he called his 'winter face' anyway – that sallow shade a faded tan produced when he hadn't been on a holiday cruise for a while. He thought it made him look Asian, which to him was ghastly, and he was always at pains to point out to people that one of his forebears had been a Spanish nobleman. He tried never to remind himself of the truth: that his parents had been market traders in Bristol and he had been born in a flat in Totterdown – in those days little better than a slum.

It had all been that bloody brat's fault. If he hadn't climbed up the ivy on the house and peered through the window he wouldn't have witnessed the group wondering what the hell they were going to do with Archer's body. Arsehole, Mansell had privately called him, a pig-thick bruiser who for the last time in his life had got his orders wrong. Georgio, who had been a real find, had strangled him. At least, Mansell consoled himself, there was no mess on the carpet. Then, after disposing of the body of the youth, they had used Georgio's car once more to drive Archer's corpse to a conveniently disused quarry and tipped it in. Rumour was that no one went there because a cow that had died of anthrax had been dumped in it. Probably not true, Mansell thought, but it suited him. Perfectly.

Normally, he would have paused to admire his reflection – in his opinion that of a well-groomed and successful businessman wearing a very expensive watch and gold rings on his fingers. But not today. To try to calm his nerves, Mansell poured himself a large shot of whisky and drank it almost in one. He didn't usually drink in the mornings – one had to keep a clear head. Then, hearing a vehicle outside, he went over and opened a window. It was the gardener.

'Adams!' he yelled as the man got out of his pick-up.

Adams, born and bred in Somerset, looked up, obviously startled.

'Rake the gravel in the drive first, would you,' Mansell ordered and slammed the window.

The window – the one where they'd seen the face staring in, the foxy features, a mouth like a slit and large blue eyes making him look like some nightmare creature in a film. Mansell had felt the hairs on the back of his neck stand on end. Livid, he had run to the window and flung it open. There had been a cry of pain as one hand had been knocked away from its grip, but the other had hung on persistently until Mansell had grabbed a poker from the fireplace and battered the clinging fingers. Then the face had no longer been there.

He had looked down and seen that the boy lying on the gravel below the window was still alive, moving a bit and uttering little cries. Georgio had seen to that too, and everything was now perfect.

James Carrick was in a depressing place. Hospital. He was no longer in pain as, he reasoned, he was dosed with morphine or something like it. His right leg was in a splint and he'd been for X-rays, but it wouldn't be until the next day that they would put it in plaster, due to swelling. He had been told that it was a displaced, oblique shaft fracture of the tibia so it would mean having a general anaesthetic as the bone would have to be put back in place. There might be muscle and tissue damage. Whatever happened, he would be hobbling around on crutches or even in a wheelchair for weeks, if not months, with what amounted to a drainpipe on his leg.

Joanna had been to see him, told him it was perfectly natural for him to feel like having a good howl, and promised every loving care when she wasn't on duty. (He had been dreading that she would say something about his being too old for contact sport, but she hadn't.) But, Carrick thought now, he could hardly expect the live-in nanny to look after him as well as Iona when Joanna wasn't there. Help him to the toilet . . .? Despite the fact that it was very warm in the ward, he shivered.

And the job! What the hell would happen? There was already a drastic nationwide shortage of CID staff, never mind in the Avon and Somerset force. Now with a murder to investigate, Lynn couldn't possibly cope on her own. Meanwhile, he was in a nil-by-mouth situation and on a drip. *I'm a drip too*, he decided, *for not recognizing that I'm too old now to play contact sport*. A real drip.

The next day, and after a vague sort of morning with a blank in the middle of it courtesy of modern medicine, he woke from a doze, still on a drip, hungry, to discover that a visitor was approaching. He knew Joanna was on duty until late afternoon and hadn't expected to see anyone.

'Can I get you anything?' Patrick Gillard asked, arriving. 'Tea? A bucket to honk in?'

He was dressed for work in a dark grey suit, white shirt and regimental tie, and placed the magazines he had brought with him on the end of the bed.

Carrick's brain still felt as sluggish as a slug in a beer trap. 'Tea, please,' he croaked, his mouth very dry.

Gillard gave him a comic-opera salute and went away. He must have met the woman with the tea trolley for he was soon back with a couple of mugs. A packet of biscuits was presented from a pocket. He then retired to a discreet distance when a nurse arrived to check on the patient and to raise the top end of the bed to enable him to sit up. Pillows were plumped, blood pressure taken and Carrick was found not to have an unduly high temperature.

His visitor reseated himself, gave Carrick his tea and said, 'With Joanna's full cooperation, we've sorted everything.'

'As in?' Carrick enquired.

'You're coming to the rectory for a couple of weeks.'

'But you don't have a spare bedroom.'

'Mother has, in the annexe. After Dad died she had his study converted into a bedroom so she could have friends to stay.'

'But she doesn't want an inert bloke in her home!'

He was smiled upon gently. 'James, old son, you aren't going to be inert. I have a first-class honours degree in walking with crutches – because I've just asked and that's what you'll be issued with. I shall give you full tuition.'

'No, sorry, I really can't impose myself on an elderly lady.'

'She offered without anyone even mentioning it. And just because my mother was a churchman's wife doesn't mean that she isn't down to earth. It won't make more work for her either because we have two home-helps and she loves cooking. Not only that, she's met you several times and regards you as almost one of the family.'

It would certainly take the pressure off Joanna, Carrick thought.

Gillard continued, 'You'll get a follow-up appointment here to make sure everything's mending in two weeks' time, but you'll be reasonably mobile by then, and after that the force will have to provide you with a car and driver if they want you to go to work.'

'I shall have to go in, though, as soon as I'm allowed out of here.'

'You'll get two weeks' sick leave. That's official because you have soft tissue and muscle damage.'

'Patrick, I simply can't!'

'Two weeks' sick leave,' was the inexorable response.

Carrick studied the other man. 'I have an idea that you're hatching a plot.'

'I knew you were a good cop. No, look, I don't want you to think I'm bouncing you into anything – because I'm not. I don't want you to give me an answer today, or even tomorrow.' He paused for a moment and then went on, 'The NCA in the form of Commander Greenway has been on at me to take on more small contracts but on a proper basis. It'll mean that I'll have to work part-time on the other job. I haven't told them yet, but I don't think it'll be much of a problem as I can do a lot of it from home. I'll say to Greenway – if you agree, that is – that my price for taking on more work for the NCA is a contract to help you out for a couple of weeks.'

'To do my job!'

'No, of course not. To be your Bloke Friday, to enable Lynn to get on with hers.'

'But you resigned from the NCA because of risks to the family.'

'It'll be on the understanding that I won't be tangling with big crime.'

'The Baker gang seem pretty hardwired, dedicated mobsters,' Carrick pointed out.

'I'll just have to shoot them,' Gillard replied with a big grin.

The DCI chose to ignore that and said, 'This is all due to a shortage of personnel in the agency as well, I take it.'

'Yes, it is.'

'I'll give it serious thought,' Carrick promised. 'And this is assuming that Avon and Somerset will agree.'

'I did work within the force for a while,' Gillard reminded him.

Carrick wondered if the NCA would be prepared to pay him for such an undertaking.

They weren't. Commander Greenway wasn't exactly hostile to the proposal but insisted that if Gillard wanted to 'moonlight', as he put it – any perceived hint of blackmail not mentioned – permission would be forthcoming, but the Avon and Somerset force would have to pick up the tab. Gillard had then told him that Carrick could hardly request that the NCA give him some assistance, so the offer must come from Greenway. The commander, who might have been thinking that he would lose one of the jewels in his particular crown if he didn't, contacted

Carrick's superintendent boss who duly referred it to higher gods at HQ in Avonmouth. Their decision was pending.

Meanwhile, Lynn Outhwaite had been concentrating on identifying the dead boy and had sent emails to all the city's comprehensive and independent schools with a photograph of the body, the worst injuries blanked out. She soon had an answer: Damien Baker had attended a comprehensive school off the Warminster Road but had not attended for several days, and they had received no notification of illness from his mother, who couldn't be contacted. The DI braced herself to give bad news and set off to the address. The area could be described as rough, so she took Constable Morris with her to make sure, if nothing else, that stones weren't thrown through the windows of their squad car when she was elsewhere.

However, the estate was quiet, the house where Damien had lived seemingly deserted. Although Bath City Council had recently spruced up the whole area, there are always people on whom such efforts are wasted, and this house appeared to be lived in by one of these. Already, the freshly painted front door had scratches and filthy handprints on it, and a full plastic rubbish bag in the tiny front garden had been torn open by dogs or foxes, the contents strewn everywhere. Flies buzzed around rotting food.

Lynn had already rung the doorbell twice and now sent Morris to knock at the back. He returned.

'The door's open, ma'am.'

'What, really open or just unlocked?' the DI asked.

'Unlocked.'

'You didn't go in?'

'No, ma'am.'

She went round there.

There was no point in knocking again. Lynn opened the door, went in and called, 'Mrs Baker? Are you there? Police.'

A TV was blaring somewhere at the front of the house.

She called again, louder, and then when there was still no response, went in, walked through a kitchen, the state of which she preferred not to examine too closely, headed towards the source of the noise and into a living room. A woman lay slumped on a sofa. She looked dead. Aware that Morris – whom, for reasons she couldn't explain, she found irritating – was right behind her,

Lynn indicated that he should kill the TV and took a closer look at her. She risked shaking her gently by the arm. The arm was cold, like the room, but there was a small, fretful movement.

'Call an ambulance,' the DI instructed into the sudden silence. 'She seems to be out of it on drink or drugs, and I don't like the look of her at all.'

The findings from the post-mortem on Damien Baker were puzzling. Stripped of medical terms, his left hand was quite badly grazed, the right severely injured, two fingers broken, and he had obviously suffered some kind of trauma injury. The grazing to the left-hand side of the face was not particularly serious, but there was a cracked jaw. The left ankle was broken and there was severe bruising to most of the left side of the body. The pathologist was at pains to point out that, in his view, the boy hadn't been hit by a car or beaten up – the latter not in any 'normal' sense. With regard to these aforementioned injuries, the only thing he could suggest was that the deceased had fallen from a height, but that didn't really explain the type of injuries to the hands. Another puzzle was that the feet, large and with long toes for a boy of his age, were calloused as though he walked barefoot a lot, even on hard ground. The actual cause of death was manual strangulation.

'Strangled!' James Carrick gasped when this was reported to him by Lynn Outhwaite in a phone call.

She said, 'He could have been climbing up the old warehouse – as boys do – and fallen, but that doesn't explain why his body was some distance from it. Or explain the cause of death. And even I can't imagine a situation where someone would come across a badly injured child and finish him off.'

'Was there any sign of sexual assault?'

'No.'

'Has that "sort of" down-and-out been located?'

'Constable Tanner followed it up. Yes, Drug Squad.'

'Had he heard or seen anything?'

'No. Nothing, but he wasn't there all night.'

Desperate to be able to get more involved, Carrick asked her to keep closely in touch.

By this time, he had been helped out of bed and was sitting

in a chair by the side of it. He had been dreading not just the wheelchair scenario but having to hop around with a Zimmer frame like some of the elderly men in the ward. Not so: Patrick was right, and a physiotherapist had arrived with an assistant bringing elbow crutches. The patient had received a crash course in getting mobile again and, as he had been encouraged to do – no, told – he now decided to go on a little journey.

It had immediately become obvious that being fit to play rugby had huge advantages now as his strong arms and shoulders coped easily and he had a good sense of balance. Not stairs on his own yet, though; he baulked at that. He was heading back when he saw someone he knew – Patrick's wife, Ingrid – approaching from the opposite direction.

When they met outside the ward, she kissed his cheek. 'I've made you a cake.'

Touched, he said, 'That probably stopped you writing at least half a chapter.'

'No, I'm stuck. And I always make Patrick cakes when he's in hospital.'

Which, he knew, had happened rather a lot over the years when he had tangled with mobsters. Most of those, however, had finished up either in prison or body bags.

'Help me with my latest case?' he cajoled as they went in, more than aware that her intuition and clear thinking had helped his and the NCA's investigations in the past.

'When you're at the rectory we can have case reviews and briefings. You are coming, aren't you?'

'If you're really sure that your mother-in-law won't mind.'

'She's looking forward to having you around. And don't forget, you can use our living room and conservatory, so you won't be under her feet at all.' She handed over the package with the cake in, saying, 'I made it in a loaf tin and cut it into slices for you.'

'Has Patrick shared the findings of the post-mortem on Damien Baker with you?'

'Yes, he did. It's utterly horrible.'

'His injuries suggested that he had fallen from a height, but the fact that he had been strangled puts a completely different angle on it.'

'Did the pathologist have any idea whether he had been killed before or after he fell?'

'No, that might not be possible. Lynn suggested that he might have been climbing the old warehouse.'

'Or was roaming around places that he shouldn't? If he climbed up a house to look into a room where a light was on, he could have happened upon people having sex. If someone saw him and lost their temper . . .' She shrugged. 'Someone having sex with the wrong partner? An affair?'

'And your famous gut feelings?' Carrick queried.

'Would anyone kill a child who had been snooping on them in bed? Probably not. But if that person was a criminal already, who knows?' She went quiet for a quarter of a minute or so, obviously thinking. Actually taking place was an author reconstructing in her imagination what might have happened – Ingrid had an almost photographic imagination. In her mind she was there, watching. Finally, she said, 'If Damien had climbed up a wall to a window there *might* have been a strong plant like a vine or tree for him to use to support his weight. He could have chosen that window – he might even have done it before – because it was easy. If he looked in and someone saw him, they could have thrown the window open, injuring one of his hands.' She paused with a grimace. 'James, this is right off the top of my head, and the last thing I want to do is muddy the waters of your investigation . . .'

'No, please, go on,' Carrick urged. He had no clear water in the case at all right now.

'If – *if* – he was still hanging on with the other hand, someone could have hit those fingers with something to make him let go. So he'd end up with one grazed hand and broken fingers on the other.'

'And then whoever it was went down and finished him off if he hadn't been killed in the fall?'

'A ghastly scenario, isn't it? Drink, drugs – who knows?' She then apologized for not staying longer as she wanted to meet the children off the school bus and left almost before he remembered to thank her for the cake.

Kayley Baker had been dead drunk but taken to hospital as a precaution when the paramedics who had arrived in response to the 999 call hadn't liked the look of her either. It hadn't taken long to establish that she was severely malnourished and suffering from pneumonia. After treatment it was still a couple of days before she recovered sufficiently to remember that she had a son called Damien and asked where he was. At this point, it was deemed she was well enough to be informed of his death and questioned by the police. Lynn Outhwaite decided this wasn't a time for the woman to be interviewed by someone wearing size-eleven boots and a sixteen-and-a-half-inch collar – the depleted CID team trying to cut themselves into several pieces already and having to rely on uniform for some jobs – and went to the hospital herself.

The woman didn't look much better than when she had first seen her. Her long brown hair, going grey at the roots, straggled across the pillow against which the skin of her face looked greyish. But her hazel eyes, right now blurred-looking possibly due to the medication she was being given, might at one time have been her finest feature. They regarded the DI questioningly.

'Who are you, then?' she wanted to know, speaking a little breathlessly.

Lynn told her.

'A detective inspector must really be at a loose end to come and make my life a misery for trying to make a little money.'

Lynn was aware of her record. 'I'm not here in connection with soliciting.'

'What, then?'

'It's about Damien.'

'What's the little sod done this time?'

There were no records of the boy ever having been in trouble with the law.

Lynn said, 'To your knowledge, did he leave the house at night when he was supposed to be in bed?'

'No, of course not!'

'But I should imagine you weren't there very much at that time of day.'

'What of it?' the woman shot back at her.

'Mrs Baker, something very serious has happened. I'm afraid Damien is dead.'

The woman's mouth formed the word 'dead' but no sound emerged. The she croaked, 'What in God's name happened?'

'We don't know yet, but his body was discovered on a building site near the river. He was wearing what could be described as blue pyjamas, but his feet were bare.'

'On a building site?' the woman repeated incredulously.

'It's about two and a half miles from where you live.'

'But that's not possible. He never went that—' She stopped speaking.

'Far? He did go wandering off, then.'

'All right. Sometimes. Did he fall off something?'

'He went climbing?'

'Oh, God,' Mrs Baker whispered. Then, 'People told me they'd seen him after dark going up the drives of big houses, climbing trees and walls. Climbing was the only thing he was good at. *Did* he fall, though?'

'He may well have done, but the cause of death was strangulation.'

'What, *murder*?'

'I'm afraid so. I'm really sorry,' Lynn added when it became apparent that the full horror had just sunk in.

'But he *wouldn't* have gone that far,' Karley Baker said through tears.

'What time was he supposed to go to bed?' Lynn asked, giving her a box of tissues from the bedside table.

'Nine o'clock. I insisted on that.'

'But were you at home four nights ago?'

'Er, no, probably not.'

'So you can't know whether he went to bed at that time or not.'

There was a whispered, 'No.'

'Have you any idea if he had a favourite place to go climbing?'

'No idea – we never talked about it. I wasn't supposed to know. I thought that if he did something he enjoyed, he'd use up some of his excess energy and behave better.'

'He was difficult, then?'

'He was a very difficult boy. Always has been. He wasn't quite right, born a bit different. I didn't like to think of him as disabled as he got around really well – just walked funny. He got a lot of teasing at school, only it was worse than that really – bullying. They called him a freak and Gollum after some character in a film 'cos of his big blue eyes. When he was a baby he was really lovely, but everything went a bit wrong as he grew.'

'Did he mention anyone at school or elsewhere who particularly had it in for him?'

'No. As I just said, we didn't talk about it.'

Lynn realized that mother and son had said very little to one another. She thanked her and rose to leave.

'He was very nosy, though,' Karley Baker said. 'Even when he was little, he liked staring through people's windows – and trying to look up women's skirts. I was always telling him off about that. I could understand someone taking issue with him over it.'

Taking issue? Lynn repressed a shudder, said goodbye and left.

'No, you're taken by a porter to your transport in a wheelchair,' Patrick Gillard said when it became apparent that Carrick was ready to leave the hospital under his own steam. 'You're on the third floor and they don't want you to break your other leg or for your nearest and dearest to drop you down a lift shaft.'

'Have you heard from HQ?' Carrick asked him.

'Your HQ? No, but Lynn Outhwaite emailed the super with a further request for assistance, so he might hurry them along. She came to see the murder victim's mother in hospital, here, yesterday. Did you know that?'

'Yes, she found out that the boy went off climbing when he should have been in bed. That might explain why he was out after dark and his injuries if he fell, but nothing else. Apparently he liked looking in people's windows.'

'Perhaps he looked in one window too many.'

'And saw something that he shouldn't? Yes, we'd already thought of that.'

'Is the name a coincidence? You have Bakers as potential suspects in the jewellery raid case. Was that lad a relation of theirs and also involved in crime?'

'Good point. I shall make a point of finding out.'

The porter and wheelchair arrived, and Carrick was transported outside to where Gillard had parked his Range Rover. It was late morning so the pair stopped for lunch at the Fox and Badger in Wellow. After a steak and kidney pie and all that came with it, Carrick suddenly felt much more like himself and the fog that had resided where his brain should be while he was in the hot and stuffy ward cleared.

'Good, you've got some colour back,' Gillard said.

'Forgetting for a moment any question of a possible connection with the Baker gang, that child could have been climbing trees and looking in windows just about anywhere,' Carrick said. 'His mother did say that he couldn't have travelled as far as the place in the city where his body was found, but how did she know? She said she couldn't talk to him about it but thought he might behave better if he let off steam like that.'

They then talked about rugby and, a little later, Gillard took Carrick to the rectory. When he was settled in – Joanna was going to bring more clothes and other things for him later – Patrick went back to work.

Carrick wished he could do that too but knew that his team were keeping him in the picture with regard to several cases. He hadn't been at his temporary home for longer than half an hour – he appeared to have the place to himself – when Lynn Outhwaite rang.

'I went to talk to the headteacher at Damien Baker's school,' she began. 'The boy was a bit of a problem apparently but didn't tick enough boxes that meant he could be placed in a Special Needs category. They really do talk about kids like that these days. He was pretty poor at all subjects with the exception of PE, at which he excelled as he was very strong in the hands and arms. The staff had tried to limit the amount of bullying he was subjected to because of his strange body shape, but the boy hadn't helped his cause by walking around muttering to himself and recently had cultivated an off-putting demeanour. His English teacher had remarked that he reminded her of a character, a hobbit, called Gollum in *The Lord of the Rings*, and that had apparently also occurred to a couple of the children in his class, who had kept whispering "Fissssh!" to him.'

Carrick, who knew nothing about gone-wrong hobbits, could

nevertheless imagine the situation. He said, 'Was she aware of his nocturnal activities?'

'No, and he didn't really communicate with anyone – not if he could help it.'

When the call had ended, Carrick took himself off down the drive for some fresh air. There was a bad moment when one of his crutches went deeper into the gravel than he would have liked and he almost lost his balance. A car came down the drive and he moved to one side. The driver's window was lowered.

'Are you sure you ought to be doing that?' Elspeth said with a smile, grey eyes like her son's on Carrick in the same steady gaze.

'Definitely,' he answered. 'You have to keep the muscles working.'

'Shall I put the kettle on?'

'Wonderful.'

'When you come in, I'll show you where everything is and then you can help yourself.'

'Having me in your home is very kind of you.'

'It's a pleasure, but you can sing for your supper. Can you do things like fixing the hinges on the doors of kitchen units so they shut properly? The lower ones, I mean. Patrick's no better at that kind of thing than his father. He once made Ingrid a wooden plant trough that she told me looked like the newly raised *Mary Rose*.'

'I'll do my best,' he promised, feeling jolly having discovered something that Patrick was no good at.

Mortimer Mansell sat down at his Regency desk – a real one, not reproduction. He didn't get the normal lift of spirits as he did so – not the usual mental picture of the discerning and epicurean businessman preparing for a morning's careful planning. Not only had there been a poor haul from the jewellery shop a couple of days ago – Georgio had just shrugged and told him stuff must have been put in the safe at night – but other things were going wrong, and he couldn't have his feel-good factor when they were. It infuriated him. For one thing, his shower had stopped working. The toaster had refused to toast. It had taken him longer than it should have done to realize that the electrics in his large bedsit were the real problem. So he had had to settle for smoked salmon with brown bread and butter after a bowl of cereal for his breakfast – the wholemeal kind, good for his insides. Mansell thought about his insides quite a lot.

Except for Georgio, the Baker lot were even more hopeless than they had been in London. Georgio had said that he was a cousin many times removed from the other lot, and it was obvious that he disassociated himself from them. Mansell was beginning to think that he wasn't quite right in the head and this suited him, although he had to be careful. But even he had screwed up this time. The body of the boy had been discovered and the police were investigating. Why, Mansell had raved at his henchmen, hadn't they got rid of his in the same quarry as Archer's? Someone had muttered something about not wanting to do the same thing twice in case they were seen, to which Mansell had bawled, hadn't their tiny minds thought of putting both bodies in the car together?

They were hopeless.

Moving out of London to Bath had been a good idea from his own point of view. This had proved to be even more sensible when another of the Baker clan – Mansell reckoned they must breed like rabbits – had been picked up by the law, literally, in London when they'd had to leave him behind after the driver of the getaway car had run him over. Luckily, he had died before he could tell the police anything. Served the stupid bastard right.

Now, though, having returned these West Country thickoes to their roots, there would have to be a change of plan. Perhaps he would put Georgio in charge. All the others were already terrified of him anyway, and with good reason. At least he had got rid of Archer – that cheered him up a bit. He too had been a distant relation of the others and had recently joined the gang from somewhere in the Midlands. Inbred, though – a moron.

Mansell's day got worse. Careless and bad-tempered following drinking too much from his cellar of fine wine the night before, he reversed his Jaguar out of one of the three garages forgetting the low stone wall around the raised bed with the giant oak tree on one side of his drive. He smashed straight into it at speed.

THREE

Scenes-of-crime evidence after the raid on the jewellery shop, one of the city's most exclusive, had been as scanty as that following the murder of Damien Baker. None of the gang seemed to have cut themselves on flying glass, so there were no bloodstains. Nor were there any fingerprints, suggesting that they must have worn gloves. In all, over three-quarters of a million pounds' worth of stock had been stolen. As far as the murder of Damien Baker was concerned, there had been no mud in which tyre tracks or footprints could have been left, as the clearing up work after the demolition of the unwanted 'add-ons' to the warehouse had been extremely thorough and most of the ground was concreted over.

James Carrick had been at the old rectory for four days now and had made it to the first floor on his own in order to use the bathroom. Elspeth had a shower room and toilet, but he hadn't liked to keep using that. Soon, he had been told, the old cloak-room on the ground floor would be refurbished – the water had had to be turned off in there due to a leak – and an en-suite installed in Ingrid and Patrick's bedroom.

At first, the children had been a little hesitant in approaching him, even though they all knew him quite well. All but Vicky, that is, who had rushed in and presented him with several of her dolls and teddy bears to keep him company when he had been seated in the Gillards' living room. If he went into Elspeth's annexe, they were brought to him there, too. At least he could make himself useful, he thought – perhaps helping the older ones with their homework or babysitting Mark if Carrie, the nanny, needed to pop out to the post office-cum-village store. The cupboard doors in Elspeth's kitchen had been the work of moments to fix with a screwdriver, and he knew she was casting her gaze around her home to see if anything else needed doing.

He had been wondering about the identity of the 'big cheese with a screw loose' mentioned by Sergeant Woods. What exactly, he asked himself, did this man – he was assuming this person *was* male – *do*? The description didn't fit any of the known villains, and although he was perfectly aware that a few of the city worthies warranted question marks – small ones – none of them were actually implicated in serious crime. Perhaps it was a newcomer.

Although he wasn't about to make it public, his leg hurt despite the painkillers he had been given. As Patrick had found out – he would, wouldn't he? – there had been a certain amount of soft tissue damage and a couple of ligaments had been seriously strained. So it ached. He was supposed to wiggle his toes occasionally but that hurt, too. To try to take his mind off everything he went through into the main part of the house – everyone seemed to be out again – and sat in the conservatory. It was full of plants. Ingrid had said she'd always wanted her very own Eden Project, but had been very careful that the plants she'd chosen weren't poisonous if chewed on by curious toddlers. Apparently, a surprising number of plants were.

After a little while, Patrick appeared, coming in from outside. It wasn't quicker than entering through the front door, but Carrick had noticed that the family seemed to use this way most of the time. Perhaps it was a subconscious decision as one was immediately decanted into a haven of scented warmth and greenery rather than the cool austerity of the hall at the front.

'Coffee?' Patrick enquired.

'Thanks, but I made myself some a little while ago,' Carrick replied.

'Fancy a trip out?'

'Aren't you at work?'

'There's nothing troubleshooter-ish on the books at the moment and I can write a report here later. Oh, Joanna rang me and asked if Ingrid and I fancy a meal at the pub tonight. I take it you do.'

'I thought she was on duty this evening.'

'No, she's just found out there was a muddle with the rota and she isn't.'

Carrick began to feel a bit happier.

'I thought you might like to go and have a look at the crime scenes of what I understand are your most serious cases right now – the break-in at the jeweller's and where that poor lad's body was discovered.'

A lot happier.

'I'll go and get changed,' Patrick said. 'Then lunch.'

After eating pasties and chips in the pub, they headed to the redevelopment site first. As directed, Gillard drove to where the fence had been damaged and parked there. The DCI had shown his ID to a constable on arrival – someone he didn't recognize, who turned out to be new. She had looked questioningly at Gillard, who had produced his NCA ID. The fact that he still had a warrant card was interesting, Carrick thought. Commander Greenway had given it to him in lieu of any other permission to carry the Glock 17 with which he had been re-issued on the grounds that he and his wife were targets for the mobsters and terrorists they had put out of business over the years. Carrick thought this situation made police history, but it did make going anywhere with him feel extremely safe as the man was an excellent shot.

Gillard assisted his passenger to disembark and they made their way to where incident tape cordoned off the place where the body had been found. It was just after two in the afternoon now and a chilly breeze was blowing off the river, bringing with it a dank, muddy smell. In the main part of the brick-built warehouse, the windows, now just holes where the rusted iron frames had been removed, looked like eye sockets. Carrick decided that even when it was redeveloped, he wouldn't live here if he was paid to.

There was nothing to see.

'Did anyone take a look inside?' Gillard wanted to know.

'Only on the ground floor as the rest's too dangerous,' Carrick replied. 'The wooden floors all have to be replaced and some of them are like cardboard as there's so much woodworm and dry rot. Someone from the Drug Squad has been squatting in an office on and off, hoping to get details of the dealers that sometimes come here. I contacted his boss in Bristol who said his man, who's been recalled now, had had a quick look round the ground floor when he first arrived and it was just dust, dust and more dust.'

'But has anyone been in between when he first went in and right now?'

'Not as far as I know. You'd have to ask Lynn.'

A sober gaze came to rest on him.

'OK, I should have asked Lynn,' Carrick admitted.

'Well, you have an excuse seeing that you were still half asleep from the anaesthetic and she's just lost a close friend. Your amanuensis will take a look.'

'The window might have been boarded up again,' Carrick pointed out.

'Plenty of wrecking tools in the battle-bus.' This was said over his shoulder as he headed back that way. 'D'you want to sit in?' he added. 'I can smell rain.'

Sure enough, a couple of minutes later big drops began to hit the windscreen. Of course, Carrick thought, Patrick had once been an undercover soldier and was attuned to weather conditions from habit. It seemed wrong to be seated in the dry when another person was doing his job for him. But then again, he wouldn't have ventured into the building himself but asked someone else to do it.

Carrick was annoyed with himself for feeling so tired. He had even been falling asleep in a chair after lunch. It didn't occur to him just then that his body was throwing everything it had into repairing the damage to his leg, never mind just having had a good meal. Sure enough, not long afterwards he felt himself dozing only to be jerked awake by approaching footsteps.

'Nothing to report,' Gillard said, getting back behind the wheel. 'Officer Drug Squad left hardly any traces of having been there other than what looks like recent footprints in the dust on the ground floor. I didn't go any further as the beams supporting the ceilings are actually sagging, but in my view nothing in that building has a connection with the crime. But that's just my opinion.'

Carrick thanked him and they drove towards the city centre.

The raided shop was still cordoned off but, as the scenes-of-crime team had completed their work, there was now frenzied activity on the part of the staff to clear the remaining stock in spite of the rain, presumably taking it to a secure warehouse. A squad car was parked on the pavement, its crew standing around, looking intimidating, no doubt to deter passers-by from helping themselves to anything shiny that was being carried to a security van, which was also parked on the pavement. Gillard followed the trend and the pair promptly had to prove who they were.

'Have the people who live in the flats over the shop been interviewed?' he asked Carrick.

The DCI nodded. 'Everyone except whoever lives on the first floor at the front, who wasn't in on the two occasions someone went there. The others said either they hadn't woken when the raid took place or their rooms overlooked the back.'

'Shall we give it a go?'

'I'd prefer not to, if you don't mind. I happen to know that the staircases in these old buildings are downright narrow and awkward for folk lumbered with crutches.'

'Would you like me to?'

'Yes, please do.'

Gillard had to show his ID yet again to a PC who was standing by a doorway at the side of the shop to gain access to the stairs and the accommodation above. True enough, within was a dark, damp-smelling hallway, the bottom steps of a flight of stone stairs just visible in the gloom. It was a spiral staircase, the sort of thing he felt belonged more fittingly in a castle. Having a right leg that below the knee wasn't the one with which he had been born, he had to be quite careful as the inner parts of the steps were extremely narrow and he had no feeling in that foot. Carrick would never have managed them.

The occupant of the apartment was a young woman and the doorbell's ring appeared to have got her out of bed as she looked sleepy and was wearing pink silk pyjamas. However, she was sufficiently awake to smile at him beguilingly.

'Police,' Gillard said, and the smile faded just a little. He produced his ID for the third time, and she took it from him to look at it carefully. 'Patrick, then,' she said, giving it back. 'I'm Hilary Manders.'

'Sorry to disturb you, Miss Manders, but I'm making enquiries into the raid on the jeweller's downstairs. Were you here that night?'

She frowned, pushing her long black hair off her face, and said, 'Yes, it woke me up.' Opening the door wide, she added, 'Come in, there's a horrible cold draught blowing up the stairs. Did you leave the front door open?'

Gillard said he hadn't.

'It's that stupid old bag who lives at the back who's left it open, then. She's a fresh-air fiend even when it's loaded with traffic fumes.' She led the way in and gestured to a sagging leather sofa. 'Take a pew. Coffee?'

He sat. 'No, sorry, I can't stay. The detective chief inspector's in the car and can't come up because he's broken his leg.'

'Those stairs are absolutely *lethal*,' she declared, plonking herself down in a tub chair. 'Oh, yes, you want to know about the raid. Look, I didn't notice the kind of things that would have sent me rushing off to tell you about it at the police station – it was nothing really, a couple of nothings.'

'Nothings can add up to something,' he said with a smile.

She smiled back. 'You know, you really don't look like a cop.'

'I save my serial killer face for interviewing hardened criminals.'

She laughed, thinking him joking, and would have been shocked if she found out he wasn't. Then she said, 'I got out of bed and looked out. My bedroom's at the front, too. There was a van parked half on the pavement, and masked men were attacking the shop front with sledgehammers or something like that. I couldn't see much of them when they were right underneath, you understand.'

'May I have a look?' he asked.

'Carry on. Turn right out of the door.'

Gillard found himself in a largish room that smelt of perfume and womankind. He opened the curtains and looked out of the window. There was actually a good view of the road below and the nearest street light was about twenty yards around to the left, a detail that he confirmed when he opened the window and leaned out. She would have observed everything that had gone on in the time she stood watching.

'There was one man who wasn't really doing anything, just shouting orders at the others,' Hilary Manders continued when he returned to the living room. 'He seemed to be shouting at one man in particular – a big lump of a bloke who didn't seem to know what he was supposed to be doing. That one wasn't masked but had a scarf or something like that tied over the lower half of his face. I know street lights can make everything look a bit funny but I'm fairly sure he had red hair.'

'Did anyone see you?'

'God, I hope not. I was peeping through a gap in the curtains.'

'And then?'

'That's it really.'

'The other nothing?'

'Oh, yes, the big lump of a bloke seemed to lose his temper at being told off and ran across the street and attacked a man I hadn't noticed until then. He kicked him. He might have been a drunk who'd been in a shop doorway. But he sobered up enough to run off, limping, and the big bloke started to chase him but came back when he was shouted at again. I rang nine-nine-nine and then dived back into bed as I was frozen by then.'

'Thank you, you've been most helpful.'

'Sure you can't stay?'

'Sure,' he answered. He asked for her full address while trying to ignore the fact that, as was only to be expected, she appeared to have nothing on under the pyjamas. Sometimes even devoted husbands yearn for their footloose and fancy-free days. Or, come to think of it, wanting nothing more right now than to respond to the come-hither messages this young woman was sending him, go back into her bedroom with her and . . .

Er . . . no.

'Phew,' he murmured as he got back in the car.

Carrick looked at him sideways. 'Was she attractive?'

'Umm.'

'Red hair,' Carrick said decidedly when in receipt of the information Gillard had been given. 'This road has white LED lights now. We might even be able to identify him if there's CCTV footage.'

'There can't be too many big lumps of blokes with red hair round here who may or may not be downright stupid,' Gillard observed and started the engine.

'Next stop, the nick.'

'No. home. You can look at mugshots online and then have a snooze, or you'll be a write-off this evening.' He chuckled.

Did Carrick mind being thus nannied? No, he didn't.

*   *   *

Three things were wrong with the tale of the dead cow in the quarry. First, it had been a bullock. Second, it hadn't died from anthrax. Third, it had fallen in when it had strayed too close to the crumbling edge, having broken out of a field half a mile away during the night. The farmer, not the most assiduous character, hadn't noticed it was missing until about three weeks later when he did a head count of his stock and, having lost several pregnant ewes to thieves the previous month, assumed that it too had been stolen. When someone spotted the dead animal and told him, he left it there. Too much bother to get it out.

It had been a favourite dumping place for rubbish, including burnt-out cars, ever since the quarry closed in the late 1980s, carried out by those intrepid souls who, like Mortimer Mansell, didn't believe the anthrax story either and were too idle to take their unwanted stuff to the tip, a matter of a few miles away in the opposite direction. Nature now covered most of the unsightliness with a healthy panoply of brambles and nettles and, right in the bottom, where there was a small lake, especially in the winter, reeds and rushes grew. The warming weather now meant that all this was green and lush, a haven for frogs, insects and small rodents. Those creatures still scraping a living in the carcass of the bullock, now little more than bones poking through the rotting black and white hide, had gladly welcomed a fresh source of nourishment when it thundered down on them. Sooner than it might have been thought possible, parts of Archer's corpse were seething masses of maggots.

Two days after Carrick and Gillard had been to the scene of the raid on the jeweller's, the haze of flies drew the attention of a sharp-eyed woman, Joan Blackley, who was a member of a rambling group. The party was on the opposite side of the quarry to what she had noticed, where the track they followed would eventually lead them back to Bathford, from where they had begun their circular walk, and then lunch in their favourite pub – they were all looking forward to that.

'Lend me your binoculars, please,' she said to a keen bird-watcher in the group.

They were very good ones and revealed all the details that she would have preferred not to see – the bloated putrefaction, the way the head rested on what looked like the remains of an animal of some kind, the wriggling holes where the eyes had been . . .

Mrs Blackley discovered that she had sat down very suddenly on the ground, a strange mist before her eyes. When they asked her what was wrong, she told them.

'Don't be silly, Joan. It's just a shop dummy,' trilled a woman new to the group who nobody liked very much.

Joan held out the binoculars for her to take a look for herself.

'Oh, I can never see anything through those things. Shall we go on? Personally, I'm starving.'

It has to be said that although Joan was sharp-eyed and fit and active, she was in her mid-eighties and a little absent-minded and forgetful. The new woman, a retired practice nurse, had already hinted to the others that she thought she was in the early stages of dementia.

'Phone the police, then,' suggested the owner of the binoculars, who didn't really believe it either and was also thinking about lunch and a pint. 'But I don't think there's much of a signal here.'

There wasn't one at all.

'Are we going to stand here messing around all day?' cried the new woman in exasperation a couple of minutes later. 'No, sorry, I'm off. I'll see you in the pub.'

'Yes, you go,' Joan urged. 'All of you.' She got to her feet and discovered that she still felt a bit shaky, the images she had just seen seemingly printed on her brain. And had it been blood on the head or red hair?

The group slowly moved off. The man with the binoculars wanted to stay with her, but Joan shooed him away, saying she would walk a little way up the slope behind them to see if there was a signal there. Then, whether she had been able to phone or not, she would catch up with them.

Having tried again and still been unable to make a call, Joan changed her mind. She wouldn't go straight to the pub – she'd follow a narrow winding path that led right around the quarry and try to phone from the other side where she knew there were buildings of some sort nearby. They'd used the path before. So surely there would be a mobile phone signal. Once started, she liked to finish things.

It took her around twenty minutes to walk round, not because it was very far but due to the path being overgrown and sometimes going too close to the edge of the hole for comfort, requiring her to undertake little detours. There was the occasional alarming glimpse of the bottom of the quarry with the lake glinting between the reeds. She had never thought it a happy place. Finally, she reached where she wanted to be, which was actually the one-time approach road to the quarry. With a pang of alarm, she realized that she was now really close to the corpse as well. Could she detect a nasty smell or was it her imagination?

Thankfully, there was a signal here and she dialled 999 but wondered immediately afterwards if the situation warranted an emergency call. Suppose she'd imagined it and it was a shop dummy after all? Still feeling wobbly – she hadn't had much for breakfast and they had had their coffee break quite early in the walk – she sat on a boulder that had probably been left over from the workings and waited. Something else that worried her was that the police, if they arrived at all, would have to walk all the way round the quarry to be able to see what she had.

After another twenty minutes had elapsed, a police car arrived and the crew got out. They seemed surprised to see Joan sitting there.

'Did you spot this body, madam?' one of them enquired, making it sound as though he wasn't sure she had seen what she'd said she had.

'Yes, it's right below the edge of the quarry. But you can't see it properly from here and please don't try to or you'll fall in – the edge is all crumbly. I'm afraid you'll *have* to walk round to the other side as I don't think there's a road over there.'

'You up for that, Fran?' the man asked his female colleague.

Fran was, and the pair, directed to the path by Joan, reported what they were doing on their radio, admitted to Joan that they didn't have any binoculars and set off, leaving her sitting on the boulder, not knowing quite what to do.

Carrick still hadn't received any kind of official notification about the possibility of an NCA assistant, but Gillard was ignoring the lack of permission and was assisting where and when necessary. The DCI was keeping right away from the nick because that was where the paperwork was, and had decided to take his two weeks' sick leave seriously. For most of the time, he remained at the rectory and rested his leg, read books from his hosts' shelves, went for short walks around the village, and tonight he was going home for a couple of days as Joanna had the weekend off.

Lynn Outhwaite rang him when, early that afternoon, the pair were on their way into the city. Gillard had to make a call there and had asked Carrick if he wanted a change of scenery.

'Someone's reported finding a body in a quarry near Bathford,' the DCI told him. 'But it hasn't yet been confirmed.'

'D'you want to go there?' was the immediate response.

'Perhaps we could go by there after your appointment. Someone should have attended by now.'

The other looked at his watch. 'I reckon we could do it now as it's a bit quicker that way round – I'll phone and tell them I've been held up. D'you know exactly where this place is?'

'Yes, for some reason I do. It's on the Bradford-on-Avon road – disused now, though.'

Despite the recent rain, a large cloud of dust was in their wake as they drove through what had been the entrance gates to the quarry, now wide open and rusting. Gillard carried on and went by some derelict sheds and an old cottage that had perhaps been used as an office. Then they spotted the parked squad car and Joan Blackley. Gillard got out and walked over to her.

'Are you from the police too?' she called a trifle nervously when he was a short way off.

'National Crime Agency,' he told her. 'I'm giving Detective Chief Inspector Carrick a hand as he's broken his leg.'

'Oh, the poor man. The other police officers left about ten minutes ago to look at it from the other side.' She went on to say where the body was.

'Is your car somewhere here?' Patrick asked, gazing around.

'No, I had a lift from home to Bathford. I'm with a walking group, you see, and spotted the body from the other side.' She waved in the general direction.

'So where's the group?'

'They went off back to Bathford for lunch. I don't think most of them believed me. But I had to come round to this side as there's no phone signal over there.'

Although trained to rapidly assess people, it didn't take any specialist knowledge for Gillard to know that this lady was too old to be hanging around here much longer, and despite being well kitted-out in outdoor clothing and boots, she was cold in the keen easterly breeze, never mind having been virtually abandoned. 'Come and sit in the car. I'll take you home.'

'Oh, you really mustn't bother. I'll get a bus.'

'There's probably two a week,' he joked.

It was a slight shock to him when he saw that he would have to give her a helping hand, but she was game enough and obviously enjoyed sitting in the back of the Range Rover.

They all introduced themselves and then Gillard said to neither of them in particular, 'Can we get over there?'

'There aren't any roads,' Joan said.

'There might be tracks, though,' Carrick offered.

Gillard grabbed a local OS map from a pocket by the driver's door. He preferred what he called 'a real map' to using one on-screen. Then, on an afterthought, rummaged in the shelf under the dash and took out a bar of Kendal Mint Cake, passing it to their passenger.

'Right!' he said after a couple of minutes' perusal.

Joan Blackley had never been in an off-road vehicle before, but in the next fifteen minutes or so enjoyed the ride bouncing over various old workings and along tracks before they finished up just above the point from where she had seen the corpse. When the vehicle came to a halt, she said, 'You know, I'm really worried that what I saw was only something like a shop dummy and I've caused you no end of trouble for nothing. That's what Mildred – I mean Mary – said it was, without even looking through the binoculars.'

Gillard had caught the embarrassed tone. 'Mildred?' he queried.

'Yes, I'm afraid that's what I call her. She's a new member of the group and rather unpleasant; she reminds me of a horrible aunt with that name I had as a child. She fell down an abyss in Switzerland hiking in the snow somewhere she shouldn't have been and that was the end of her. I was told off for being regrettably happy about it.'

Also regrettably, both men burst out laughing.

The crew of the squad car toiled into view – their walk was uphill – and Gillard, having suggested to Carrick that he stay right where he was, or at most disembark and stay with the vehicle, collected his binoculars and went down to speak to them.

'But shop dummies don't have red hair, do they?' Joan said almost to herself. 'Nor flies buzzing round them.'

Carrick had been about to open his door. 'Red hair?' he repeated.

'Well, I *think* so. It didn't really look like blood. A big fat man – although that might have been because of . . .' No, she didn't want to think about putrefaction anymore.

'We won't keep you long,' the DCI promised. He had looked at mugshots but only those of people with criminal records in the force's area. Three had had red hair – two women and a teenager convicted of arson.

There was no doubt in the observers' minds as to what they were looking at; Carrick able to make out the corpse from where he was standing by the car. He put into action the difficult operation of retrieving it, and then Joan Blackley was taken home.

'Does your group have a leader?' Gillard asked as he saw her to her front door – just to be on the safe side.

'No,' Joan replied, finding her door key. 'We just meet and wander along. It's all very casual.'

'You ought to. And they should have stayed with you even if it meant you had to change your plans for lunch.'

Joan smiled up at him. 'I think it's a good idea, but couldn't stand it if Mildred was bossing us all about. I might even have to leave, you know. She really is insufferable. Just about her only topic of conversation is her big house and garden and how she has to have a cleaner and a gardener. The gardener's just been given the sack by another employer because he was accused of reversing his van into the man's car, even though he insisted he had nothing to do with it. Oh, I'm so sorry, wittering on like this. But I do want to thank you both so, so much for looking after me.'

'Who is this person?' Gillard enquired, his nose for fraud twitching.

'Sorry, I've no idea – and please don't suggest I go and ask Mildred about it.'

'Not a chance.'

Once indoors, Joan went straight into the kitchen to find some much-delayed lunch. Corpses apart, what a gorgeous morning, she thought.

'Gorgeous men, too,' she whispered.

The Bristol and Bath newspapers were questioning why no one had been arrested in connection with the death of Damien Baker. An open-and-shut case, one hack suggested in roundabout fashion; he might have been a runner for drugs dealers and dispensed with. Neighbours reported that someone, probably a journalist, perhaps even the same individual, had knocked on Mrs Baker's door, but she wasn't at home, still in hospital as her recovery from pneumonia was protracted due to being malnourished and generally poorly. Others ambushed DI Outhwaite as she left work the following Monday and demanded a progress report. Carrick gathered that her reply had been short and not very sweet.

He had been giving thought to what Ingrid had said about a possible sequence of events in the boy's death. One had to be wary, of course – it was the product of a vivid imagination. But he was tempted to believe that something along those lines had occurred. It would do no harm at all, he reasoned, to keep it in mind.

Now, of course, they had a possible connection between the raid on the jeweller's shop and the corpse in the quarry. The remains had been identified as those of Robin Archer, known as 'Hoodie' to his friends for reasons that didn't need to be explained. Carrick had conferred with Derek Woods about this, but the sergeant hadn't heard the name before. That wasn't to say that the man hadn't been a recent addition to the Baker gang, but no information was forthcoming as to where he had lived.

A few more days went by and the DCI had to oversee various other cases, mostly over the phone and on email from the rectory, although Ingrid did drive him into the city one afternoon when Lynn needed his help. Patrick took him to the address of DC Gascoign's parents where he spoke and had tea with them for just under an hour. Patrick stayed in the car outside, listening to the radio. That wasn't anything to do with him.

FOUR

When, after the weekend, early on Monday morning, Carrick got the post-mortem results on Robin Archer, he was so stirred up he rang Patrick Gillard's mobile number. The pair could not be described as muddling along, but there had still been no official permission from HQ for the one-time army officer to give him a hand, and the following Friday was the end of Carrick's sick leave. No notification had been forthcoming as to whether he'd get a police driver either. This morning, he had no idea where Gillard was – not at home anyway – and he was all ready to apologize if he was engaged on the job for which he was actually being paid.

'Archer was strangled,' Carrick said when Patrick had answered and assured him that he'd just left someone's house.

'That *is* interesting,' he said. 'But it's dangerous to jump to the conclusion that the crime was connected with Damien's death.'

'But if Archer was the man Hilary Manders saw taking part in the robbery, there's a chance that he was got rid of because he screwed up and attacked whoever it was over the road. We don't yet know the estimated time of death but red heads aren't all that common.'

'Has that person been traced?'

'No, but we have tried to locate him. Rough sleepers tend to move on if there's been any bother.'

'And probably had the living daylights frightened out of him. Do you think Miss Manders would be able to identify Archer as the man she saw from a mortuary photo?'

'Unlikely as he had a scarf over the lower half of his face. She only really saw his hair. Besides which, decomposition was quite advanced. I wouldn't wish it on her.'

'Do you need to go anywhere? I'm free for about an hour.'

All Carrick really wanted to do was go to the nick and work

on cases first-hand, especially to discover where Archer had lived, but he thanked Gillard and said he'd try to fix Elspeth's iron which was stubbornly remaining stone cold.

'I think you'll find that it set sail with Noah,' Gillard said. 'See you later.'

Carrick had a look at the iron, which was indeed old, the kind where the plug could be removed. There was a loose wire in this and he felt that he had triumphed, but when he plugged it in and switched on, there was a small but significant explosion in its works accompanied by a strong smell of burning.

'Well, it *was* old,' said Elspeth when she got home a little later. She considered. 'At least twenty years, come to think of it.'

He had already ordered her a new lightweight one as a thank-you for her hospitality.

Lynn Outhwaite had made it one of her priorities to find out where Robin Archer had lived, and decided that although his connection with any other local gang wasn't known, it might be worth questioning several usual suspects other than the elusive Bakers. After all, there had been four or five men who had raided the jeweller's. To choose from, there were the North brothers from Twerton, although the eldest, William, Bill, was serving time for serious assault and burglary. Another possible was Caroline Davidson, an alias – she used others – who had a rag-tag group of unemployable hangers-on. They specialized in housebreaking, picking pockets during Bath race meetings and casual burglary, walking along a residential road trying doors to see if any had been left unlocked and, if so, going in and helping themselves to whatever they could quickly sell. It was stretching it a bit to connect them with a raid on a jeweller's that involved violence with sledgehammers, but sometimes those questioned were pleased to pass on information about others to get the pressure off themselves. The other possibility was the Bakers, but they had been very quiet of late – there was a rumour they had been in London – some of their number behind bars. Lynn wasn't silly enough to think that those remaining had retired from crime and gone to live in Frinton.

Standing five foot two without shoes, she took a couple of burly uniformed constables with her and visited several last-known addresses in Bath and Bristol. She wanted to do this job herself, partly because there was, as yet, no replacement for DC Gascoign – his funeral was in a couple of days' time with full police honours, and she was dreading it – and also because she felt a need to prove that she was worthy of her new promotion. This might have been due to the fact that her father had been a domineering man who believed, to the day he died, that a woman's place was in the kitchen, so Lynn was desperate to show that she could do the job. This was sad as she was highly thought of.

But she learned nothing really useful. No one admitted to knowing a Robin Archer – at the addresses where anyone answered the door, that is. The only address for the Baker clan, the main reason for her escort, was on a council estate on the outskirts of Bristol. She already knew that at this end of the terrace house there were usually a couple of caravans in what at one time had been a large, L-shaped garden – now little more than worn grass and mud. A lone tree could be glimpsed to the rear, a rope tied to one of the few remaining branches, obviously used as a makeshift swing. Several children who ought to have been at school were either swinging on it or kicking a football around amidst a lot of shouting and screaming.

Having navigated her way around various rubbish in order to reach the front door, Lynn then spotted a woman hanging grey-looking washing on a line stretched between the tree and something out of sight. She led the way down the side of the house, noting that two of the children, who had stopped what they were doing when they saw the visitors, had red hair. The woman paused in her hanging out of the washing.

'I'm looking for the home of Robin Archer,' said Lynn, having introduced herself.

'He didn't really 'ave one,' the woman said. She looked beyond tired.

'But you did know him.'

'*Of* him,' she corrected. 'My 'usband used to say that he was the next worst thing to useless.'

'Was he a relation?'

'A distant cousin on my husband's side. My family doesn't have morons like that.'

'And you are?'

'Doreen Baker.'

'Did Archer live here?'

'No, he had a place on a caravan site on the Lower Bristol Road.'

'You do know he's dead then.'

'Yes, I do.'

'D'you mind telling me how you knew?'

'Gossip,' was the tight-lipped reply. 'The bloody man should've stayed right where he was in Stoke.'

'Do you know why he came to the West Country?'

'He got wind of a job.'

'D'you know what it was?'

'No.'

'There's been no official identification.'

'Well, don't look at me. I don't do dead people.'

'Is there anyone you know of who might identify him?'

'No. His girlfriend in Stoke left him ages ago.'

'No family at all, then?'

'Yeah, them two kids with ginger hair over there. He brought them with him to dump them on us after a while, and they're going into care when social services get round to it. We can't afford to feed 'em.'

'Is a woman by the name of Karley Baker a relation of yours?'

'She might be another one on my husband's side but I don't know her.'

'Is your husband at work?'

'At *work*?' the woman crowed. 'That'll be the day. No, he walked out on me. So it's just me, my sister and these kids while the menfolk get drunk, take drugs and give bother to you lot.'

'They must hang out somewhere.'

'God knows where, then. In a squat, p'raps – or that caravan site.'

Going back to where they had left the car, Lynn said quietly to her companions, 'Bear in mind that situation when you next get involved with criminal and so-called dysfunctional families and are all ready to condemn all of them out of hand.'

They found the caravan site in the Lower Bristol Road and

made enquiries there. It was semi-derelict. A sad-looking, elderly man emerged from a caravan by the entrance and told them that the rent for the pitch in question hadn't been paid in weeks. Someone had collected two children that had been abandoned there, who he and his wife had been looking after as they kept saying that their father was coming back. Lynn then had to tell him that he wasn't.

'Have you any idea if he had a job?' she went on to enquire.

The man endeavoured to straighten his stooping posture. 'No, and you didn't ask. He was a big brute of a bloke and he could have picked me up in one hand and thrown me into that rubbish bin over there. He was pretty stupid too, and they're always the most dangerous. I met some of those in the army.'

'Did you notice anyone calling on him?'

'No. In this game, it pays to shut the curtains and mind your own business.'

Lynn surveyed half a dozen or so grubby-looking caravans. 'Who else is living here?'

'Only an old biddy in one of them. That one,' he added, pointing. 'A bit nutty if you ask me, but she pays the rent all right. She can't stay much longer – the council are bulldozing the whole area for housing.'

'Where will you go?'

'The missus and me have arranged a pitch on a farm near Peasedown. There's no running water and electricity right now, but the farmer said he'd fix something up for us.'

'I'm going to have to have Archer's caravan cordoned off so it can be examined,' Lynn told him. Surely, she thought, these people could apply for council accommodation – strictly speaking, they were homeless.

'Good luck with that – there's a right old mess in there.'

They had a look for themselves without going inside and all three were perfectly content to leave further investigations to a forensic team as it was so filthy. But Lynn wasn't finished. She knocked on the door of the 'old biddy's' van and prepared herself for another onslaught of urban squalor. A smartly dressed and petite elderly lady opened the door.

'Are you from the council?' she asked before Lynn could say anything.

The DI introduced herself and asked her back-up to return to the car.

'Do come in,' said the old lady. 'I'm Phyllis Taylor. At one time, I seem to remember being a lot younger and managing a building society office. But memory can play tricks, can't it? Or I might have worked in Woolworths or been a Playboy Bunny.' She trilled with laughter. 'Take a seat, my dear. Have you come about that awful man who abandoned his children? Nigel – he's the old man who runs this place – and I fed them and tried to keep them amused, but after a few days he reported their situation to social services, who I *think* took them to stay with relatives. Would you like some tea? I buy estate teas and mix them to a brew I like.'

Lynn would have preferred coffee but smiled and said she'd love some. Then she said, 'Can you tell me anything about Mr Archer? He's dead, you see.'

Phyllis paused in filling a kettle from a large jug of water that she had to use two hands to lift. 'Dead!' she exclaimed. 'Now there's a thing. I said to myself only yesterday that he was the sort to come to a bad end.' Eyes bright, she whispered, 'Did someone kill him?'

'Yes,' Lynn answered.

'It's dreadful to be glad, but I didn't feel at all safe, you know. He used to pace around smoking at all hours of the night and, once, even looked in one of my windows. And the shifty sorts that visited him! Once or twice I peeped out if I heard voices – this was always at night, you understand – and there they'd be, smoking and drinking from tins that they threw everywhere. Horrible people. And now he's gone. Good.'

'Can you tell me anything at all about these visitors?'

'Well, there's only one of those awful orange street lights that make everyone look half dead. Sorry, I didn't hear any names mentioned. I've nothing else to tell you, I'm afraid, but I'd have a little bet on most of them being related. Like a pack of wolves – or hyenas.'

Lynn stayed for her tea and a chat, and then left feeling strangely buoyant. She wanted to dance around. Good tea that.

'You OK, ma'am?' one of her escorts asked politely when she got back to the car.

'Why do you ask?'

He hesitated before saying, 'You look a bit spaced out, that's all.'

'I had a very strange cup of tea,' Lynn told him, just preventing a giggle. 'And if you put it all round the nick, you're toast.'

'I've applied to transfer to CID,' Joanna told her husband when she called in at the rectory on her way home. It had actually involved making a short detour. 'But, as you know, it'll take several weeks, if not months, to grind through the system.' She unpinned her long Titian hair from the bun she wore it in for work and shook it free. 'The bad news is that Frome don't want to lose me.'

'There's only an inspector in charge there, isn't there?' Carrick said.

'She makes up in firepower what she lacks in rank, though,' Joanna observed.

'We'll see about that,' Carrick said grimly.

'When are you coming home for good? Surely you can manage now. Iona's missing you.'

'As long as you don't mind having a few microwaved meals when I'm doing the dinner.'

'Yes, I do – we'll go to the pub. Have they organized a driver for you yet?'

'They don't seem to have done. I intend to raise hell.'

'What about Patrick?'

'There's been no official response. Meanwhile, I get the impression he's fitting me in with his other job. I don't like to ask really, as he's not been very forthcoming about that side of it.'

'And the work situation?'

'Bad. No real evidence in connection with Damien Baker's death or the raid in Milsom Street. The only things we do have are that both Damien and Robin Archer were strangled and the latter *might* have been the red-haired man in the robbery.'

Without hesitation, Joanna said, 'I'd want to work on the theory that it was him taking part in the raid and that he was killed because they were fed up with him making a mess of things – such as attacking passers-by. Whether he was connected to the gang or not, Damien witnessed Robin being killed so they killed him too and dumped his body at that old warehouse site before or after chucking Archer's in the quarry.'

'That isn't the way CID is supposed to work,' he told her severely.

'No, I expect I caught it from Ingrid, don't you?'

'Have you been discussing it with her?'

'No.'

Carrick then found himself staring at thin air.

She came back and put her head round the door. 'Be very careful; you've got a nasty strangler out there.'

A little later, DI Outhwaite called him and reported what she had learned at the Baker address and caravan site. She said nothing about her strange cup of tea, the effects of which seemed to be wearing off.

There were other cases to work on as well, of course – mostly not Carrick's personal responsibility, but he didn't want to load too much on to Lynn. There were jobs he could do online, even 'paperwork' of the tick-box variety such as surveys and staff assessment reports. But at the nick he knew the pile in his tray was getting ever higher . . .

Patrick came upon him in the conservatory, thus engaged, a little later when he came home. 'I took the liberty of going back and having a poke around in that quarry,' he said, having dumped the things he was carrying in various places. 'Damaged vegetation suggests the body was removed from the top – that was the most practical way.'

'Yes, it was,' Carrick replied.

'There's a narrow track down into the bottom of it not far from that point that was just about doable and, having almost slithered into the small lake at the bottom – tons of frogs – I went to a spot roughly below where the body was found. Other than a cow's skull, which for a full two seconds I seriously thought of bringing home and nailing over the front door, I found a shoe – a man's trainer, actually. It had come to rest under a small tree. I'm not saying it's Archer's, and you probably have his shoes already, but it didn't look as though it had been there for very long, so—'

'We haven't,' Carrick interrupted him by saying. 'The body wasn't wearing shoes.'

'I didn't touch it with bare hands but got it in an evidence bag I happened to have in my pocket.'

Carrick had an idea that all kinds of bits of police kit were residing in the Range Rover, just in case. 'He had quite small feet for a big man.'

'This is around a nine.'

'I'm indebted to you. And for your hospitality, of course.'

'Fancy a tot in the pub tonight?'

The Assembly Rooms in Bath, designed by John Wood the Younger in 1769, were described when completed in 1771 as 'the most elegant and noble in the kingdom'. Today, visited by tourists in their thousands, they are not just for looking at but can be hired for special occasions. They also possess what are regarded as the finest eighteenth-century chandeliers in the world, which the United States tried – but failed – to buy in 1950 for the White House.

On the evening of the day Patrick Gillard found a shoe, Mortimer Mansell, owner of a small chain of exclusive restaurants, one of which was in the city, was getting ready to go out. The occasion, a gala dinner held at the Assembly Rooms organized by the Chamber of Commerce and hosted by the mayor, was to celebrate the city's ongoing success in commercially difficult times. The historical details of the venue were going through Mansell's mind as he studied his reflection in one of his long mirrors. Yes, an ideal setting for those successful in life. He thought he looked really good in white tie. It suited him. To perfection.

It suited him, too, to be a good distance from his next target, a large manor house some five miles from the city's eastern boundary. It was the home of Lord and Lady Atworth, and Mansell knew His Lordship to be a rude and insufferable bore. His wife merely went round with her nose in the air and spoke to no one she regarded as of inferior class to herself – that is, nearly everybody. It had been reported to him by the manager that they had been difficult and obnoxious customers in his city-centre restaurant, demanding a table that was already booked, openly laughing at other diners and, finally, having ordered extremely expensive wine, refusing to pay the full bill, saying that the service had been poor.

Although he had planned to expand his other, more lucrative, business when he left London, this was the first occasion Mansell had gone for a private house, and the Atworths were an extremely gratifying target. Better than that, he knew they had been invited to the dinner on the grounds that Atworth – Mansell privately described him as 'filthy stinking rich' – put a lot of funds into city projects such as the restoration of one of the old Roman baths. Gossip of the malicious variety had it that his wealth involved money laundering. He had every faith in gossip from this particular source as he was no stranger to this method of dealing with money that had no legitimate origins. That apart, the pair of them stuck in his gullet.

One slight concern – no, more than slight – was the calibre of those doing the job for him. There had been no problem in hiring new people in the capital – who had refused to move to the West Country with him – but here, in the Bath area, they seemed thin on the ground, so all he had were the Bakers, some of whom he had originally taken to the capital with him as they had been useful in the past. Now, despite their failings and lack of savvy, he had been forced to bring them back because recruiting replacements was so difficult here. He stood still as it occurred to him that one reason for this – *the* reason – might be that the police were better at their job here, never mind that they hadn't yet come knocking on his front door. There was a chance that it was also because, unlike the Metropolitan and City of London Police, they weren't overwhelmed by gang culture and suffering from lack of financial resources.

Mansell had researched, as far as was possible, the local Avon and Somerset force. There was always the possibility of cultivating a weak link, someone with money worries, perhaps a debt problem, a member of the CID team with a drug habit or an individual sometimes referred to as a 'bent copper'. It was always worthwhile listening to his sources of this kind of information. He knew from a reliable one that the local detective chief inspector, James Carrick, had recently broken his right leg playing rugby. Not an effete character wearing shades and a designer mac, then. The fact that he was Scottish was also worrying. Personal experience had demonstrated that Scottish cops could be bloody horrible when they so chose. This Carrick would have to be kept an eye on. And who the hell was the dangerous-looking character who had been seen ferrying him around in his Range Rover? Not merely a police driver, that was for sure.

But for now he determined to put all that out of his mind and go and enjoy himself, content in the knowledge that the Atworths' house would soon be ransacked for stuff for which he had more than one dealer ready and waiting.

Carrick had already ordered a more extensive search of the quarry area, telling them to take a dog with them this time as he was keen to find Robin Archer's other shoe, if indeed it had been Archer's. He had been told that the first one fitted the body's left foot perfectly. Cautious to a fault, though, he knew he would have to wait for the results of DNA tests before he had a source of clues as to where Archer might have met his death. Tests on various samples – rather a lot of them – that had been gathered in the murder victim's caravan would probably take longer as the interior of it, as described by Lynn, had been filthy. She had been back to the only known address for the Baker clan and checked on the ages of the two children, ostensibly Archer's. They were five and four – too young, in everyone's view, to be questioned.

It was raining again, and Carrick's short journey from the rectory to the village pub, having negotiated the rectory's gravel drive, would have involved a choice between crossing the waterlogged village green or using the unmade road that surrounded it in the presence of only two street lights. He and Gillard had therefore come by car.

'I shall have to go to the funeral tomorrow and then pop into the nick to do some paperwork,' Carrick said. 'But there's no need for you to drive me in. I'll get a taxi to the funeral and someone can give me a lift to work afterwards.'

Patrick Gillard placed a couple of tots of single malt on the table along with with Carrick's change. 'Thanks, and your health.'

They had the public bar of the old inn to themselves but for a couple of gnarled elderly locals who were regulars and had their favourite stools at the end of the counter. The old inn was still sticking to the tradition of gleaming brasswork, bits of horse harness and framed old prints of the village. No music, and the single gaming machine had been banished several weeks previously. That's how most people liked it. Those that didn't could go elsewhere.

'Your two weeks' sick leave is up, isn't it?' Gillard queried. 'Tomorrow?'

'Yes, but I've loads of paperwork to do – it just means sitting at my desk, reading,' he was told.

'When's your next hospital check-up and X-ray?'

'Thursday morning at ten.'

'Fine, I'll put it in my diary.'

'Your company's happy with the part-time working, then?'

'At the moment. As I think I've already said, a lot of it is writing reports, which I can do at home, and if I make calls on people, they all tend to be within the county, and if it isn't another branch deals with it.' After a pause, he added, 'But I still feel like a guy who goes round measuring up windows for blinds.'

Carrick regarded the other sympathetically. 'It's a real come-down for you, isn't it – not working full-time for the NCA?'

Gillard shrugged. 'There are three kids who don't need a dad six feet under and another two who don't need a *second* dad six feet under.' Then he smiled and tossed back the rest of his tot. 'Another?'

'Please.'

When he was again seated, Carrick said, 'I told you about what Sergeant Woods said to me, didn't I?'

'Yes, you did.'

'I've been thinking about this character he described as wealthy and "a big cheese with a screw loose" who's rumoured to be a backer for the Baker gang. I can't do anything about it right now as I've absolutely nothing else to go on, but it's interesting nonetheless.'

'He could be a local businessman with a secret hobby.'

Carrick grimaced. 'Someone who's good at keeping a low profile.'

'Have you approached the Met yet to see if they have any missing big cheeses? As you're more than aware, criminals do move out into the provinces thinking the police there are likely to have straw in their hair.'

'No, but I will.'

'I'll check with Greenway. Who knows, the NCA might have a couple of names for you to follow up.'

FIVE

The call from Lynn Outhwaite came at a little after ten that night, just as Carrick, who had discovered that walking on crutches was extremely tiring, was thinking of going to bed. He promised to ring her back and, having been sitting in his room in the annexe reading as he didn't like to be under either Elspeth's or the Gillards' feet all the time, made his way into the main house. By this time all the children were in bed, of course, and there was no sign of Ingrid, but Patrick was in the conservatory playing the guitar, which he had recently taken up again.

'Please don't let me stop you,' Carrick said.

'It's OK. Turning in?'

'Well, I was. But Lynn's rung me to say she's just been told that there's been a burglary at the home of Lord and Lady Atworth. A gang literally smashed their way in and ran through the house snatching up anything that looked as though it might be valuable. But the body of a woman's just been discovered in a back room. It would appear that she was the housekeeper, Mrs Mary Cawston, who lived in a top-floor flat with her son. He called the police.'

'D'you want to go out there?'

'If you really don't mind.'

Gillard got to his feet. 'Not at all, but I must be over the limit.'

'No, you aren't.'

Carrick contacted Lynn to tell her that he was on his way, with assistance, and asked her for directions, but just then she couldn't help him. No matter, he assured her, she could stay put and they'd watch out for blue lights.

Gillard, having stayed assiduously within speed limits, arrived at imposing entrance gates flanked by even more imposing stone lions on plinths. The DI had rung Carrick back with the postcode which had duly been fed into the Range Rover's satnav. This was just as well as the mansion was right out in the countryside down a very long drive.

Several squad cars were parked by the house, the front of which was illuminated by 'heritage-style' lamps, also on stone plinths. The house itself looked huge, and it wasn't until later they discovered that in fact it was only one room deep and had originally been built by someone with a desperate need to impress but limited funds.

'The Atworths aren't back yet,' rapped out a tall, fair-haired young woman who emerged from a group who had been standing in the porticoed entrance. 'And, by the way, who the hell are you?'

Gillard, in his present role of Bloke Friday, bodyguard if necessary, tea-wallah and putter-in-their-place-of-stroppy-cops, introduced the pair of them.

The DI, Alison Pewsey from Midsomer Norton, mellowed and found her good manners. 'I'm waiting for a pathologist and scenes-of-crime people to turn up, sir,' she went on to say. 'There's a lot of damage. They didn't just steal property but threw things around, so the fewer people who go in there the better. There's one potential lead: blood on the floor near a smashed glass vase and smeared on the edge of a door.'

'And the Atworths aren't back?' Carrick queried. 'From where?'

'According to the son of the murder victim, Philip Cawston, they've gone to some kind of gala dinner in Bath.'

'How old is Philip?'

'I'd say in his early twenties. He's employed here on a part-time basis, but his main job is at an electrical shop in Bear Flat.'

'I'll speak to him in a minute, but meanwhile I'd like to have a look at the body.'

She led the way, and Carrick managed the several steps up to the front door, again inwardly cursing his pride for carrying on playing rugby when he was too damned old. He didn't notice that Patrick walked behind him in case he lost his balance.

The 'back room' was actually a study at the extreme left-hand end of the house, a small and snug hideaway that had proved to be no refuge for Philip Cawston's mother. The woman looked as though she had been in her mid-fifties, and her body was lying face up on the floor, clad in a pink fluffy dressing gown and matching slippers. There were no obvious signs of injury, but the position of the body suggested to Carrick, rightly or wrongly, that it had been flung down with some violence. He found himself wondering if she had been strangled and then thrown aside.

'Philip said she must have run in here to try to escape them,' said Pewsey. 'He was in his room watching television when he heard a racket downstairs and his mother shouted that she was going down to investigate.'

'Didn't he go with her?'

'No, his leg's in plaster with a broken ankle. He said he fell down a high curb.'

'So where is he now?'

'He's made it to the kitchen. He doesn't like to go into the Atworths' rooms.'

Philip Cawston was sitting at a huge wooden table, huddled around a mug containing what looked like tea, in just about the largest kitchen that Carrick had ever been in. It made the young man look small. There was nothing 'heritage' in here, though – the overall impression was of polished stainless steel and seemingly every gadget known to cooks. A female uniformed constable was with him.

'This is Annie,' Philip said. 'She's looking after me.'

Carrick seated himself mostly because the sound leg that was doing all the work ached. He was touched by the young man's good manners and said who he was. 'Please tell me what happened,' he requested.

Philip pushed his long dark hair off his face. 'Well, I've said all there is to say really as I wasn't present when it happened. I heard a noise, banging and crashing as though a tornado was going through downstairs, and then Mum shouted that there was a break-in. She'd been getting ready for bed. She's always tired – she works too hard. I grabbed my crutches – I see you've got the same problem – and went to the top of the stairs. But our flat's at the top, on the third floor, so I couldn't see anything, just heard shouting and then I heard Mum' – he gulped – 'scream. I started to go down the stairs – the Atworths are too mean to put in a lift – but when I got to the next floor I realized that people were running all over the ground floor, throwing things around. I feel a coward really . . .'

'No, you're not,' Carrick said gently. 'What could you have done?'

'I must be a coward because she's dead,' Philip muttered. 'The second floor's mostly guest bedrooms, and I went in the best one with the four-poster bed that I knew had a phone and called the police. I stayed in there and locked myself in the en-suite until I heard sirens. I'm a coward. I wasn't there to help Mum or stop them . . .' His voice broke.

Gillard said, 'But you'd have probably been lying dead somewhere now. You said you heard shouting. What were they saying?'

Philip roused a little from his misery. 'Oh. It was sort of "In here, mate!" and "Look at this lot!" Not exactly those words, you understand. It was mostly swearing.'

'No names?'

Philip pondered for a few moments and then said, 'Yes, I remember now. One of them yelled, "What do I do with this, Steve?" and another man answered, "God knows. Ask Georgio."'

'D'you reckon he was the boss?'

'He could have been.'

'Do you have somewhere else to go?' Gillard enquired. 'Or do you want to stay here?'

'I can go to a mate's place until I find somewhere else. Obviously, I can't stay here. Mum was going to chuck me out anyway; breaking my ankle sort of put that on hold.'

'Didn't you get on?'

'No, she was always comparing me with my dad. He was a portrait painter. She said I was useless. I am. I just have a job in an electrical shop.'

'I understand you have a role here, too,' Carrick said.

'Yes, I'm a sort of handyman. I fix things and wash their cars.'

'We'll take you to your mate's place,' Gillard murmured.

There was a commotion somewhere outside and a red-faced, white-haired and obviously not sober elderly man strode unsteadily into the room. 'What the bloody hell's going on?

My front door's been smashed in and my belongings are all over the floor in the hall. Did you do that – carry out a raid? What d'you think my home is, a bloody drugs den?'

'Lord Atworth?' Carrick enquired.

'Who the hell else could it be?' the man retorted, his gaze on Carrick's crutches.

'It looks as though your housekeeper was murdered during a break-in.'

'Looks as though? Is the woman dead, then?'

'I'm afraid she is, sir.'

'Are you sure?'

'The detective chief's inspector's just said so, hasn't he?' Gillard interposed. He had remained standing and now had the demeanour, a natural one as it happened, of a retired lieutenant colonel who didn't feel driven to be polite to a rude peer of the realm.

Atworth looked taken aback and then caught sight of Philip. 'You can clear out. It's bad enough having crippled cops without you unable to work as well.' He stalked out, more unsteadily, on hearing a shrill female shriek somewhere in the house, and this was followed by a roar of rage as he must have looked in through the doorway of his main sitting room on the next floor, which was actually cordoned off.

'You *were* about to tell him about the thefts and worse damage upstairs, weren't you?' Gillard said to Carrick.

'But he didn't stay around,' the DCI lamented. 'Do go and tell him that I shall want a full inventory of what's missing – as soon as possible.'

'It's a pleasure.'

Carrick had a good idea how the request might be phrased. Still, Gillard wasn't an employee of the Avon and Somerset force, was he?

They were at the house until just after one the next morning. Philip, openly crying, had been taken to his friend's home in a squad car, having been told the police would want to speak to him again. Lord and Lady Atworth had refused to be interviewed and, with police permission, mainly to get rid of them, had packed overnight bags and departed to a hotel, His Lordship demanding frequent progress reports on the investigation into the theft of his possessions, and claiming he didn't have time to provide an inventory. Following a request from Carrick, Patrick Gillard had walked around all non-restricted areas of the house looking for anything that might give them a lead into the identities of those responsible. He didn't find anything. A daylight search would take place as soon as it was practical.

'Who knew he would be at the dinner?' Carrick said on the way home, thinking aloud. 'If the idea was to raid the place when they weren't here, that is.'

'They're the sort to blab it all over the county,' Gillard said sourly.

'The first thing I'll do tomorrow – today – is to get a full guest list from whoever organized it.'

'I'm on hand later to take you to that funeral should you wish me to.'

Carrick turned to smile at the driver. 'And after that, I'm minded to forget the paperwork and carry on being footloose and fancy-free. I want to follow up DI Outhwaite's visit to the Baker address with regard to the Steve and Georgio who were mentioned. Lynn said it just seems to be women and children living there, but a slightly heavier approach might bring rewards.'

'D'you reckon the housekeeper was strangled? '

'Let's put it this way: if she wasn't, I'll be quite surprised.'

It was at just after eleven thirty that morning when Patrick Gillard parked outside the Baker 'sty', as he referred to it on seeing the general state of the property with its split and overflowing bags of rubbish at the front of the house. These had been joined by a stained and faded three-piece suite. He didn't normally leave his own vehicle close to a house where 'suspects' were known to live, or had lived, but had had to think of Carrick. He had also observed that there was another vehicle parked there already, a small red Ford that gave every impression of being an MOT failure. Carrick, he noticed, also gave it a calculating look.

'Bald tyres at the back?' the DCI queried under his breath.

'Bald tyres at the back,' Gillard agreed.

'Please make a note of the number as I don't have a hand free.'

They were both feeling very down after attending the funeral of Detective Constable Gascoign, a young man who had had such a bright future.

'Doreen Baker?' Carrick said when the front door was opened, Lynn Outhwaite having given him a description of the woman to whom she had spoken. A smell like boiled onions wafted out.

'Yes – Mrs.'

'I'm Detective Chief Inspector James Carrick and this is my colleague who works for the National Crime Agency. We're—'

'Why don't you bloody lot leave us alone, eh?' she yelled. 'Someone was here the other day nosing around.'

'I'm looking for two men,' Carrick continued, as though she hadn't spoken. 'But I only have first names – Steve and Georgio.'

'There's millions of Steves,' she scoffed. 'And my family don't go in for fancy foreign names.'

'How about plain George?'

'Lots of Georges as well, aren't there?' That with a triumphant smile revealing those teeth she had remaining.

In the back of the house somewhere, a man sneezed loudly.

'You and who else?' Carrick asked.

'None of your business!'

'We don't have a search warrant,' Carrick said quickly to Gillard, perceiving that he was all for going in to investigate.

'*You* don't,' said Patrick. Gently pushing past Doreen Baker, he went in.

'Oi!' she shouted. 'I'll report you to the chief constable!'

'Not my boss,' Gillard's receding voice replied.

A few moments later, turmoil erupted within and a large, bearded man came lumbering down the hallway. He was hoiked to a standstill from the rear, no doubt by a hand grasping his dirty sweatshirt, somehow turned round inside it and took a wild swing at the man who was endeavouring to apprehend him. He missed, caught a heel on the worn carpet and thundered over backwards on to the floor.

'Police! I need to ask you a few questions,' Carrick shouted to put this transaction on an official footing.

'He's hurt and you've made it bleed again!' Doreen Baker cried. 'I'll report you for that, too!'

Gillard oversaw the man getting to his feet and said, 'I did tell him that his arm needed looking at.'

Again, Carrick said who they were and then asked the man his name.

He got a mouthful of obscenities by way of a reply.

'Call up a squad car, would you?' Carrick asked his temporary and still unpaid assistant. And, eyeing the makeshift bandage oozing blood on the man's forearm, added, 'We'll carry on with this down at the nick after a short trip to A and E.'

'Tell him!' Mrs Baker ordered her sullen housemate. 'They'll only paste hell out of you otherwise.'

Neither Carrick nor Gillard refuted this, merely exchanged glances, Gillard then finding his mobile.

'Steven Baker,' the man ground out.

'How did you hurt yourself?' Carrick wanted to know.

'He was mending a broken window,' put in Mrs Baker.

'Shut up, Ma!' Baker bawled and then said, 'I cut myself on a broken bottle. It's out the back – here.'

His mother flounced off down the hallway, muttering, and went from sight.

'We do have smears of blood at a crime scene to compare with yours,' Carrick told him. 'And if there's a DNA match . . .' He left the rest unsaid but resolved to have a watch put on the house in the event of any stolen property being spirited away before he could obtain a search warrant.

The unthinkable happened: Steven Baker made a sudden bid for freedom. A flying fist caught Gillard unawares on the side of the face and he lost his balance, stumbled, hit his head on the doorpost and fell into a bush to one side of the front door. Baker then gave Carrick a violent shove, with a predictable result, and fled down the front path to his car. After a few fumbling seconds with ignition keys, it sped away. There was a loud clang as a section of the exhaust pipe fell off, the resulting throaty roar fading into the distance.

'What the hell were the pair of you doing acting like that without telling anyone?' Joanna demanded to know when Carrick called her later and related what had happened. 'The pair of you could've been *killed*.'

'Hardly,' her husband argued. 'Patrick's armed.'

'And was half in a bush by the front door while you were flat on your back on an old sofa.'

'We got a sample of Baker's blood, though.'

'How?'

'On Patrick's sweater during their set-to in the hall.'

'Did he get right away?'

'For now, but he'll probably have to ditch the car as it's a wreck and the silencer fell off. It was making a hell of a racket. We'll find him.'

'James could have been really hurt,' Ingrid scolded her husband that evening. 'Damaged his broken leg or even broken something else.'

'Look, I'm just the driver,' Patrick said, his other half not appearing to be wildly upset about the burgeoning bruise on his forehead. 'He wanted to go there. I took him.'

'You're just like a pair of *kids*. And this man escaped?'

'For the time being. We got a sample of his blood on my woolly pully, in case you were wondering where it was.'

'Sorry, but I simply don't understand how he got past you.'

Gillard had a headache and also an idea that he was now too old and slow for stopping eighteen-stone hulks. 'He got past me because he caught me unawares. I'm not infallible, you know.'

She gave him a big smile. Admitting that must have hurt.

'What's for dinner?'

'Chicken casserole, rice and asparagus. It's almost ready, the kids are starving, so hurry up and have a shower – you reek of something horrible that was on that sofa James ended up on. He's having dinner with Elspeth, by the way.' Heading for the kitchen, she added, 'It's probably in that damned quarry by now.'

'Eh?'

'The car he drove off in. He might dump it there if he *was* part of the gang that got rid of Archer's body and there was no publicity when the police found it . . .'

This was the first thing Patrick said to the DCI when they met after an early breakfast the following morning, Carrick having had tea, toast and marmalade in the annexe. It was the day of his hospital check-up.

'I'll send someone out there,' Carrick said. 'Now. Oh, by the way, I'm really fit enough to go home permanently now, so I was thinking of getting Joanna to pick me up tomorrow as it's her day off.'

'Have they fixed up a driver for you, then?'

This omission was why Carrick was still at the rectory.

'I think someone's being drafted over from Bristol.'

'Bristol! Someone is coming over from Bristol every day to run you around?'

'Crazy, isn't it?'

'You might be better sticking with the present arrangement.'

'Yes, and I really appreciate it, but you have a job to do.'

'I'm actually doing everything that I have to in between. D'you want to pop into the nick on our way to the Royal United?'

'D'you think I should, then?'

Gillard looked annoyed. 'James, I'm not telling you what to do.'

Carrick chuckled. 'No, but whatever the story, you still work for the NCA. Yes, right, good idea.'

This paid off, Lynn Outhwaite appearing to be pleased to see him.

'I was going to give you a ring. It might not be the same bloke, guv, but last night the A and E department of the hospital asked for assistance to deal with a violent drunk who had a deep cut to his right arm. The crew who attended ended up arresting him as he'd done quite a lot of damage and for the safety of everyone concerned. He fits the description of the man who gave you the slip yesterday.'

'Was his injury dealt with?' Carrick asked.

'Yes, after a struggle.'

'I'd like him brought here, this afternoon if possible – if he's sobered up by then.'

Later, at the hospital, Carrick had an X-ray and saw the orthopedic specialist for around five minutes. He was told that everything was mending well and to come back in a month's time.

'I don't normally feel like chucking myself in a quarry,' he said as he made his way, with difficulty, towards the exit, down a corridor almost blocked with wheelchairs, trolleys and equipment, the purpose of some of which couldn't even be guessed at. He'd hoped for better news.

His escort, who had had far too much experience of leg injuries, just smiled. Magic wands didn't exist.

Steven Baker had sobered up by late afternoon but definitely wasn't smiling. He was slumped in a chair in the interview room. His solicitor, who looked as though his client might not have been his first choice if he'd had one, sat on his right at one end of the table. As he was closely involved with the case, Carrick had decided to be present and was praying that this unseemly individual would give him a much-needed lead. Patrick had said he would hang around and get a cup of tea somewhere.

A couple of minutes later, the DI entered and officially opened the proceedings, explained Baker's legal rights and then said, 'You were arrested last night for causing criminal damage in the Accident and Emergency department at the Royal United Hospital and, earlier, resisting arrest and assaulting a police officer. However, Detective Chief Inspector Carrick isn't going to press charges with regard to that, which means he's permitted to be present.'

'I don't remember none of that,' Baker mumbled.

'How did you cut your arm?'

'As I said, on a broken bottle.'

'You remember that bit, then.'

'Yeah, that was before I went out for a few drinks.'

'When you were arrested you had over two hundred pounds in used notes in your jeans pocket. Was that wages?'

'Yeah.'

'Really?' Carrick said heavily. 'Most people get paid on Fridays.'

'Well, I do jobs and get paid by the day, don't I?'

'What kind of jobs?'

'Any jobs.'

'For which you get paid more than two hundred pounds a day?'

'No, it was, like . . . several days' money.'

'Why did you run off when I said I wanted you to answer questions?'

'Well, I panicked, didn't I?'

Lynn said, 'To the extent of dumping your car – which we've just found – in a quarry not all that far from here?'

With the unkempt hair and beard, it was almost impossible to gauge this man's facial reactions, but Carrick thought he detected a look of alarm flicker through his eyes.

'It got stolen,' Baker said after a long pause. 'Last night – after I left Ma's.'

'Where from?'

'Where I live.'

'You said when you were brought in that you're of no fixed address.'

'That's right.'

'Yet you were at your mother's house.'

'Yeah. But she won't have me living there. There's no room for me with her sister and all the kids.'

'So where *are* you living?'

'Right now, in a squat.'

'Where was your car when it was stolen?'

'Er . . . I should have said from outside the pub.'

'*Which* pub?'

'Dunno – can't remember.'

'Please explain why anyone would want to steal that wreck.'

'Well, I don't know, do I? Yobbo joyriders p'raps. Look, you don't have anything you can pin on me.'

'I agree with my client there,' said the solicitor primly.

'We have a murder victim at a country house where there was a violent burglary,' the DI continued to Baker, as though no one else had spoken. 'The PM report has just confirmed that she'd been strangled. Your car was found at a quarry where, several days previously, a man's body was discovered. He had been strangled too, and a man answering his description has been found to have been previously caught on security cameras as a member of a gang that carried out a violent robbery here in the city. We have identified him as Robin Archer, who, according to criminal records, was known as Hoodie.'

'Nothin' to do with me.'

'But you must have known of him.'

Baker shook his head. 'Nope.'

'But your mother does. She told us that he was a distant cousin on her husband's side.'

'Oh . . . right.'

'Your car will be removed from the quarry and taken to a forensic lab. Then we might know a—'

There was a knock at the door and someone said that Lynn was wanted.

'Is it about this case or another one?' she snapped.

'Another one, ma'am. He said it was very important.'

'All right. Sit in with the DCI for a while, will you.'

She left the tape running.

The 'someone else' came in and sat down.

'Oh, it's you,' said Baker.

Patrick Gillard smothered a yawn, apologized and then introduced himself. 'I actually turned up to run DCI Carrick home,' he explained. 'But as I'm not pressing charges after you took a swipe at me, I might just ask you a few questions.'

'So your role is what, other than taxi driver?' the solicitor wanted to know.

'I work for the National Crime Agency,' Gillard answered. Then, having completely ignored Baker, he said to Carrick, 'I've just had a conversation with Commander Greenway. We were making enquiries about a guy by the name of Georgio earlier. On the off-chance I contacted him and asked about cases where violent robberies have resulted in the deaths of either witnesses or residents of the properties involved. That rang a bell as chums in the Met share info with him. In most cases mentioned, victims were strangled and snouts were freaking out that a madman using the name Georgio was on the loose.'

'He might have turned up in Bath then,' Carrick mused, suspecting that a plot had been hatched by Lynn to get this arch-inquisitor on board. He felt that he ought to feel resentful at being thus sidelined but wasn't: she had probably done it on the spur of the moment because the opportunity had been too good to miss.

There was a little silence.

Gillard's gaze came to rest on Baker and he smiled happily before saying, 'I don't fancy your chances when you go back to that lot.'

'I ain't going back to any lot,' Baker retorted.

'Very sensible. What the hell had Hoodie done to deserve death? Oh, we do have a witness to the jewellery raid who said he didn't seem to know what he was supposed to be doing and then set about some poor devil sleeping rough in a shop doorway across the street. Was that his crime? Is Georgio this strangling nutter? Does he obey orders or is he out of control and kills for the hell of it?'

Carrick didn't think Baker had sufficient intellect to cope with all this, but it had the effect of making him swallow nervously.

'And then there's the lad who might have witnessed Hoodie being killed. He was strangled too, so we're working on the possibility that there's a connection. What does it feel like to be an accessory to the murder of a child?'

This hit the target. 'I weren't there!' Baker shouted.

Gillard frowned. 'How was that, then?'

'I weren't, that's all. They all went and done that. It was nothin' to do with me.'

'They?' Carrick queried.

'The – the others.'

'*What* others?'

Baker let out an explosive sigh. 'Some of my family are bad boys. They're in with a gang.'

'Like Archer, for example.'

'We didn't count him as family.'

'But he was in with the rest of the bunch.'

'S'pose so.'

'Is Georgio part of the same bunch?' Gillard asked.

The solicitor held up a hand. 'I think this aggressive questioning is highly irregular.'

'Three murders are highly irregular,' Carrick told him angrily.

'Georgio?' Gillard sweetly prompted Baker.

'Well, he ain't the boss, but all the others are shit-scared of him.'

'Who is he?'

'Dunno . . . just Georgio.'

'Who's the boss?'

'Dunno that either.'

'You don't know?' Gillard said incredulously.

'No, they won't say. Said it's more than their lives are worth to tell me.'

'So they know him, then. Is that because they go to gang meetings and you don't?'

Carrick thought this question inspired.

Baker nodded.

'Please make a vocal reply for the benefit of the recording,' the DCI requested. 'It's for your own protection.'

'Yus,' said Baker.

'Any idea where they go for these meetings?'

'No, they won't say that either. But I got the idea it's a posh kind of place.'

'Were you on that raid at the country house the other night?'

'No.'

'You're lying,' Gillard told him. 'That's where you cut your arm and DNA testing will soon confirm it.'

'That's why so much money was in your pocket,' Carrick added. 'You went through drawers and found it.'

'No, it was my wages! I told you that just now.'

'For the job.'

'Oh, all right. Yus.'

'So you *were* on the raid at the house and then they told you to disappear.'

'Er . . .'

'Same arrangement at the jewellery shop job, too?' Gillard asked. 'You provided muscle and then Georgio, or whoever, told you to sod off.'

Alarmed, Baker looked at the solicitor.

'You are permitted to answer, "no comment",' the man told him.

'No comment,' Baker said.

Gillard gave him a huge smile and said, 'Were you told to sod off after you helped dispose of Archer's body in the quarry and then they called you back for another job?'

'I keep tellin' you, I weren't there.'

'You'll probably get police bail,' Gillard went on to say uninterestedly. 'Yes?' he asked Carrick.

Carrick nodded, aware of another ruse. 'Possibly.'

No, actually, he wouldn't.

'Then what?' Gillard barked at Baker. 'What will you say to them when you go back? Sorry, I was arrested, but don't worry, mates, I ran rings round the stupid bastards? Will they believe that or get Georgio to make sure you never come to court should we eventually charge you with robbery and murder?'

The suspect squirmed in his seat. 'OK,' he then mumbled. 'I helped with the big-house job and the jewellery shop one, but honest, I really weren't there when the child was killed. Only the big boys go to meetings and that happened after the shop one. I don't know what actually happened, like. Georgio told them not to blab to *anyone*.'

Carrick charged him with two counts of robbery with violence and remanded him in custody for his own protection.

'It's James for you,' Ingrid said. 'He said your mobile was off.'

'Must have forgotten to charge it,' Patrick muttered, putting down his tea mug.

It was early in the Gillard household, seven fifteen, just before the three eldest children would be down for breakfast. Vicky, soon to start school and regarded by everyone in the family as a born saint, had gone into her grandmother's annexe and Elspeth was giving her breakfast. This happened quite often. The youngest, Mark, had just been put in his highchair by Ingrid and trusted not to drop slices of banana on the floor while his egg was boiled.

'Result!' Carrick's voice said. 'I know that Steven Baker's admitted being there, but a silver picture frame was found under the driver's seat in his car. I'm sending someone off to the Atworths' to confirm that it's theirs. It has to be, or from another similiar job, as there's a photo of an old lady in it – perhaps Atworth's mother. Just thought you'd like to be kept in the frame, too.'

Gillard thanked him and then asked if he wanted to be given a lift to anywhere.

'No, from today I have my driver. But I'll keep in touch.'

'I hope you didn't mind my input yesterday.'

'Not at all. I'll let you know if anyone else needs terrorizing.'

'That's what I call incriminating evidence,' Ingrid commented when informed of the find. 'Have any forensic results come in on the shoe you found?'

'No, not yet. Did I tell you that the other one had been found?'

'No.'

'It was in a clump of reeds on the edge of the pond. I reckon someone threw them both in after the body was dumped. God knows how they'd both come off.'

'I can imagine one of the gang taking a fancy to them and being told to forget it.'

'That sounds plausible.'

Gillard had a call to make because of a disputed insurance claim. It was in connection with someone's gardener being accused of reversing into his employer's Jaguar but denying he'd had anything to do with the damage. Hadn't he heard something like this before?

SIX

Mortimer Mansell was incensed with rage. He had never had this kind of trouble in London. These Bakers – scum – he had brought back with him were even more useless than before. Word had it – he had several informers – that not only had Archer's body been discovered in a quarry but Steven Baker, who had dumped his car in the same quarry, had been arrested. And why the hell had Georgio killed that woman at the Atworths' place? They had all worn hoods, so she would have been of no value to the police as a witness. This was the penalty, Mansell knew, of no longer overseeing jobs himself. But he daren't, not now, not now his face was quite well known in the city. If someone pulled his hood off . . . That was the problem with working in a smaller place – in the capital you could disappear if you wanted to.

The jewellery job *should* have netted around half a million pounds' worth – retail that is, not the price he would get for them – of gold items, diamond rings, bracelets and necklaces, several Rolex watches, which he had specifically asked for. But it hadn't. Mansell had worked it all out beforehand and given Georgio a list, telling him to memorize and then destroy it. The problem was he was expecting two or three dealers to visit him this evening but had only a fraction of what he had been expecting to show them. Georgio had merely shrugged and told him that they'd done their best. Mansell wasn't sure that he believed him.

Having planned to use the best living room for the dealers and wondering whether he should take the throw off the blue sofa before proudly showing what was on offer, it would now be an anticlimax. He couldn't contact them when they were on their way and never knew at exactly what time they would arrive or even who would turn up. They lived their lives like that: never predictable – they couldn't afford to be.

The haul from the Atworths' house was not as much as he

had hoped for either, and would have to be much more carefully handled. Different dealers, much lower profiles, shady, mostly from abroad and with complicated methods of getting stuff out of the country. They paid well but their shifty behaviour made Mansell himself feel nervous. If he wined and dined them well, things might not be so tense . . .

Positively the last straw was damaging the Jag. He had thought he was safe, specifying on the insurance claim that his gardener, Adams, had reversed his truck into it. Why should Mansell lose his no-claims bonus? But the old fool had denied it even though he had damaged his vehicle on other occasions trying to reverse in the drive and hit a wall. Mansell had sacked him for rudeness – he was getting too old to do the job properly anyway, and it had been a good excuse. Then the insurance company had sent someone to look at the damage to both vehicles and take photographs – Mansell had already sent one of the 'boys' to inflict a bit more on the idiot's already battered pick-up – and the company was *still* nit-picking. Now, to cap it all, they were sending another member of staff to review the case the following day.

It was time, though, to plan the next job. He had orders for certain pictures and Chinese artefacts from people who knew exactly where they were in private collections and art galleries . . .

Patrick Gillard wasn't quite sure if he was in the right place, but nevertheless glad as he headed down a narrow single-track lane somewhere in the Somerset countryside that he was driving a Range Rover. An ordinary saloon car would have grounded in more than one place in the deep ruts, and twice he had had to pull over on to the rocky verges to allow first a post office van and then a private car to come the other way. The satnav didn't seem to be too sure where he was either. But eventually he reached a wooden gate that had had the name *Rose Cottage* burned into it with a hot iron, went through it, obeyed the handwritten notice to please shut it, and rolled down an even narrower track to park in front of an old house that looked as though it had been there in the Middle Ages.

A woman emerged from the front door. Arms folded, her face creased into a frown, she didn't look particularly welcoming.

'They said someone called Gillard was coming. Is that you?' she called as he disembarked.

'Yes, good morning,' Gillard said.

'You come to browbeat my Bobby as well?'

'Indeed I have not,' he replied.

'Only we had some other bloke here a few days ago. He made out that my husband was lying. Proper upset I was about that.'

Gillard had an idea who that person was and guessed that that gentleman had been beside himself at the state of the access lane as he had an upmarket sports car. Lord only knew what make it was; Gillard wasn't remotely interested in cars, only their practical value.

'I assure you, Mrs Adams, that I'm only intent on getting to the truth,' he said. 'May I come in?'

Grudgingly, she stood aside and waved him into the cottage. He had to duck beneath a climbing rose, heavy with buds, around the door and, once within, watched where he went as the room was quite dark and very small with a lot of knick-knacks arrayed around the brick-built fireplace and on the wooden furniture. It was very cool inside – the reason, no doubt, for the small log fire in the hearth. A black-and-white cat curled up on the rug in front of the fire opened its eyes to give him a good hard stare and then went back to sleep.

'Bobby's out in the barn. I'll get him,' said Mrs Adams, going away.

Gillard gazed around. This could be a film set for a dramatic adaptation of something along the lines of *Cold Comfort Farm*. There was nothing in this room that appeared to date from after the sixties, perhaps when these two had got married. It was all very clean, though.

'He's coming,' Mrs Adams said, returning. 'You'd better sit down.'

Gillard sat on a rock-hard two-seater Chesterfield.

'You know this Mr Mansell, then?' she asked cagily.

'No. If I did I wouldn't be permitted to take the case,' Gillard replied, opening his briefcase. 'I'm seeing him tomorrow.'

'Oh.' Then, 'He's given Bobby the sack. Said he was rude to him.'

'Things do get a bit heated when there are disputes like this.' The remark sounded very trite to him, but what else could he have said?

'And the man's only going to lose his no-claims bonus – if he did it himself, that is.'

'How long had your husband been working for him?'

'Around three years, I reckon. But he was away abroad and in London for a lot of the time and hasn't been back in Bath for long. When he came back, he set about doing a lot to the garden.'

At this point, Mr Adams appeared and Gillard was immediately reminded of Geoff Hamilton of TV gardening fame. Here was a man in tune with green things that grew and everything that nurtured them. He was probably in his late sixties or early seventies and walked with a slight stoop, probably as a result of bending down to tend to plants for most of his life. The overall impression, though, was of strength, both of body and character.

Gillard got to his feet, introduced himself and offered a hand which, a little reluctantly, the man took. 'Have you always been involved with gardening?' he asked in an effort to break the ice.

'I was an assistant to the under-gardener at Stourhead at sixteen,' replied Mr Adams. 'Worked my way up and finished in charge. When I retired, I wanted to carry on but doing small jobs – keep my hand in, kind of thing – although I hadn't really been getting them dirty for years. Bath's a good place for that – plenty of folk with big gardens but no spare time.' He smiled wryly. 'Some too busy partying and making money.'

'Tell me about your job with Mr Mansell.'

'If I'm not polite about him it'll go against me, won't it?'

'No, you can say what you like to me. I'll just write down the bare details.'

'Well, he's a right bastard.'

'Bobby!' his wife whispered.

'No, Maggie. He was do this, do that, without ever a "please" or "thank you". Spoke to me like I was rubbish. I had to do all kinds of things that a labourer should have done. Putting in plants, trimming grass and hedges is one thing – that's my job

– but shovelling a lot of gravel down in the drive, getting in and taking out his bins, clearing up the mess on the patio after a party? No.'

'He's saying you reversed your truck into his Jag.'

'Well, he's a liar, too. I didn't. It's nearly always in the garage and he must have done it himself. I've got no evidence but—'

'But what?' Gillard prompted when he stopped speaking.

'You might be making trouble for yourself,' Mrs Adams warned her husband.

'I know.' The man sighed.

'Please tell me and I can use my own discretion,' Gillard urged.

Mr Adams said, 'I used to park my pick-up at the top of the lane here and carry down the tools as it's a pig to get down to the house and turn. So I didn't hear anything, but one night someone did some more damage to it – bashed it with something heavy like a sledgehammer. I'll admit that the vehicle's old and already knocked about as I have to get it to some really out-of-the-way places, but this is different.'

'I didn't notice it on the way in,' Gillard said.

'No, you wouldn't have done, sir. Since that happened, I've brought it down and put it in the barn. Only two jobs to go to now, you see.'

'May I have a look?'

Mr Adams sighed again. 'Is it worth it, though? I shall probably have to get rid of it soon anyway – go for scrap, likely – and give up doing jobs. What I'll have to pay to insure it'll probably go up if he succeeds in his claim, won't it?'

'It's a matter of principle,' Gillard said. 'But it's your decision.'

'Yes, you're right. Come with me.'

The kitchen they walked through was a study of rural home management of fifty years ago. A large pot on the old Rayburn stove was bubbling gently, wisps of steam emanating from beneath the lid. Gillard's nose told him that it was bones simmering with vegetables to make stock for soup. There was a modern refrigerator and even a microwave, both looking incongruous with the ropes of different varieties of onions hanging from hooks in a beam above. Another cat, a ginger one, sat looking out of the window, having squeezed itself between pots of crimson geraniums on the ledge.

Outside, there was a small yard – in which it was obviously very difficult to turn a vehicle that wasn't actually a pony and trap – and opposite the cottage a long, low barn. Missing slates on the roof had been replaced with sheets of corrugated iron, which Gillard knew, having lived there, was rudely referred to in Devon as 'Cornish thatch'. But it was warm and dry inside.

'It's a damned nuisance having it inside,' Mr Adams was saying. 'But if someone can bash it, they can torch it, can't they?'

'Please point out the deliberate damage,' Gillard requested, gazing at the rear of the battered vehicle.

'The corner dents are my fault,' said Mr Adams, pointing. 'That reversing lamp got broken a couple of weeks ago and that *was* at Mr Mansell's place. The rest, those big dents on the number plate, were done by someone. And I do have to point out, sir, that it recently passed its MOT.'

Gillard had already spotted the dents. Caused by reversing into another vehicle? Very unlikely, and he didn't count himself as being any kind of expert on the matter. 'D'you know how much the repairs to the Jag are going to cost?' he asked.

'Mr Mansell said it was thousands. He said if I paid him in cash, he wouldn't claim on my insurance. I got really angry then and said I'd see him in hell first, and that's when he fired me. He said I was pretty useless anyway . . .' His voice petered out sadly and then he said, 'He owes me some wages, too.'

Gillard couldn't remember ever feeling before that he wanted to give another man a hug. 'How d'you reckon he did the damage?'

'Well, if he did it at home, it was likely by reversing out of the garage he keeps the car in and forgetting the little wall round the oak tree at the end of the drive. But I can't be sure, of course.'

Gillard wondered if it was worth getting an expert in vehicle damage to take a look. It wasn't as though any possible flaw in the manufacture of either vehicle was involved. But the circumstances of this case were disturbing.

'I couldn't fault the way he planned the garden, though,'

Mr Adams added. 'I don't want to blacken the man completely. All the best trees and shrubs from the best nurseries. That part of it, planting them, was actually a great pleasure for me. But he had the wrong kind of gravel to put down in the drive. It didn't bed – it's like walking on a beach and I had to keep raking and rolling it, especially after he'd had visitors.'

'Did he have many visitors?' Gillard asked for something to say.

'I can only speak of the lighter evenings recently, you understand, as I work later then. Can't say as I liked the look of 'em, though – but I guess that's just me being old-fashioned and out of touch. At the time, I simply couldn't believe that they were *friends* of his.'

When you've been a senior army officer and then in the police you know how important it is to listen to what people say.

James Carrick wasn't too pleased with his driver. In his twenties, not long out of his probationary period, PC Alan Warren could drive a car well enough but otherwise it was like being in the company of some kind of puppet. In a word, wooden. The DCI didn't like his staff to be wooden. The possibility that the man was scared stiff of driving a DCI around didn't occur to him.

He reckoned that he was getting pretty handy with his elbow crutches, although getting in and out of cars could be a bit awkward. It had been much easier with Patrick's Range Rover. Warren at least gave him a hand if he needed it.

On this particular morning he arrived at the nick at around eight thirty with the priority of switching on his coffee machine and asking someone to find him something to eat. That was going to be another problem – people turning up at his home with ferocious punctuality to pick him up. This morning, he hadn't had any breakfast as he'd slept late, and Joanna, who would have roused him, had not been at home. *No, I won't be ratty to everyone*, he inwardly promised. *It's my fault for refusing to accept that I'm too damned old to play rugby*.

Having told Warren that he wouldn't need him until much later that day unless he phoned to indicate otherwise, he headed for his office. He supposed he could have asked to use another on the ground floor but bloody-mindedly told himself that the exercise to get up to the first floor did him good. It was depressing, then, to arrive at his destination feeling completely wiped out.

Lynn Outhwaite, perhaps having anticipated a certain degree of angst on his part, had already switched on the coffee machine and placed a forensic report on his desk. It held the results of testing on the first training shoe that Patrick had found in the quarry. The second one was still undergoing investigation. Carrick made his coffee, found the packet of biscuits he suddenly remembered was in a desk drawer and sat down, munching, to read it.

The list of minute bits and pieces found embedded in the sole of the shoe was mind-blowing, even to an experienced policeman. There was mud, traces of what was thought to be used motor oil, dog excrement, seeds (collectively described as weed seeds but further work could be done on request), greasy cooked potato (it was friskily suggested that the wearer might have trodden on a chip) and bits of grass and other plants (which again could be further investigated if necessary). The Velcro fastenings, always providing a rich harvest, had more grass (some green, some dried), fluff from any number of sources and various hairs stuck to them. The latter were mostly human (DNA testing would establish if they had belonged to the wearer), but there were also dog hairs and a few large white ones that, so far, had not been identified. If the officer in charge of the case required the animal source of these to be established, they could phone a number at the top of the report.

Carrick reached for his desk phone and did just that. He also asked if it had been possible for any DNA to be extracted from the part-eaten chocolate bar that had been found on the floor of the jeweller's shop after the raid. No, said the person to whom he spoke; there was too much dirt and bits of broken glass ground into it.

The wire tray with the paperwork in it was piled even higher with paperwork, so he groaned and made a start.

Just after lunch, a sandwich that a kind soul had fetched for him, there was a tap on his slightly open door and Patrick Gillard put his head round it. 'May I make improper use of police records?' he enquired.

'Well, you are an improper sort of cop,' Carrick replied.

Gillard came right in and sat down in one of the two spare chairs. 'Yes, but this is in connection with a case of mine.'

'You sniffed out a rotten apple, then?'

'Just someone called a bastard and a liar who might have dodgy friends. Or perhaps I'm just suffering from withdrawal symptoms.'

Carrick swivelled his computer round. 'Help yourself.'

'You might have to put in your security clearance.'

'You mean you don't have one now?'

'Dunno. I'm only a casual labourer with the NCA.'

He discovered that he did.

'What's this person's name or is it confidential?' Carrick asked after a couple of minutes had elapsed.

'Mansell. For some reason I didn't notice his first name.'

'Doesn't mean anything to me.'

It didn't mean anything to Records either. The only Mansells with criminal records were a female who was dead, a youth of seventeen and an old lady who had been convicted of shoplifting but let off with a caution. Patrick, thinking of his own slightly absent-minded mother, was of the opinion that this sort of thing should never come to court.

Although his stint at helping Carrick was, strictly speaking, at an end, Gillard trotted the latest developments in these cases past Ingrid when he got home late in the afternoon. He had come across Matthew, Katie and Justin in the kitchen busy with bread, butter and strawberry jam to keep them going before sitting down some time later for dinner at the big kitchen table. Their parents refused to countenance them eating with it on their laps in front of a television. Ingrid was in her writing room with baby Mark shunting around the floor with a wooden toy train. She didn't usually mind being disturbed.

'You're early,' she observed when she saw him.

'Shall I go away again?' he asked with a smile.

'Don't be silly.' Having shut down her Mac, she said, 'I think I heard James say that he was requesting a full guest list of those at that gala dinner the Atworths attended. Has he received it yet?'

'Pass.'

'Only I was wondering if whoever was behind the robbery at their home knew for a fact that they wouldn't be there that evening.'

Patrick scooped Mark on to his lap whereupon his son wanted to go back on the floor and was duly reunited with his train. 'Does Vicky know he's got one of her dolls in the tender?'

'I think she's donated that one to him.'

'It's a good point about the guest list. I'll mention it to James when I contact him next.'

'That journalist in the *Chronicle* is still raving that the police have got nowhere in finding Damien Baker's murderer, heavily hinting at incompetence on the part of the CID. There's even a snide remark – described as coming from someone he interviewed who wanted to remain anonymous – that Carrick having broken his leg means the investigation has come to a standstill. "Are Bath's innocent children safe?" he's asking.'

'They'll say anything to sell newspapers. By the way, that shoe I found had everything but the kitchen sink embedded in the sole.'

'I should imagine most people's have.' She was thoughtful for a few moments and then went on: 'The situation is still roughly the same, then. Setting aside the fact that he was also called Baker, there's a murdered boy, strangled, who may or may not have been surprised witnessing a murder, presumably in a house he'd climbed because he liked doing that kind of thing – his mother said so. Then there's the body of the man in the quarry who'd also been strangled and who could have been the victim of the murder Damien witnessed. Then the housekeeper was strangled at the Atworths' house. *Then* that Baker character dumped his car in the same place. If there's a connection, is he that stupid?'

'Definitely,' Patrick said.

'And you told me earlier that a silver picture frame was found in this car. Has it been confirmed as belonging to the Atworths?'

'Not yet. They've gone to the South of France to get over the shock.'

'How helpful of them. Can't they be contacted?'

'They refused to give mobile numbers or email addresses as they want to be left in peace.'

'Why do I detest these people? For goodness' sake, they could have been sent a photo of the picture frame!'

'What's for dinner?'

Ingrid hadn't finished. 'And what about this rumour from Sergeant Woods that someone described as a big cheese is bankrolling the Bakers in return for services rendered? He could be behind these crimes – big house in Bath, dealers and fences on the end of the phone.' She shrugged. 'So why can't he be found?'

Patrick also shrugged and then said he'd go and get out of his work clothes. But first he went back into the kitchen where Katie fixed him a jam butty.

Mortimer Mansell had risen a little earlier than usual as he wanted to plan his next job, something different again so there was no fixed pattern. He had hoped to be able to do it before now but hadn't been able to think straight on account of the damage to his car and everything else going wrong. He'd brought the car home after the garage had given him an estimate for repair – it was perfectly drivable – but if there was one thing he hated it was being behind the wheel of a car that had even a scratch on it. His first priority had been to speak to his rep from the insurance company and put him in the picture regarding the general incompetence of his one-time gardener. It was obvious, he would say again to this insurance person – his usual rep had been to see him already, driving a very nice red sports car, too, that Mansell thought must be new – that the old man was over the hill. This next one was due in an hour or so and it would be interesting to see what he was like. He knew his usual rep. Apparently, this other rep was being sent along because Adams was denying that he was responsible for the damage – a complete waste of everyone's time, in Mansell's view.

Another irritation, something that he was becoming more and more angry about, was that he hadn't got the prices that he'd wanted from the dealers for the fewer than expected items taken in the raid. They had sat there, on his prized sofa, shaking their heads and drawing in their breath through their teeth like a bunch of donkeys. They had colluded, he was convinced – created a ring as they no doubt did at auctions. Next time he would contact others he knew.

Mansell had been tempted to employ a butler when he moved to this house so he wouldn't have to answer the door himself. But that would have been too risky – a pair of eyes and ears that could have snooped on everything that went on. That was the last thing he wanted. So he made a point of being downstairs at around the expected time so that he didn't have to travel all the way from his office on the second floor. He was hoping that this Gillard would be punctual. He was, and the first thing he noticed was the man's mode of transport, glimpsed when he opened the door. Did an insurance dogsbody's salary run to that? Or did they get an allowance from the sky-high premiums the company charged? He began to feel even more annoyed.

'Good morning,' said his visitor, introducing himself.

Mansell stiffly returned the greeting and invited him to come up to his office where they could discuss the matter.

'Is the car here or somewhere else?' was the opening question.

'Oh, here. Would you prefer to see it first?'

'Yes, please. We've seen the estimate for repair,' he continued as they walked towards the garage. 'And, of course, it's high as Jaguars are expensive cars. But you're fully comprehensive, so why aren't you content to claim on your policy?'

'Because I don't see why I should have to pay higher premiums having lost my no-claims bonus on account of someone else's carelessness.'

The car had been driven into the garage so that the rear faced the doors.

'As you can see,' Mansell said, 'The damage is ghastly. A big dent and the boot lid no longer shuts properly so I've had to tie it down with string. It's insufferable.'

Gillard bent down to have a look. The back of the vehicle was indeed badly damaged, scratched as well as dented, but there was no hint of flakes of paint from Mr Adams's bright blue pick-up. His fellow worker of the red sports car, whom he had never met, had said in his report that in his view the car had been rammed into by another vehicle. Probably not true.

'Has anyone else been driving this?' he asked, straightening up.

'No, of course not! No one drives it but me.'

'Did you witness what happened?'

'No, I just heard the crash. The car was parked outside the doors here and Adams was on his way home. As I said to the other man from your outfit, I gave him the sack there and then as he flatly refused to accept responsibility and was damned rude.'

'Quite a lot of people deny responsibility,' he was calmly told. 'Now, if you don't mind, I'd like to see where you were when you heard the crash.'

This man in his expensively tailored suit was making Mansell feel very unsettled. 'I get the impression that you don't believe me,' he said angrily.

'I don't want you to think that,' was the reply. 'It's something I'm required to do, that's all.'

The only room that Mansell felt he could take him to that had a good view of where they were now was the one on the first floor – the one where he had his meetings with what he referred to as his 'scum'. He felt two eyes boring into his back all the way up the stairs.

'Here,' he said when they arrived. 'That window over there.'

He wanted to scream when the window was opened and Gillard looked out, pausing to carefully look down.

'Yes, I see,' he murmured and closed it again. 'Well, thank you, Mr Mansell. The company will be in touch in due course.'

'Aren't you going to give me some idea what the decision will be?' Mansell demanded to know.

'No, I'm afraid I can't discuss it with you, and the decision won't be mine anyway. And because Mr Adams is still vehemently denying that it's his fault I'm minded to call in an expert on vehicle bodywork damage.'

'Look, Adams hit things with that wreck of his all the time,' Mansell blustered. 'Any fool can see that – it's covered in dents. He's over the hill. Ought to retire before he kills someone.'

'There is a slight complication,' Gillard told him with a polite frown. 'Since this happened, his vehicle's been vandalized.'

'So *he* said, no doubt.'

'Even I can tell the difference between damage resulting from careless driving and blows with a sledgehammer.'

Mansell didn't argue further with this man who had a gaze that made his knees turn to jelly.

Having let him out he went back upstairs and watched as Gillard went towards his car. He then became alarmed as he observed a slight detour made to carry out a careful examination of the low wall around the oak tree. Having brushed away most of the marks on the stonework himself, Mansell was fairly sure that there was nothing to see, but the wretched man then went on to take photographs with his phone. Did insurance companies really go to these lengths? Being unable to remember having claimed for anything in the past, he was beginning to think he'd been a fool to assume otherwise.

I don't like feeling a fool, he thought, almost grinding his teeth in his fury. What had started out as a whim to show Adams who was boss – he had been hoping the man would beg to get his job back, in which case he would have acceded – was beginning to be more nuisance than it was worth.

He resolved to try to discover where this insurance dogsbody lived.

SEVEN

'Really?' Carrick exclaimed. 'Are you sure?'

It was just after seven the next morning and Lynn Outhwaite had phoned to tell him that PC Alan Warren, his driver, who had been on his way back to Bristol, had had his squad car deliberately rammed into by a motorist who was being pursued by other police, a man suspected of being involved in a housebreaking. Warren was in hospital with a broken arm and suspected concussion.

'Is he in real danger?' Carrick asked after she'd told him the news.

'I don't think so, guv, but he's being kept in for observation as he was rather knocked about.'

'I'll go and see him as soon as I can.'

'Shall I find someone to come and collect you?'

'No, we can't spare people. I'll get a taxi.'

Joanna found him slumped gloomily at the table in their old farmhouse kitchen. 'Is that tea cold?' she asked, always one to give practicalities priority.

'Probably,' he muttered and related the news.

'I can take you on my way in – I'm not due to start until ten.'

'Frome happens to be in the opposite direction to Bath from here.'

'So I'm just being helpful,' she retorted, and switched on the kettle to make another brew.

'Sorry, Jo. But I'm going to raise hell – again.'

'Make sure it's with the right people,' she warned, aware that once the wild Scot in him was unleashed, just about anything could happen.

Later, sitting at his desk at work, he discovered that PC Warren would be kept in hospital for at least another twenty-four hours. The medics were carrying out further tests as there was concern about possible internal injuries. Common sense told him that the man would then need a few days' sick leave, never mind not be able to do any driving. Raising hell had to be temporarily delayed, though, as he had to conduct a debriefing on another case, then interview someone with a grievance and, another priority, finish writing a report that should have been delivered the previous week. After all this had been attended to, he got on the phone to HQ. Pointing out, politely, that if he didn't get more support, there was a risk that he'd end up having to go on indefinite sick leave suffering from stress appeared to rattle the bars of the cage of a super he'd never heard of. He was promised a driver while it was deemed necessary.

He wondered if he ought to interview Steven Baker again, the only confirmed link with the raids on the jeweller's and the Atworths' home. He had now received the full inventory of items stolen from the former, and it was all high-end merchandise with a retail value of about half a million pounds, including diamond rings and bracelets, other gold jewellery and Rolex watches. Just a few items of lower value were missing, and there was the suspicion that the gang had quietly put a few things in their pockets. Perhaps the rumour was correct and there was a big cheese behind it, although whether he, or she, had a screw loose was another matter. Whoever it was, he or she was certainly discerning and/or had a ready market for the goods.

He was organizing coffee for himself when Lynn looked in and said, 'I've just been told that a woman's gone into the One Stop Shop and said that she's been away on holiday, but before she went she was certain that she spotted Damien Baker one night. She can't remember exactly which night it was, but he was somewhere near the bottom of Brassknocker Hill. Asked how she could be so sure it was him she said that although he couldn't really be described as disabled – apparently, she lives on the same estate so was familiar with the lad – he had a distinctive way of walking so it's highly unlikely it was anyone else. Shall I send someone along to talk to her? She said she was going straight home.'

'Please do,' Carrick replied. 'Coffee?'

'Thanks, I've got one.'

The day dragged by as the DCI submerged himself in outreach programmes, diversity questionnaires and training schedules.

Both his legs ached. When he got to a booklet entitled *How Green Is Your Nick?* he hurled it into the farthest corner of the room and, as fast as was possible right now, stormed out. Not for the first time recently he then beheld his wife coming towards him.

'Reporting for duty, sir,' she said.

'Funny, ha-ha,' Carrick growled.

'No, seriously, I'm your new driver.'

'You are? That's wonderful!'

'I think it's someone's idea of a joke. But not everyone knows we're married.'

Like Ingrid, she had kept her maiden name, Mackenzie, so this was perfectly possible, even though Carrick was listed as her next of kin.

He said, 'But you can't just sit around waiting to take me places.'

'No, of course not. But you're a CID bod short, aren't you? I'm volunteering. Look, I'm only here on a temporary basis.'

'It means all your shift patterns will have to be changed.'

'James, you're the DCI. Fix.'

Lynn appeared and Carrick explained the latest development.

'I heard a rumour that you assaulted the DS who took over your job when you left the police,' the DI said to the new arrival.

'Yes, ma'am, I punched him on the nose.'

'I'd like to know why.'

'I was working as a private investigator and one of my clients was murdered so the police had to be involved. The DS made inappropriate remarks.'

'Sexist, you mean.'

'Yes, he'd already asked me if sir here was a good screw and then followed it up by telling me where he was if I fancied a quick one.'

Carrick felt the warmth climb to his face but kept quiet.

With her boss's permission, Lynn then asked Joanna to go and interview the woman who had reported seeing Damien as she simply didn't have anyone else free. Outside the door, she lost her battle with laughter and cackled all the way back to her desk.

'Off you go, then,' Carrick, straight-faced, said to his wife.

'I told him sir was fantastic, better than him even if he got a new set of everything in the charity shop he was found in,' she said with a smile and briskly walked off.

Mrs Stanton not only lived on the same estate as had Damien, but her house was virtually opposite. The woman, probably in her fifties, answered the door, expertly fielding a small terrier of some kind as she did so.

'Come in,' she called from somewhere within having taken her wriggling armful away and shut it in a room. 'Sorry about that,' she said returning. 'She will run and jump all over people at the door, and not everyone welcomes that.' She ushered Joanna into a front room. 'Do sit down. Someone said you were coming.'

Joanna produced her warrant card. 'CID have borrowed me for a little while,' she explained.

'I had a horrible feeling about Damien as soon as I moved here,' Mrs Stanton began without being prompted. 'I mean, his mother was hardly ever at home, especially at night, and I think he had to fend for himself. He was a strange lad, would say hello if you spoke to him first but not otherwise. Yes, I worried about him. He seemed so vulnerable somehow – but you can't interfere.'

'I understand that he used to go wandering around at night.'

'That's what Mr Tonkin next door told me soon after I moved in. He sometimes works nights so is around then. He said he actually saw him in the city centre one night, just walking down Union Street.'

'Can you remember exactly when it was that you saw him?'

'Yes, I've had a good think. It was the night before the morning I went on holiday. I sometimes work night shifts, too – in a care home quite close to here. I'll get my diary and tell you the exact date . . .' She went from the room.

'Would you like some tea?' she called.

'Only if you're having one too,' Joanna replied.

The room was comfortably furnished in a somewhat dated style but she noticed that there were no recent family photographs, just an old black-and-white one of a couple on their wedding day – her parents perhaps. The reproduction furniture might have belonged to them too, as perhaps had the floral china plates on the walls. In a way, it was a sad room. Memories.

A few minutes later, in receipt of a mug of tea and the information she wanted, which she had made a note of, Joanna said, 'So you saw him walking along the A36, the Warminster Road at the bottom of Brassknocker Hill, at what time?'

'It must have been at around nine thirty. I was on my way back from work. And there he was, loping along as though he had somewhere to go. But I don't know whether he went up the hill, of course.'

'He wasn't just wandering along then but walking as though he had a plan or destination in mind.'

'That's right.'

'Was he carrying anything?'

'Not that I noticed.'

After a further short chat with Mrs Stanton, mostly about the weather and Bath City Council's total uselessness at sorting out the traffic problems, Joanna left. She didn't go straight back to the nick as James wouldn't need to go home yet, but drove along the Warminster Road and, turning into Brassknocker Hill, found a place to park and went for a walk.

Ingrid was proofreading her soon-to-be-published previous novel. She had come to the conclusion years previously that although no doubt dripping with degrees in English and all qualifications necessary for working in publishing, her editor didn't necessarily know about what Matthew and Katie would call 'stuff'. In the past, she had crossed out her perfectly correct 'staging' in reference to the interior of a greenhouse and inserted 'shelves'. Now, something had been queried that had already been explained in the previous but one paragraph.

'I hate you!' she said out loud.

'Sticking pins in effigies again?' said a voice she recognized.

'Hi,' she called.

Patrick, just returned from work, came in but, in receipt of a look from his wife, didn't drop everything he was carrying on to a small armchair. Going away for a few moments, he deposited his car keys, mobile phone, bulging briefcase, jacket, a paper file, laptop and newspaper in the hall.

'James has received the guest list for the gala dinner,' he said when he came back.

'Any interesting persons thereon?'

'I'm not sure. Your cat's whiskers would be doing their thing right now, but we have to be careful – or rather James has.'

'And?' she said hopefully. This was a reference to the intuition she sometimes had about people and situations.

'I went to see someone who's claiming on his gardener's insurance because he maintains that the man reversed his truck into his car. The gardener is insisting that he didn't and that his one-time employer was a real bastard and had dodgy friends. This character's name is on the guest list.'

'Even my cat's whiskers would be a bit cautious with that one,' Ingrid told him.

'I agree, it's more than fragile. Another thing is that Joanna has been temporarily assigned to be James's driver and she's giving a hand generally in between. Lynn asked her to interview a woman who had reported seeing the murdered boy near the bottom of Brassknocker Hill one night. That's been presumed to be the night he died as his body was found the next morning. This character we're talking about lives there.'

'Umm. Quite a lot of houses in that area.'

'Not only that, after she'd spoken to her, Joanna sniffed out a possible lead and went for a walk up the hill until it peters out into mostly countryside and then came back on the other side of the road. Nothing stirred really, except that she noticed a woman inside a shrub who appeared to be looking for something and stared at her in hostile fashion, and a man leaning out of an upper window of a house cutting the creeper off the wall below it as far as he could reach. She noted the name of the house and that's the one I went to in connection with the claim.'

'It's still called circumstantial evidence.'

'There's more. When I was there I asked if I could look out of the window as this man said he had done just after he heard the crash when the gardener reversed into his car. I did happen to notice that the ivy just below the window frame had been torn off in places.'

'You're thinking that Damien had climbed up and been thrown or fallen off.'

'It's possible.'

'It still wouldn't hold up in court.'

'There's another little bit. Among all the stuff on the shoe belonging to Steven Baker that I found in the quarry were a few large white hairs. They're not from a dog and tests are ongoing. On the floor of the room I was taken to, there was a polar bearskin rug.'

'What, a real one?'

'Looked like it.'

'He is a bastard, then.' She tidied her desk and then glanced up. 'Your case still wouldn't hang anyone.'

'I know. Where are the kids?'

'Carrie's taken the three youngest to an after-school birthday party in the village hall. They should be back at any minute. Katie asked Matthew to go with her to check on the horses as she had a bag of carrots to take and it was quite heavy. I didn't like them going on foot as the road is so narrow and was going to drive them, but Elspeth volunteered. They should be back soon, too.'

Patrick's horse and Katie's Exmoor pony were kept at livery stables locally.

'And now I have to cook dinner for seven as Elspeth's eating with us tonight and it's later than I thought!' Ingrid exclaimed after a quick look at her watch.

'I'll give you a hand,' Patrick offered.

'OK, a very large risotto with leftover chicken plus anything I can find in the fridge that is *remotely* suitable,' she said as she fled from her writing room.

The extensive recreation ground by the side of the River Avon in the centre of the city, home of Bath Rugby Club, brings a rural ambience to the urban Regency buildings but actually represents a flood plain. Situated quite close to Pulteney Bridge and the weir on the river it seems to stretch as far as the eye can see. A wide waterside footpath that borders it makes for pleasant summertime strolling and is a favourite place for both residents and visitors. This morning though, with a thin mist swirling through the arches of the bridge, bringing with it a light but chilly drizzle, it wasn't really a place to linger. It was a little after seven a.m.

Sam Whittle had been going for his early-morning walk for years – 'taking the air', as he laughingly referred to it – and gloomy weather wasn't going to stop him. He had walked in heavy rain, thick fog (care needed here even with railings on the riverbank), ice and, once, a blizzard. Being outside was, for him, being alive. Even in the middle of the city there was wildlife to be seen if one was quiet: foxes, waterbirds and, on one occasion, a badger. He liked the smell of rivers too – that wet earthy scent with a hint of crushed reeds and water plants.

It wasn't sufficiently light yet for the lamps lining the footpath to have gone out which meant that the woman's bare leg protruding from beneath an evergreen shrub of some kind looked almost white in the illumination. Sam immediately thought of hoaxes and student pranks, and almost went right by without investigating. But, after hesitating, he pushed aside the greenery for a closer look.

She was dead all right.

'Do we know who she was yet?' Carrick asked. He had just arrived for work.

'No, guv,' Lynn said. She always seemed to be in before him, however early he turned up. 'She was naked; nothing to go on from an identification point of view other than a small tattoo of a bird on the back of her neck. She was found by a Mr Whittle. He goes for a walk along by the river every morning, early, as, of course, do quite a few other people a bit later on, so the body must have been dumped there overnight. I can't see that she was killed there as anyone could have witnessed the crime from Grand Parade overlooking the weir.'

Carrick thought that would apply to someone dumping the body as well but merely asked, 'Description?'

'Five feet five inches tall, long brown hair that was loose at the time of discovery, about twenty-two years of age. Initial findings are that she hadn't been dead for very long, between three and five hours. Signs of fairly violent sexual activity.'

'Rape, then.'

'Possibly, but that wasn't how it was worded.'

'Has anyone been reported missing?'

'No, not yet.'

'It's a priority to find out who this woman was.'

'I've asked for photographs to be taken so they can be released to the media.'

Carrick was praying that more would be learned from forensics. Otherwise, he would finish up with another criminal investigation that had come to a standstill.

Five minutes or so later, Joanna, who had dropped him outside the nick and gone off to find somewhere to park, tapped on the door and looked in. 'D'you need me for anything, sir?'

She and Carrick were keeping everything on a very professional footing, and he assumed that another person was in earshot for her to address him thus.

He gave her a naughty smile that obviously no one else could witness and said, 'No, I don't think so, thank you. You might give Lynn a hand with our new murder case. She'll explain.'

As Joanna went off down the corridor, he heard her say, 'I wonder if she was strangled.'

Lisette Hornby was identified almost immediately because her mother, nervous for her safety, phoned to report that her daughter was missing as she hadn't come home the previous night. Lisette, she said, worked as a part-time barmaid and hostess at a wine bar-cum-night club in a basement under a shop in Stall Street, and had said nothing about staying the night with friends. Close to tears, Mrs Hornby went on to say that she had always hated her working there and knew something terrible had happened to her.

After recent events Carrick felt that he really couldn't ask Lynn to be closely involved with yet more death by sending her to tell the woman that her worst fears might have been realized. He would go himself. Notwithstanding that it was his normal practice to take a female officer with him on such occasions, he asked his driver to accompany him into the house. This was situated in a tiny mews off the lower end of Bathwick Hill, the terraced cottage seemingly squeezed between a picture-framers and another larger house, the front of which was almost completely hidden by creepers.

'Mrs Hornby?' Joanna enquired when a middle-aged woman answered her ring at the door.

Wordlessly, she opened the door wide and they entered, Carrick apologizing for his temporary awkwardness.

'You have come to tell me something terrible,' Mrs Hornby said with a strong French accent.

'Not necessarily,' Carrick told her. 'There's been no identification yet, but a young woman's body has been found in the city centre. I must point out that it might not be your daughter but—'

'You want me to come and see her?' the woman cried. 'I will come. I must *know*.'

'May we sit down for a few minutes?' Joanna ask quietly.

'Yes, sit. I am rude with being upset.' She took a deep breath. 'I should make you coffee.'

'Would you like me to do it?' Joanna offered.

'Can you make proper coffee?'

'She can,' Carrick said.

When Mrs Hornby had returned, Joanna having been shown where everything was, she said, 'I didn't want her to take the job. She is having what I think is called a year out from university. Since my husband died she has been living with me as it is just right for her at the moment. But if only she could travel the world – I can't afford to help her with that and I'm not very well so she decided to stay with mother. I love her for that. And now . . .' Tears threatened.

'Do you have a recent photograph of her?' Carrick requested.

'I look.' She went away again.

Carrick gazed around the room. There were a lot of photographs on a sideboard, some of a man in British Army uniform, several of a baby at various early stages, a couple of large groups, perhaps taken at conferences or symposiums.

Mrs Hornby returned and handed over an A5-sized envelope. 'She was at a friend's wedding and had these printed for me as I don't have a computer.'

The DCI only had Lynn Outhwaite's description of the murder victim, but indeed the bridesmaid standing with the bride and groom in one of the photos looked as though she was of medium height and her brunette hair was styled in what Joanna had once told him was called an 'up-do', twined with narrow pink ribbons and tiny matching roses. She was very pretty.

'May I have this one for a while?' Carrick asked, holding it out.

'Of course.' She frowned darkly and then muttered, 'It's the boyfriend – I know it's the boyfriend. She was going to leave him. He didn't like it.'

'What was his name?'

'Georgio someone or other. I never met him. I think she thought I wouldn't approve. I didn't because I knew he didn't make her happy.' She fixed Carrick with a hard stare. 'When can I see her?'

He promised to arrange it, and later that day Mrs Hornby was taken to the mortuary where, weeping, she identified her daughter's body.

Lisette had been strangled. The body was so bruised it was clear she had suffered a savage and sustained assault before being killed. The manager of the establishment where she had worked, the nightclub, which to Lynn Outhwaite's certain knowledge – and she had double-checked – had never given the police any cause for concern, was on the premises when the DI called in.

'How long had she been working here?' Lynn asked him. She had taken Joanna with her. Her thinking on this had been that if the woman was running the DCI around she could also drive the DI when she wasn't otherwise required. There might have been a small degree of waspishness in this decision, but she couldn't fault the professional behaviour of the two. Her plan had immediately fallen foul of practicalities when Joanna had pointed out that it was actually quicker to walk and asked if she could come along anyway.

The manager, who had introduced himself as Tony d'Artanonne – Lynn wondered if it was his real name as he had a strong Estuary accent – was about fifty years of age, dark-haired, and wearing a tracksuit. He had, he had told them, just come back from the gym. They went into his office, which seemed to be little more than a place to put broken and unwanted furrniture and store disposables; a vast pile of boxes of what might have been toilet rolls threatening to avalanche on to the floor.

'Only for a few weeks,' d'Artanonne replied in response to the question. 'She was a student. Look, this is dreadful. She was a good kid. I kept an eye on her, made sure she wasn't bothered by the customers.'

'She had a boyfriend by the name of Georgio,' Lynn told him.

'Oh, *him.*'

'You know him?'

'*Of* him. I stuck my nose in and told her she was mad, but you know what it's like with these youngsters – never listen.'

'Who is he?'

'Trouble. He's been barred from nearly all the pubs in Bath – at this end of the city anyway. Always ready to pick a fight.'

'But do you know his *name*?'

'No, it's best not to.'

'We *can* carry on with this conversation down at the nick.'

The man did the male equivalent of freaking out. 'No! It's true! I really don't know who he is. All I know is that he was making her life miserable, not actually stalking her but always in her life, waiting for her outside after work to escort her home – or so he said.'

'Who did he say that to?'

'Another girl who works in the club. I can't remember who.'

'Can you describe him?'

'I only saw him once and it was dark.'

'The street lights are pretty good here, though. What did he look like?'

The manager looked sullen.

'Please *think*.'

After several moments, he said, 'I suppose he's a bit taller than me, fair-haired but it might be bleached as it's dark at the roots, medium weight but broad across the shoulders as though he does weight training.'

'Did Lisette ever mention where he works?'

'No. He's the sort that might not.'

Lynn could never understand why young women would countenance, for one second, such men.

Joanna said, 'You must have been quite close to him if you saw that his hair was growing out dark at the roots.'

'Er . . . no, not really.'

Suddenly, Lynn realized why her boss so valued this young woman's professional ability, never mind anything else. She was looking at d'Artanonne as though, if she could, she'd take him down the nearest dark alley and batter his brains out.

'OK, OK,' he said hurriedly. 'I spoke to him one night – just the one occasion, you understand. He asked me if anyone I knew, any of my customers, in his words, "bought stuff". I told him no, of course not. I knew he meant stolen property. Then he said that if I did know someone, there'd be something in it for me. I told him again that I didn't. He muttered, "Think about it," and slouched off to where he'd been waiting for Lisette.'

'Did you tell her about this?' Lynn asked.

'No. I didn't think it was any of my business.'

'But surely Lisette's safety was!'

He just shrugged.

Joanna wasn't about to let it drop and said, 'I really, really want you to tell me if you did in fact point this man in the direction of anyone. I have to tell you that he's a suspect in her murder.'

Again, he shrugged.

Joanna turned to Lynn. 'Nick him on suspicion, ma'am?'

'All right!' the man yelped. 'I'll tell you! There's a guy who sometimes drops in at about eleven at night. Someone whispered to me that he was dodgy, connected with crime, but they didn't know what. Then the barman, Karl, mentioned that he'd heard he was a fence. When this bloke and Georgio were both around one night, I gave him the nod. That's all, nothing else. What happened after that, I couldn't tell you.'

'How much did Georgio give you?' Lynn wanted to know, glad that she hadn't come on her own as this man now had the demeanour of a hunted animal.

'No money.'

'What, then? A hot tip for the three thirty?'

'Nothing like that.'

'*What?*'

Joanna moved over to a position by the door and stood with arms crossed.

'Just some spoons,' d'Artanonne muttered, eyeing her. And when both women carried on glowering at him, added, 'Little ones in a box. They're not shiny though, so most likely they're rubbish. I almost threw them away.'

'Where are they now?' Joanna enquired.

'Here, in my desk.'

He tossed a large and sagging plastic bag containing metal coat hangers into a corner with a crash, opened the top drawer of a flatpack something or other that hardly earned the description 'furniture' and handed over a small box.

'Hallmarked coffee spoons,' Lynn said, having put on a pair of nitrile gloves, opened the box and taken one out to look at the reverse. And to d'Artanonne, 'In other words, solid silver.'

'But they're black!'

'That's because they need cleaning!' Joanna snorted.

Lynn arrested him on suspicion of handling stolen property.

'I want this man found!' James Carrick raged when Lynn reported to him a little later. 'Where is he hiding out? Come to that, where the hell's the rest of the gang?'

There was a tap at the door and a constable entered.

'If that's more rubbish I have to read you can take it away again,' Carrick told him darkly.

'It's a forensic report, sir.'

'OK. Give it to the DI.'

She glanced through its two pages, then said, 'In a nutshell, the human hairs found on Robin Archer's trainer were his and the white hairs were from a polar bear.'

'What! When on earth was he last in polar regions?'

'Rug?' she suggested politely.

EIGHT

By dint of exerting patience and charm, Patrick Gillard had arranged, at short notice, for a vehicle damage expert from Bristol to look at Mortimer Mansell's Jaguar and the other vehicle in question. When asked for an interim verbal report, the man had said he thought the car had been reversed into a stone wall, possibly the one in the driveway of the property. Samples from the scratches and dents on both vehicles had been taken for analysis. He had added, with an Irish lilt of humour in his voice, that stone walls didn't normally run into the backs of vehicles. The gentleman whose car it was, he had gone on to say, had initially been obstructive but reluctantly agreed to the examination when told that he was hindering his own claim.

Now Gillard was in a quandary as his part in this case was done. Nothing daunted, he rang Michael Greenway who, by some miracle, was not in a meeting and free to talk.

'How important is it to the NCA to find the strangler who might have ended up here?' Patrick asked.

'If you don't mind my saying so, coming from you that's a damned silly question,' the commander snapped. 'All police forces want him brought to justice.'

Gillard had deliberately asked a damned silly question. 'Do I get the case, then – to work with the Avon and Somerset force?'

'Do they want you?'

'I'll soon find out.'

'And your reasons?'

'We have another murder case where a woman, who was the girlfriend of the man calling himself Georgio, was strangled. As I said to you the other day, he *appears* to have killed three times already.'

'I'd need a bit more convincing.'

'I *might* – and I'm being extremely careful here – have met the man running this lot in connection with my job. He's almost certainly put in a false insurance claim against his impoverished one-time gardener, saying he reversed his truck into his Jag. He didn't. This man is a gold-plated bastard.'

'Does Ingrid have any of her funny feelings about this character?'

'She's never met him and isn't going to.'

'Umm.'

'DCI Carrick's just rung me to say that one of the murder victims had polar bear hairs on a shoe that was found near the body. There's a polar bearskin rug on the floor in this man's study.'

'That wouldn't stand a snowflake's chance in court and you know it!'

'Mike, I want this man and his pet strangler behind bars!'

'I'll think about it.'

Even Gillard didn't tend to swear at commanders and merely observed a quarter of a minute's silence.

'Oh, all right! But I'll need quick results! And don't kill him!'

'I'd prefer to be paid by the NCA this time.'

The commander merely breathed out hard.

It occurred to Patrick that it might be a good idea to trot this arrangement past James Carrick before he did anything else.

The DCI seemed pleased to see him and, before Patrick could explain the reason for his presence at the nick, related Lynn's arrest of the manager of the night club where Lisette had worked. Carrick then handed over the evidence bag containing the box of silver coffee spoons, one of which had been deliberately left loose in the bag to aid identification.

'Probably from the Atworth job, or one similar,' Gillard commented. 'New ones from a jewellery heist wouldn't have been tarnished like this. These haven't been cleaned for years.'

'Joanna had gone along with Lynn,' Carrick went on. 'Which was just as well as she didn't like the way things were developing with this man.'

'Those two and Ingrid once pulverized a twenty-stone yob who resisted arrest and attacked them,' Gillard recollected with a laugh. 'He couldn't wait to be taken into custody when they'd finished with him.'

'Don't remind me. I thought Joanna was going to be done for assault. She wasn't even in the job then.'

'I've just been talking to Greenway. I asked him if I could carry on giving you a hand with your murder and robbery cases – which might all be connected, of course.'

There was quite a long silence.

'This Mansell character, who, as you know is involved in a case of mine,' Gillard continued, 'is what Matthew would call a disease.'

'That doesn't mean you can hang crimes on him,' Carrick pointed out infuriatingly.

'And I told Greenway that I'd prefer to be paid by the NCA this time,' said Gillard. He hadn't reached the rank of lieutenant colonel by throwing things at people who argued with him.

'Sorry, but I think the first claim with us is still grinding through the system.' Another silence, a shorter one this time, and then Carrick said, 'Delighted.'

The proofreading completed, Ingrid cast around for something to do for a while that didn't involve reading from either a screen or paper. Her eyes were tired. OK, there were some small domestic jobs to do, although none of these were hanging heavily on her conscience.

She missed working with Patrick dreadfully. For some years they had made a good partnership, although they had come close to being killed on several occasions. This was a new phase in their lives, she kept telling herself, and she'd have to get used to it. Except that . . .

Who *was* this man Patrick suspected of being a criminal? No doubt client confidentiality would prevent him from telling her. But James might. She rang him and he did, immediately, and went on to say that he'd been curious about him after what Patrick had said and had looked up an account of the gala dinner in the local paper. Mansell, it appeared, owned a small chain of upmarket restaurants in Chelsea, Richmond and Harrogate. There was also one in Bath, in Regency Street. A spin-off outside catering company operated only in Bath.

'Patrick mentioned Brassknocker Hill, but do you know the house where he lives?' Ingrid asked.

'Yes, but I ken you shouldn't go calling on him,' Carrick replied with a chuckle.

She could hardly badger him about this and they spoke for a little longer about general things. Afterwards, she realized how depressed he was with being forced into inactivity. Dinner with him and Joanna at the Ring o' Bells might help to cheer him up. She rang him back and then booked a table for four the next evening. It briefly occurred to her that they seemed to be spending rather a lot of time in the pub . . .

Mansell, then, Ingrid mused a little later. A man with a facade of genteel respectability who lived in a big house? Paraded himself as a successful businessman of taste while heading a gang and plotting his next raid on businesses and private homes? Perhaps that was fanciful on her part, the stuff of crime fiction. She could write a book about someone like that. What Patrick had said, though, when she thought about it, did hang together.

Perhaps she'd go for a stroll up Brassknocker Hill.

The opportunity came the next day when she had to go into the city. Borrowing Carrie's car, she spent part of the afternoon buying fruit and vegetables at a farm shop, which was on the way into the city, and then went on to Sainsbury's. Then, with a slight change of plan as there were perishables in the car, she drove straight to where she thought Mansell's home might be and, after careful reconnaissance, eventually parked near the entrance of a house not far from the bottom of the hill. Ivy was growing up the wall on the side that was visible from the road. This place was a possible.

There were four cars parked in the drive, the gravel surface of which was obviously unsuitable as the vehicles had ploughed deep ruts in it. It was like a shingle beach. She couldn't take the registration numbers of the parked vehicles as they were parked sideways on to her as she crunched her way, on foot, towards the front door. At least those inside could hear visitors approaching. This proved to be true when it was opened before she had a chance to ring the bell.

'Oh,' said a man. 'We're just leavin'.' He gave her a leery smile that she didn't need at all and headed towards the parked cars.

Four more men traipsed out after him, putting up the hoods

of their sweatshirts even though it wasn't raining. None of them registered her presence.

'Mr Mansell?' Ingrid enquired of a portly man who had remained in the hallway within.

'What do you want?'

Smiling into his rudeness, she said, 'I'm interested in your house actually. It's so historic and I'm an author and write articles for a rural magazine. I was wondering if I could include yours.'

This was perfectly true: when copy was short, she did just that for Hinton Littlemoor's parish magazine, *Roundabout.*

'No. I don't give interviews.'

'I don't want to interview you; I was just wondering if I could walk round the outside and perhaps take a few photographs.'

'No. How did you know my name?'

'You were at the gala dinner. I understand that you're a local businessman.'

He came out. 'But I don't bandy my address around.'

'I was there too and chatting to Lord Atworth. He knew. Said what a lovely residence you have.'

'Is he a friend of yours, then?'

'Not at all. We were just being sociable.'

'He's not so sociable now, though, is he?' the man jeered. 'Not since his house was turned over and some of his shiny treasures stolen. Sod off.'

She left.

Ingrid and Patrick met at school, and although she had good exam results, she had only really made a name for herself because of nabbing the Head Boy. Over an unusually long hot summer, they had walked the dogs on Dartmoor, had picnics and, in dells and other hidden places, made love. Suffering a crisis of conscience one day, Patrick had asked her to marry him and, on being told that she was only fifteen, had attained a shade of paleness that, up until then, she had thought impossible.

Right now, though, he almost achieved an action replay.

'You *went* there?' he exclaimed when he had recovered from the initial shock. 'But—'

'I was curious and in absolutely no danger,' she interrupted him to say. 'I'd have outrun him easily – especially as I think he'd been drinking.'

'But had those other blokes gone by then?'

'No, but they were in their cars. Patrick—'

It was his turn to butt in. 'I hope to God you didn't give him your name.'

'Of course not!'

'It was a really stupid thing to do. You knew this man was suspect.'

They didn't say a lot more to each other before they went out.

The saloon bar of the old pub, which was now mostly a restaurant, was quiet as there was a football match on the TV in the other bar. The nights were still chilly so there were logs crackling in the inglenook fireplace.

The reaction from James Carrick to what Ingrid had done was roughly the same, but the admonishment – 'Ingrid, that wasn't at all sensible' – more polite. But as he was still a boiled-in-the-tartan cop, he added, 'Can you describe any of the men you saw leaving?'

'Not really; they all put up the hoods of their sweatshirts,' Ingrid replied. 'But the one who opened the door was about five foot ten inches tall, of medium build, broad-shouldered and had fair hair that was probably not his natural colour. I seem to remember that it looked darker at the roots.'

'Oh, God,' the DCI muttered. 'That description fits Lisette's boyfriend, Georgio.'

Somehow saying nothing, Patrick took a fierce swig of his pint of Jail Ale.

Joanna ruined this male consternation by laughing and gave Ingrid the thumbs up. Then she said, 'What you pair don't seem to realize with all your frowning and tut-tutting is that Ingrid's turned up potential evidence. Why were those men there? What was the man who answers Georgio's description doing there? Were they planning their next job? Constructive thinking, please.'

Right now, though, that was in short supply as both men buried their noses in their tankards.

* * *

The next job – if indeed, with all due police caution, those responsible were the same gang – took place at just after two a.m. two days later. Despite the fact that Carrick had introduced round-the-clock foot patrols in the main shopping and tourist areas, an international jeweller's on the corner of Milsom Street and Green Street was targeted. The method was roughly the same as on the previous city-centre raid, the gang succeeding in smashing their way through the metal grilles on the right-hand side of the main entrance of the shop with axes and sledgehammers. They failed on the other side and, in a panic as, quite by chance, an ambulance on an emergency call with blue lights and sirens raced down the street towards them, they grabbed what they could and, to the howling of various alarms, bolted.

Their getaway car had been parked halfway down Green Street, and the gang took out their frustration at being practically empty-handed – they had dropped most of what they had succeeded in grabbing – by smashing as many shop windows as they could as they ran. A man returning home from work in a nightclub had tried to run but didn't get out of their way quickly enough and was killed with one vicious blow from an axe. A couple of men heading for shift work thought of trying to stop them but, wisely, ran for their lives.

The getaway car roared away, those inside it laughing at the pathetic scramble of the doomed bartender as he had tried to escape.

Police were at the crime scene in around two minutes as the crew of a patrol car called to the same traffic accident in Walcot Street as the ambulance heard the alarms go off. They arrived at the same time as the nightworkers who had returned, one of them having taken the registration number of the getaway car. It wasn't until a little later that the body of the barman was found inside the recessed shop doorway where he had run to hide. The axe blade was still embedded in his head.

All this was deemed serious enough for senior CID officers to be informed, and Carrick's work mobile number was rung. Joanna took the call, the phone for some reason having been left on her bedside table, and she moved to rouse him. He was already awake. He thought it vital, with only a skeleton staff at the nick, to promise to go in as soon as he could.

'Phone Patrick,' he said to his wife. 'He wanted to be on board – now he is.'

Fifteen minutes later, Joanna dropped off her husband at the rectory in Hinton Littlemoor where Gillard hurried from the house and they drove off in the Range Rover. The valley where the village was situated was full of thick mist, so they proceeded carefully, not speaking after Carrick had given Gillard a quick résumé of what had occurred. The DCI remained silent when they did not take a direct route into the city centre but drove along the Warminster Road and, for a short distance, up Brassknocker Hill. But he did break his silence when they parked outside what looked, in the street lighting, to be quite a large house that could be glimpsed through the new foliage of the trees.

'Is this your Mr Mansell's place?' he enquired.

Gillard killed the lights and grunted by way of an answer, but then said, 'Do I have your authorization to do a little quiet investigating?'

'Yes, but for God's sake be careful.'

'Please stay in the car. If it comes to trouble, I'm a bit more mobile than you are.'

Which was a really tactful way of putting it.

Gillard opened Carrick's window about halfway to enable him to hear any 'trouble' and silently got out of the vehicle, leaving the driver's door just pushed to. As he already knew, the driveway was gravelled, which didn't make for a silent approach – unless one stepped through the shrubbery surrounding the front garden and then walked on to the small central lawn, that is. His main concern was triggering security lights, but so far nothing had happened, the entire place seemingly in total darkness – everywhere so dark, in fact, that it was impossible to tell if any cars were parked at the side of the house. For a couple of minutes, he stood quite still by the house wall, listening and waiting until his eyes had got used to the gloom.

Silence but for a little traffic on the main road.

If Mansell was indeed involved in crime and these violent robberies in particular, it nevertheless seemed inconceivable that the gang would come back here. Then, when he was wondering about the wisdom of going down the wide driveway, he heard a door open and close – it had squeaky hinges – somewhere in that direction. There was the crunch of footsteps on the gravel and then a car door slammed. Flattening himself back to the wall in the lee of the rampant ivy growing up it, he stayed motionless as the car was started and headlights beamed down the drive. The car, Mansell's Jaguar, passed him, and, barely pausing, turned left and accelerated towards the main road, where he was just in time, having risked breaking into a trot, to see it again turn left.

Gillard went back to the Range Rover, praying that whoever was driving – presumably Mansell – hadn't noticed it. He thought that unlikely as he had been in too much of a hurry. Following this car seemed to be too good an opportunity to miss.

'Do we find out where he's going?' he fired at Carrick as he climbed back in.

'Yes, I'll phone and say I'm following a lead,' Carrick replied, thinking that, at the speed it had been going, they'd probably lost it already.

Not so. It had been caught by a red light at roadworks some half a mile away from the junction. There were three cars behind it so Gillard wasn't too concerned that the driver of the Jag, Mansell or not, might spot them. Several cars came the other way and still they sat there. Then, after someone flashed their headlights at them, the lights changed. A couple of the cars in front turned off but the Jag kept to the main road.

'Don't tell me he's going back to that bloody quarry,' Gillard said.

Several miles farther on, that was exactly where the car in front appeared to be going, indicating right and entering the now familiar unmade road. Gillard drove by, did a U-turn, killed the lights and bumped on to the verge near where the car had gone from their sight. Carrick thought he intended to follow on foot and was about to voice his alarm at such a hazardous move when, a quarter of a minute or so later, Gillard started the car again and, without putting on any lights, followed at a distance.

'When he stops, I shall stop,' he muttered.

'I hope you've cats' eyes,' Carrick said, no louder.

Cats' eyes weren't necessary; the rear lamps of the vehicle in front were perfectly visible. It was a clear night, and although there was no moon, bright starlight and the whiteness of the quarry road ensured that they wouldn't hit a large rock or disappear into a deep one-time working at one side of it. Then, as they approached the sheds and old cottage, the twin red lights disappeared.

'He's parked!' the DCI exclaimed.

But Gillard was already pulling over behind what appeared to be a gone-wild hedge and into the lee of a leaning tree, and they came to an abrupt halt. Again silently, he got out and then turned to whisper, 'I'm not intending to undertake any stupid heroics but I must see what Mansell, if it is him, is up to. The fact that he's here at all is deeply suspect.'

'If you're not back in ten minutes, I'll call in.'

'Make it fifteen.'

Gillard moved around the tree and then stood by it, listening. There would be more difficulty here than standing by a house wall with the faint background illumination of street lighting. Beneath his feet was rough grass and other mostly dead vegetation that was tall and weedy due to the lack of daylight beneath the tree. For someone with sensation in only one foot, this was a problem, and the only safe way to walk was on the road itself and hope not to trip over any wayward rocks. He decided to risk this rather than catch his feet and fall flat on his face, the thought going through his mind, again, that, hell, he was too old for this kind of thing.

The buildings – actually, wooden sheds, discernible as darker humps against the paler piles of discarded spoil from the quarry – were only a matter of fifty yards from him now, and after more careful and – although he didn't know it – catlike steps, he could make out the vehicle they had been following. It was parked at the front of the cottage, the doorway of which had a chink of light down one edge, suggesting that the door was ajar. Pausing by the side of the first of the sheds, all of which on his previous visit had looked as though they were on the point of collapse, he waited once again. On a slight breeze coming from the direction of the cottage, now some thirty yards away, came the smell of cigarette smoke and, faintly, the sound of voices. There was no sign of any other vehicles; perhaps, he thought, they were somewhere round the back.

It was now three forty-five and there was a hint of lightness in the sky to the east. It would soon be a lot brighter. Coming to a decision, he picked his way round to the rear of the shed and from there along to the next one, expecting, at any moment, to fall down a hole in the ground or encounter a similar disaster. Nothing happened, except that he hit his head on what was probably a section of dislodged guttering. This must have loosened it further, and he froze as it fell to the ground behind him with a loud thump. But there was no break in whatever was going on inside the cottage, the voices now louder but not at a volume that enabled him to hear what was being said. Then someone started shouting, a rasping voice that he recognized as Mansell's. It was mostly obscene abuse telling whoever was within that the job had been another failure and yet another person had been murdered. The emphasis was on the former rather than the latter.

Gillard decided to stay put for another couple of minutes to see what transpired. An awesome reputation he might have had during his service days and afterwards, but he hoped he had never been what used to be called 'gung-ho'. Thinking soldiers tend to stay alive, and this one had no desire to argue with that.

The shouting went on and then Mansell, presumably having run out of expletives, roared, 'That was crap! Give me what you did manage to grab and get out! All of you! Lose yourselves! When I've thought what to do with you, I'll let you know. And no, you're not getting paid for that total, total screw-up!'

They might even kill him, was the thought that went through Gillard's mind.

Mansell might have suspected this as well as he left the building briskly, got in his car having thrown something on to the back seat, drove to where he could turn and then sped back and away, scattering stones. Gillard, mentally telling the man that he knew where he lived, was more interested in what his gang would do now. Slowly and carefully, he made his way back towards the car. There was no point in getting Carrick to call out assistance – not yet. More might be quietly discovered right now.

Virtually within touching distance of the Range Rover, he paused to listen but could hear no sound of any activity behind him. Where were their cars? Had they come with just the getaway car and left it somewhere on the main road in order to walk the rest of the way? That seemed unlikely and would be downright stupid. But these men didn't appear to be over-endowed with brains.

'God, you startled me!' Carrick whispered when he got back in the Range Rover, the interior light having, wisely, been switched off. 'Was that Mansell in the Jag?'

'Most definitely,' Gillard answered. He quickly reported what he had heard and seen. 'Your move, boss.'

'I reckon I've got grounds to arrest him,' Carrick said and found his mobile. 'I'll get him picked up when he returns home and call up support to grab this lot.' He made the arrangements and then said, 'You do realize that DCIs aren't supposed to do things like this.'

Somewhere close by, there was a loud crash, followed by another, the sound melding with that of breaking glass, and then, finally, another crash just before a protracted sliding roar as though a roof had fallen off.

'Bloody hell,' Patrick muttered and opened the car door to get out.

Almost immediately, he heard and saw that they weren't the only ones roused. A rectangle of light sprawled from the cottage as the door was flung open. He pressed himself back against the tree and peered at what was happening through the greenery. Four – no, five – men emerged and stared at the newly presented bonfire where the sheds had stood. They then appeared to panic and dashed back within, slamming and, by the sound of it, bolting the door.

'Is there a lane behind the house?' he asked, having hurried back to the car.

'No idea,' Carrick replied.

This question was soon answered as somewhere below and behind the cottage lights appeared and at least one car was started and driven away.

Both Gillard and Carrick swore.

They swore again later when it was reported that Mansell hadn't gone home.

* * *

'You're not supposed to do things like that – sir,' Lynn said, having been given an account of what had happened.

Carrick had been late for work after a dental appointment and took it from her use of the formality that she was really annoyed with him. But having had only a couple of hours' sleep, he wasn't about to get confrontational. Anyway, she was quite right.

'We have at least connected Mansell with the crime,' he countered. 'Any progress otherwise?'

'Some – and, of course, the investigation's in full swing. The getaway car was found this morning abandoned near the racecourse. They'd had a go at torching it but failed, so perhaps they were disturbed. It's being taken to the lab for forensic testing. Best or worst of all, depending on how you look at it, are fingerprints that were found on the helve of the axe that was used to kill the man they encountered. It would appear that he got in the way.'

'Any matches for them?'

'Not so far.'

'Do we have an identity for the man they killed?'

'Yes. According to a driving licence found in his wallet, he was Leonard Littleman. His sister, with whom he was living, said he had a job as a barman in a nightclub. He would have been going home from work.'

'What about the cottage?'

'I was just coming to that. There's a scenes-of-crime team still there, but, as you know, their findings, if any, will be a while coming through.'

'And the witnesses you mentioned?'

'They were a couple of men going to shift work at the postal sorting office. They've been interviewed but couldn't tell us a lot, other than that one of them took the registration number of the car they used. Needless to say, it had been stolen. The raiders, as before, wore masks, so the only lines of enquiry are the fingerprints I've just mentioned and possibly others at the crime scene. Oh, plus any DNA found there. I sent a crew out to find that lane you mentioned, and it turns out that it's a disused track that went to the farm where the quarry now is. The house was demolished a long time ago but the access lane still exists and comes out near the village of Attlebury, not far from Bradford-on-Avon. Impressions of tyre tracks found below the rear of the cottage have been taken, but what good that'll do, other than possibly connect them with the vehicle abandoned near the racecourse, I don't know.'

'Thank you, that's pretty comprehensive,' the DCI said. 'Coffee?'

After glancing at her watch, she sat down in a spare chair. 'Please. Then I must get down to Green Street again. D'you know where Patrick Gilllard is?'

'Yes, sorry, I forgot to mention it. He said he'd go and have a look at that lane. The man was trained as a tracker so might be able to tell us a bit more.'

The trained tracker, in fact, found nothing. He was very careful not to contaminate what had to be regarded part of a crime scene and noted that the police personnel on site up at the cottage had marked the area where there were a couple of footprints on the bare earth bordering the verge. Looking up, he saw that the rear wall of the house appeared to be so close to the gully with the lane at the bottom of it that it might slither into it at any moment. Indeed, there were a couple of cracks that went from the ground to a couple of feet below the roof.

He went up to speak to those above and enquired if they'd had any significant finds. The woman in charge told him that if he wanted to come any closer he'd have to don a protection suit, and actually, she was busy.

Gillard, who could have the patience of several saints when necessary, then asked, 'Were they hiding out here, d'you reckon?'

'I can't be sure of anything yet.'

'Signs of activity? Drink cans, remains of takeaways, things like that?' he persevered.

'Yes,' she answered grudgingly.

He wished her happy hunting and took himself back to the nick. There, he too was given coffee by the man in charge and they settled down to do a little brainstorming.

'There *are* grounds for arresting Mansell,' Gillard pointed out a while later, when they had been through the various ostensibly connecting cases without the DCI coming to any decisions.

Carrick fidgeted. No one had told him that his leg inside the plaster cast would itch so much. 'If he's not around, I think I'd prefer to let him brew for a little while,' he said. 'Lull him into a false sense of security.'

'As long as he doesn't plan something else in the meantime.'

'I still want some real evidence.'

Gillard knew they wouldn't get anywhere and rose to leave. 'Knitting needles,' he said as he went out of the door.

'Eh?'

'Charity shops usually have 'em – long ones.'

Carrick referred this to Lynn shortly afterwards, the enigmatic smile on Gillard's face and his remarks annoying him slightly. But the man didn't normally say anything downright stupid.

'Is your leg itching then?' she immediately asked.

'This shouldn't happen to a dog!' Mansell raged a few days later.

On top of the extremely ghastly result of his latest project – that is, almost nothing to show for it and the fact that Georgio had killed someone, again – he had just received a phone call from the insurance company to the effect that they were rejecting his claim for damage to his car. There was absolutely no evidence, a woman's voice had continued, that his one-time gardener's vehicle had caused it. Achingly polite, she had then pointed out that fraudulent claims could result in prosecution. A formal letter would follow.

'He didn't have the guts to sign it himself, but I know that bastard Gillard was behind this,' Mansell muttered. He thought of phoning back to complain but changed his mind. Perhaps he could lure the man to his home and ensure that he was mugged nearby. No, that was stupid. Far better to do it in the vicinity of the office where he worked – Mansell knew where the Bath branch of the insurance company was situated – otherwise he himself would risk being implicated. And he had gone to all the expense of staying at a hotel for a while afterwards – where he was right now, bored out of his mind – in case anyone, mainly the police, had seen him near the quarry that night. Had the gang been arrested? He had heard nothing. They were absolutely useless and he was beginning to think of going back to London. Where you could disappear.

NINE

Lynn Outhwaite knew that her boss hadn't lost heart; he was just exhausted from struggling on crutches. He shouldn't be at work at all. It was so frustrating not to be able to grab this Mansell character and ask him more than a few questions. Feeling bloody-minded, she requested, and received, a search warrant for the only address they had for the Baker family, something that she thought ought to have been done before. OK, a watch – intermittent, it had to be admitted – had been put on the place and nothing suspicious observed but . . .

This time, Doreen Baker tried to bar the way into the house, all the while shouting abuse. Lynn, who had, wisely or not, led from the front, tried to remind the woman calmly that obstructing the police was a criminal offence. But she saw the fear in her eyes, the reason for which was soon discovered when suspected stolen property was found in a plastic sack under a couple of bicycles, also removed by the police, in a shed, possibly from either of the city-centre jewellery robberies. A very old woman – apparently, Mrs Baker's mother – who also had a good selection of non-complimentary epithets, was gently assisted to her feet from an armchair by Lynn and Joanna – who had gone along to add to the back-up – and found to have been sitting on a small hoard of stolen property hidden beneath a cushion. It consisted of some old jewellery, perhaps from the Atworths' home, a small silver trophy, now dented, with *Best in Show* engraved on it, a couple of ladies' gold watches and a solitary gold cufflink. Asked afterwards why she suspected something like that, Lynn replied that part of a necklace was actually visible poking out from under the edge of the cushion.

Lynn charged the two women with handling stolen property and they were released on police bail. To the DI, they were an irrelevance in that they did not really further the investigation at all and had answered 'No comment' to all questions. Nothing else of note had been found at the house so far, but a team was still working there.

Then there was a breakthrough. Lynn didn't believe in coincidences, but the scenes-of-crime team at the quarry cottage, who were on the verge of finishing, found a diamond earring that had fallen down a gap in the rotten floorboards and this was immediately identified by the manager of the jeweller's as missing stock. He had the other earring of the pair, which had been dropped on the shop floor, to prove it. And, just as the picture frame found in Steven Baker's car would most likely tie him in with the first of these raids when the Atworths returned, this connected Mansell with the latest as he had been heard and seen going to and leaving the cottage.

'OK, see if Mansell's returned home,' Carrick said. 'If he has, do you want to question him yourself?'

'Too right,' the DI replied.

'Make sure someone like Sergeant Woods is with you. Until we get another DC we'll have to use those personnel we have. You know where I am if you want me.'

'May I take Joanna with me as well to arrest him?'

'Of course, if she isn't involved with anything else. *And* the crew of a squad car in case he has company.'

'I know she has a useful right hook,' said Lynn as she went out.

Then, having what seemed to be a good idea, Carrick rang Patrick Gillard's mobile number. 'Where are you?' he asked without preamble.

'At home, catching up on my main job,' he was told.

'We're pulling in Mansell – if he's back at home. A diamond earring identified as stolen on the latest raid was found at the quarry cottage. D'you want to be around when he's questioned?'

'I don't mind being *around*, but don't forget, I've already met him in the course of *this* job. That represents a conflict of interest, doesn't it?'

Carrick had forgotten this. 'Is Ingrid still involved with the NCA?'

'Only in the sense that she sometimes lends me a hand.'

'But does she have a warrant?'

'Just an ID. She has no powers of arrest now.'

'Please find out if she can question suspects. I really could do with her help when we succeed in getting hold of him. If it's today we have enough evidence to hold him until tomorrow morning.'

But when Patrick spoke to her Ingrid wasn't at all happy with the prospect of questioning Mansell as she also had already met him. Not only that, her family and mother-in-law had previously been targeted by local villains who were suspects in other cases so nowadays she preferred to be involved with those crimes that weren't on her own doorstep. He understood that. So be it.

As it happened, Mansell still didn't appear to be at home, and this situation continued for the next few days. Then Lynn Outhwaite, returning from another job with Sergeant Woods, whom she had again 'borrowed', made a short detour on her way back into the city and parked outside Mansell's house. Resolving to ring the doorbell – more, it must be said, so that she could write in the case file that she had than from any hope of an answer – she saw a movement behind the upper glass panels of the front door. Still within sight of Woods as she had parked right across the driveway, she beckoned urgently to him and hurried. There was a small van parked in the driveway.

Ringing the bell brought no result, so, seeing a large, black-painted iron knocker that she hadn't previously noticed, she pounded on the door with that. Moments later, it was snatched open.

'Yes?' said a short woman with one hand on the business end of a vacuum cleaner.

'Is Mr Mansell at home?' Lynn enquired.

'No, sorry.'

'D'you know where he is?'

'No again. We're just cleaners. There's three of us here.'

'I'd like to speak to you all, please.'

This she did but learned nothing. Mansell apparently didn't speak to the cleaners at all, other than to tell them to stop talking and get on with it.

Patrick Gillard nearly always left his Range Rover in Charlotte

Street car park. It was a short walk to his office from there if he cut through some of the historic narrow side roads, most just wide enough for horse-drawn carts or the Hansom cabs that had been the town and city transport when the houses were built. On this particular evening, and unusually for him, he returned the same way as on his morning journey. This was because it was quicker and he was a bit later than usual due to an end-of-week meeting to review claims that he had had no choice but to attend.

The more interesting and, in his opinion, more important investigations into police cases involving murder and the jewellery heists seemed to have come to a halt. It was true that they had arrested Steven Baker, but he was little more than hired muscle as he had nothing more to offer. Another member of the gang, Robin Archer, was dead, and what evidence the police possessed suggested that he had been even more stupid. And this character calling himself Georgio: where was he hiding out?

Turning left into Upper Borough Walls, he went a short distance before crossing the road and going under Trim Bridge, which is actually part of a house, into Queen Street. It was damp and overcast, a chilly breeze funnelling into his face down the narrow way, the only sign of human activity the lights in the Italian restaurant halfway up on the right-hand side. But, no, he couldn't take himself in there and sit down to a big serving of delicious, steaming and creamy pasta, preferably with squid and other things in it that Ingrid said made her feel quite ill even to look at. She said squid was like eating a cross between jellyfish and spiders. But God, he was hungry. And, having left home that morning in a lightweight jacket, cold.

Mansell's name had come up at the meeting. To the manager, he was no more than someone who had tried to make a false claim and been found out. Gillard had kept quiet about police suspicions about the man; it was no business of the insurance company. The MI5 part of him that still beguilingly lingered urged him to break into that house and look for—

Three men rushed at him from a recessed doorway, one lashing out with a kick aimed at the stomach. This didn't land as the intended victim, always more alert when cold and hungry, suddenly wasn't there. The second man, a foot raised to slam into someone he'd assumed would be on the ground by now, lost his balance when that also met thin air and he collided heavily with the first attacker. He tripped up the kerb and then, off balance, found himself caught and hurled several yards, hitting his head hard enough on a wall to lose consciousness.

They had worked out a Plan B beforehand and the remaining two located their target and went in together, aiming to slam punches into him. After landing a couple, one ran straight into a fist that broke his nose which fountained blood. He staggered away, screaming with pain and fright, fell over the unconscious man on the pavement and ended up in the gutter, stunning himself on the kerb. Shocked into immobility by this, the remaining man lined himself up for a flying set of knuckles that immediately sent him into oblivion.

By this time there was a small audience but Gillard ignored them and, having retrieved his briefcase from where he had dropped it, sat on the kerb, gasping for breath as he had taken a blow that winded him, and found his mobile to call his emergency NCA number. Then he took his Italian throwing knife from his jacket pocket, flicked the blade and, feeling ridiculously chuffed, told those to whom it applied and were fully conscious – that is, none of them – that they were under arrest.

'Two Bakers, one Smithson!' James Carrick exclaimed happily the next morning. 'Respectively Zak, Ben and Jez. That's just about all they'll tell us that's useful right now. Oh, and they said they'd only been after your wallet and watch.' He fixed his gaze on the reason for his upbeat mood and added, more soberly, 'You weren't meant to know who they were, though. You might even have been left half dead.'

Gillard had a couple of bruised ribs, but had dutifully taken the painkillers Ingrid had presented to him with a look that told him it was a Good Idea if he did. He took a sip from the coffee that Carrick had just given him and said, 'Or even fully dead. Were they intent on softening me up for Georgio?'

'We might even find out. But you won't be able to question them yourself.'

'To my great regret. D'you reckon those three—'

'One of whom, Jez Smithson, is in hospital with concussion and likely to stay there for another twenty-four hours.'

'Do you want me to apologize to him?'

'Keep your hair on. No, of course not. Just stating fact.'

'D'you reckon they're active members of the gang – if they're in the gang we think they are – or reserves, so to speak?'

'They're denying being part of any gang; just wanted some cash for drink. All they'd say after that was that they'd come to Bath from Bristol, which is where they usually hang out.'

'The fact that they're admitting they were intent on mugging me suggests otherwise.'

'I too had thought of that,' Carrick commented urbanely, before realizing that he was now being a bit superior. 'Now, if you'll excuse me, I want to sit in as Lynn questions the two who are fit to be interviewed here.'

Gillard had called in to the nick on his way to work. After the high of the arrest of his attackers the previous evening, his mood was now distinctly flat. They still hadn't found Mansell, the evidence they had didn't build a really watertight case against him, and the questioning of the three who had waylaid him would not be conducted by those he was confident would get results. The DCI and his team were very good cops, but right now Carrick was exhausted and the gravity of these cases was wearing him down. Patrick groaned inwardly, finished his coffee and followed the man in charge out of the room.

Zak Baker was in his early forties and thought it about time the police left him alone. Other than the fact that his jaw ached where a big bruise was emerging, this conviction was at the top of his mind right now, and he sat in the interview room glowering at the young woman who intended to question him. In his view, women had no business being cops; they should be at home looking after the kids. The fact that he had never had a proper job in his life didn't enter the equation, and he didn't wonder either where the money might come from to buy these hypothetical kids their Honey Monsters breakfast cereal. It went without saying that Zak didn't do an awful lot of thinking at all. His confidence, however, had caused him to refuse legal representation and wear a smirk on his face.

Lynn had formally opened the interview when Carrick entered, and for one heart-stopping moment Baker thought this tall man on crutches was the one he and his chums had tried to kill the previous night. But this bloke had fair hair, didn't he? Their target in the city centre had been dark.

Lynn opened the interview with, 'You're Zak Baker and you're of no fixed address. Why did you assault that man in Queen Street last night?'

'I've already said – we needed some dosh to buy a drink.'

'Yet you had just over fifty pounds on you when you were arrested. Was that as a result of having already mugged someone else?'

'No! That was money I owed someone.'

'Who?'

'Oh . . . er . . . my brother Ben. He wanted it as he said he was skint.'

'The one with the broken nose.'

The man just carried on staring at her, so Lynn reckoned that meant yes.

'You're lying,' Carrick said. 'He was arrested before he was taken to A and E and found to have just under seventy pounds on him.'

'Well, *he* was lying, wasn't he?' Baker bawled.

'Who set you up to do it? Georgio?'

'No!'

'You do know someone with that name, then,' Lynn said.

'No.'

'He's the main suspect in a murder investigation and we're fairly sure he's killed others. Bit of a serial killer, is he?'

'No idea.'

'You might find yourself charged with being an accessory to more serious crimes. Were you there when Georgio strangled Archer?'

'No!'

'And the child who might have witnessed it?'

'No!'

Carrick said, 'And then there's the business of a suspect who appears to be in overall charge. We'd already suspected him of having connections with crime and one gang in particular. After the jewellery raid on the corner of Milsom Street and Green Street, police personnel followed his car to a cottage at the disused quarry on the main road to Bradford-on-Avon. He was heard shouting at those inside. It appeared, apart from the fact that a perfectly innocent passer-by had been left dead with an axe embedded in his skull, that the job had gone very badly. So the whole lot of you screwed up, didn't you?'

'I'm not in a gang,' Zak said.

'An independent group of three, then – you and your brother Ben and Jez Smithson, with Georgio hiring you for certain little jobs. How much did he pay you to beat up that man the other night?'

'Nothing. We weren't paid. I've said that all along.'

'But didn't he give you a reason for wanting him done over?' Lynn enquired.

'No. I mean . . . Look, you're trying to trick me!'

The questioning went on, but they got no further.

Although there wasn't a permanent watch on Mansell's house, only spasmodic surveillance, he hadn't been seen to leave his home. It wasn't difficult, Patrick Gillard thought, to come to the conclusion that, unbeknown to the cleaners, Mansell had gone to ground in his own house. In an attic? Were there cellars? Or was he merely not answering the door? Gillard decided that it was time the softly-softly approach or war of nerves, whichever way you looked at it, was abandoned and he himself wore his NCA hat. It being Saturday, he drove over there and having shopped for a few things for Ingrid at a supermarket, parked outside the house on Brassknocker Hill and rang the doorbell.

Part of the lack of evidence problem was that although Ingrid had seen men emerging from this house, including one that fitted the description of the one calling himself Georgio – he was the exception as he was the chief suspect in a murder case, as well – there was no proof that those particular individuals were connected with crime or crimes. They might merely have been labourers being briefed for a job. Along with other people Gillard didn't think so and the whole situation was getting extremely frustrating, watches on railway and bus stations having so far yielded nothing.

But Mansell was different. He and Carrick had seen and heard him at the quarry.

Although he could hear the bell ringing somewhere within, no one came. Right, it would have to be a covert operation – definitely not fuelled by what had happened to him personally, even though Mansell might not have been behind it. He had already noted that the house wasn't overlooked by neighbouring properties as the gardens here were surrounded by mature trees, some of them conifers, and there didn't seem to be any security cameras either, which was surprising. He relied on a one-time colleague, Terry Meadows, who now had a security company that also supplied armed guards for merchant shipping, to keep him abreast of information on the latest gizmos. But having slowly gone down the side of the house and round to the rear looking out for small and therefore difficult-to-see state-of-the-art surveillance equipment, there appeared to be nothing.

The place had been built, he thought, in the Regency period – the late eighteenth and early nineteenth centuries. Bath had become fashionable and enjoyed a building boom during that time, houses and mansions constructed of the honey-coloured local stone. Those who owned quarries had made a fortune burrowing ever more extensively under the growing city which, in modern times, led to collapsing roads and subsidence to houses. This had required some very expensive remedial work.

At the rear, there was a large conservatory, perhaps a Victorian addition. It was in very poor condition, and although it appeared to contain the conventional sort of cane furniture, there were no plants. He looked in and saw that everything appeared to be unused and a bit dusty. Mr Adams, Mansell's former gardener, had mentioned a patio that he had had to clear after social gatherings, and it was here, in front of the conservatory. A wide lawn extended to a yew hedge that may or may not mark the boundary of the garden; the former needing cutting. Mansell hadn't yet got another gardener, then. Gillard took this all in at a glance and then returned his attention to the house. He couldn't see any cameras at all, not even tiny ones.

Walking around the entire property – the garden on the opposite side of the house to the drive was narrow and shady, planted mostly with ferns – yielded no evidence of an alarm system either, so perhaps, he surmised, they were all indoors. Having had no intention of creeping about at night with a torch like a common thief, he looked for places of potential easy entry. Who knew what was happening within? Mansell might have had a heart attack in there. Or a stroke. Or – and this with only a trace of black humour – Georgio might have strangled him after the bollocking he had given them at the quarry cottage.

The next problem was the possible presence of an internal alarm system; he couldn't believe there wasn't one. Increasingly these days, most systems were too sophisticated for his small but very handy 'knackering' device. A squaddie had given it to him when he left the army and got a job at a security company. It was designed to silence alarm systems that had gone haywire. This had been a weird thank-you – had he thought his senior officer was about to turn himself into a house-breaker? – for Gillard who had got him out of serious trouble for some misdemeanour or other – he had forgotten exactly what.

The outer conservatory door had an old-fashioned lock that had probably been in situ since new and the key wasn't on the inside. He had a set of what Ingrid called his 'burglar's keys' that would open this but, having donned a pair of nitrile gloves, he discovered that it had been left unlocked. Silently, he went in, very mindful that this might be what he, or anyone else, was expected to do. A quick look round told him that there were no intruder detectors. He turned his attention to the inner, modern, double-glazed French doors, the curtains on the other side of which were drawn. When he carefully tried the handle of one, he discovered that these were also unlocked. He opened the door. No alarms went off.

Perhaps being married to Ingrid had given him some of her 'cat's whiskers' intuition because *something* was screaming caution at him right now. The room within, possibly a large dining or withdrawing room in the days when the house was built, looked as though it was never used, with chairs and a table pushed against a wall, leaving the centre of the room empty. A massive sideboard was on another wall. The heavy curtains being closed made it dim so he slid one open a little, freezing when the rings it was hanging on clattered on the metal pole. But nothing happened.

Silence.

There were movement detectors, but if the tiny red lights in them were making contact with a central control unit he couldn't hear any alarms being triggered. Slowly, he crossed to a door on the other side of the room, one of two which were around eight feet apart, and opened it. It was a very large cupboard. He tried the other one. Beyond was a wide passageway with daylight coming through open doorways on both sides. Straight ahead, the passage appeared to widen out into a larger area – the entrance hall perhaps. He silently headed towards it, caution causing him to draw his Glock. The side rooms, with the exception of two, appeared to be used only for storage. What was inside all those cardboard boxes, he wondered, itching to have a look. But not now. Of the other two rooms, one gave every impression of being a large kitchen with further rooms off; the other, smaller, was being used as a general dumping place for coats, hats and shoes. There was a huge fitted cupboard along one wall; one of its double doors was ajar, seemingly because of the pressure of what was inside. He went over to it, didn't touch anything as he feared an avalanche, just peered around the slightly open door. All he could make out were box files, cardboard boxes and folded fabrics – curtains and towels perhaps.

When he reached the wider area, he saw that it was indeed the entrance hall, and the first thing he noticed was a set of muddy footprints on the black-and-white tiled floor. It looked as though someone had entered through the front door, which was to the right. The traces of mud petered out a few steps up the stairs. Carefully, not going too close, Gillard bent down and scrutinized them. Something wasn't quite right.

Mentally noting this, he headed up the stairs, walking close to the bannisters on the right-hand side. How many times had he done this sort of thing during army and MI5 training sessions in the past? Then, there might have been trip wires, electrically live door handles, concealed assailants waiting to ambush, even cold-water drenchings to make trainees lose concentration. Not to mention snipers armed with live ammunition. And the training officers with a fine line in well-tuned abuse.

'Is anyone there?' a weak voice called.

The skin on the back of his neck tingling with shock, Gillard nevertheless didn't go rushing up to where he thought the voice might have come from. He had been taught the hard way about that, too. He did not respond and carried on with his surreptitious ascent, pausing on the first-floor landing. This was where Mansell had brought him when he called round about the insurance claim – the room with a door to the right of him now. It was closed. Another door further down the landing was ajar. Then he heard a slight sound coming from within, perhaps a groan or a deep sigh. Going over, he pushed the door right back and looked in.

An elderly man lay on the floor, moving just a little, restlessly, blood on his head and face. Straight ahead of Gillard, a body was slumped on a blue sofa. Identification was almost impossible as most of the face was just a jumble of blood, teeth and bone, an avalanche of more of the same down the front of the corpse. But who else could it be but Mansell? A bloodstained long-handled spade – Gillard recognized it as a Devon shovel – lay on the carpet.

Rapidly checking the room for anyone else, Gillard holstered the Glock and went over to the old man.

'Mr Adams?' he said quietly. He appeared to be unconscious now.

The pale blue eyes opened. 'I didn't do it,' he whispered. 'Oh, it's you, sir – the insurance man. Please tell them I didn't do it.'

Having just entered the room and observed the murder victim, Carrick swore very quietly and then said, 'I'm not going to ask you why you were here, and if anyone asks me I'll tell them that the deceased was a client of yours and you'd called round on an insurance matter. I'll then remind them that the law permits anyone to break into a premises if they think there is danger to life or limb with regard to those inside.'

He had been speaking crisply and in the manner of an Elder of the Kirk delivering the sermon as the minister had just been arrested for drink-driving, so, just then, Gillard merely thanked him.

'And you reckon this was Mortimer Mansell?' Carrick went on to say, gesturing to the corpse.

'As far as identification's possible, yes.'

Mr Adams had just been taken to hospital, the sound of the siren still audible in the distance as the driver fought their way through the city's traffic. Waiting scenes-of-crime people had followed the DCI in and now started work. A pathologist was expected at any moment.

'What the *hell* happened here?' Carrick burst out. 'Can you really carve someone's face half off with something like a shovel? There's enough blood on it to point to it having been the murder weapon. The old man, Mr Adams, is his one-time gardener, you say?'

Gillard nodded.

'D'you know his first name?'

'His wife calls him Bobby.'

'Probably Robert, then. He gives every impression of having been beaten over the head with the poker that's near Mansell's right hand, so did he try to fight him off?'

'Trying to answer a previous question, would anyone really try to kill someone with the blade of a shovel? Far easier surely to bash them over the head with it.'

'Someone's gone to speak to Mrs Adams, so we won't know any more for a while. Are you aware of anything else that might be important?'

'Not right now, but I'd like to remind you that Mansell appears to have been involved with crime and criminals. His gardener doesn't seem to fit into that. Oh, and I hope your team has noticed the muddy footprints in the hallway leading towards the stairs. Adams was wearing shoes; the prints were made by someone with boots, and – this a guess from my tracking days – they weren't on anyone's feet but on their hands, to make it look as though someone had worn them when they came in the front door.' He moved to leave.

'I'll pass on the message,' Carrick said. 'Where's your next appointment?'

'Hinton Charterhouse.'

'For God's sake, don't find any more mutilated corpses.'

'The man *was* responsible for Adams losing his job, and Adams might even have blamed him for the added damage to his pick-up,' James Carrick pointed out on Monday morning. 'Mrs Adams has been spoken to and said she was present when her husband received a phone call from Mansell to say that he owed him wages and was minded to give him his job back. So he went over there by bus as his vehicle had a puncture. As you can imagine, she's very upset.'

Patrick Gillard said, 'Although Adams did say that Mansell owed him wages when I first spoke to him, that rings alarm bells with me straight away. I simply cannot imagine Mansell offering to pay anything he owed him. How is Adams, by the way?'

'In intensive care with a fractured skull, a broken left arm and severe general bruising. He might not survive.'

'He probably will. I got the impression that he's tough.'

'As we saw, Mansell's body had a bloodstained poker near the right hand, which does give the impression that he put up a fight. But, of course, we won't know any more until forensic reports come in and we can interview Adams.'

'He told me that he didn't do it.'

'Did you believe him?'

'Yes, I did, actually.'

'You don't think he might have gone over there, in good faith, to get the money owed to him and then Mansell taunted him, perhaps refused to pay, and he lost his temper?'

'That's possible,' Gillard conceded.

'And why, for God's sake, did he take that long-handled shovel with him?'

'We don't know that he did.'

'I simply can't believe that thing belonged to Mansell.'

They were talking in Carrick's office, Gillard having called in to find out if there had been any developments overnight. But right now, he didn't think the DCI looked at all well.

'James, are you feeling all right?' he asked.

'No, I don't actually.'

'One moment.' He went into the corridor to find Lynn Outhwaite and almost immediately came upon her. 'Lynn, I think you ought to get a first-aider and possibly a paramedic to the boss – he's not well.'

'Flu?' she queried.

'He might have an infection.'

Carrick was found to have a high temperature and was taken to hospital as a precaution. When the ambulance had departed, Gillard sought out the DI and offered his assistance.

'We're still hunting high and low for this Georgio character and his mob,' she said. 'And now everything's been complicated by Mansell being murdered, so we won't be able to question *him*. Anyway,' she went on to say, 'don't you have other obligations?'

Gillard had never been able to work out whether she liked him or not. Ingrid had no problem with her; they got on amazingly well, in fact, as they appeared to have the same sense of humour, and, seemingly, that also applied to Joanna. Carrick thought Lynn was the best cop on the premises, which was probably true. But she had been promoted to DI only recently.

'Would you rather I went away?' he asked quietly.

'No! I didn't mean it like that. Perhaps . . .' She shrugged sadly.

'Have you contacted Joanna?'

'The boss did before he was taken off. I asked her to go and talk to Mrs Adams, so that's where she is right now.'

'Has Adams actually been arrested and charged?'

'No, he was just about unconscious by the time the paramedics arrived.'

'I did try to keep him awake,' Gillard murmured. 'Does Mrs Adams know that Mansell's dead?'

'I don't see how she can, but I told Joanna she could tell her if it seemed appropriate and depending on her mental state.'

'I think that old man might have been set up and they intended to kill him. It would have been very neatly sewn up for them, wouldn't it? Mansell dead, obviously murdered, suspect dead too, with injuries that suggested the murder victim had fought back.'

'Evidence?' Lynn asked.

'Absolutely none right now.'

'You probably won't agree, but I'm going to get a warrant and search Adams's place. He *is* the main suspect right now and it's something I ought to do. I'll be asked why I didn't otherwise.'

'It's not for me to agree or not with what you're doing, Lynn,' Patrick said. 'Coffee courtesy of Carrick's whizz-machine?'

She smiled. 'Why not?'

Like Gillard, Joanna had had a problem finding Rose Cottage and, having finally arrived, was hoping that Mrs Adams wasn't actually at the Royal United Hospital hoping to see her husband. There were no cars parked at the top of the narrow lane that led down to the house and only a pick-up with a flat tyre could be glimpsed in the yard to the rear of the house. Perhaps the old lady had to go everywhere by bus.

'Rural idylls aren't necessarily that good when you're getting on in life,' Joanna whispered to herself. She knew that Elspeth Gillard was very grateful for her own circumstances, still able to drive and living in a pretty village with the security of a loving and, it had to be said, reasonably wealthy family literally on her doorstep. But this couple . . .

A dog was barking somewhere within when Mrs Adams answered her knock at the door almost immediately. 'Oh, I've already answered questions, you know.'

'This is more of a friendly visit to offer help and support,' Joanna replied, having just decided that's exactly what it was.

'You'd better come in, then,' Mrs Adams said reluctantly. 'Wait a sec and I'll put the dog out the back.'

Invited, moments later, to seat herself in the living room, Joanna wondered why the woman seemed to be on the defensive. Perhaps she just didn't like the police.

'Have you heard how your husband is?' she began by asking.

'Poorly, but what else can we expect? It baffles me utterly. What on earth happened?'

'You said yesterday that he got a phone call from Mr Mansell saying that he owed him wages.'

'Yes, that's right, and said perhaps he ought to give him his job back. Didn't actually apologize but said he regretted what had happened.'

'And your husband had to go into Bath on the bus?'

'Yes, we had to sell the car. Now he's talking of selling the truck as it's getting too old and expensive to run. The good Lord knows what'll happen then.'

'Did he go into Bath on the same day, Saturday, as the call?'

'That same afternoon – the call came in the morning.'

'Mrs Adams, did your husband take anything with him to Bath? Any tools?'

'No, of course not. Why would he? It was only going to be a chat.'

'Only he was found in the same room as what was described to me as a Devon shovel.'

'What, one of those long-handled things? I can't see my Bobby taking one of those on a bus. Folk would think he was a labourer, wouldn't they? No, come to think of it, I saw him walking up the lane and he didn't have it then.'

'Do you know if your husband owns a shovel like that?'

'Well, he may well do, but I don't know about all his tools.'

'So where would it be if he had one?'

'Out in the barn, I should imagine.'

'Do you think you could look for it in a minute?'

'I suppose I could. But what I want to know is who did this terrible thing to him. Mansell?'

'We don't know yet. But I have to tell you that Mr Mansell's dead. He was murdered.'

'*Dead!*' She fell silent for a few moments and then said, 'And you think Bobby killed him? What, with the shovel?' Her voice had risen to a hoarse shriek.

'No one's come to any conclusions yet,' Joanna hastened to say.

'But my Bobby wouldn't hurt a fly – not even a nasty piece of work like Mansell. So who found him, then?'

'The insurance man who came to see you. He had to go back to talk to Mr Mansell about something.'

Sometimes you have to tell tiny white lies.

'I have him to thank, then,' Mrs Adams said thoughtfully. 'And we got a letter to say that the claim on the damage for Mr Mansell's car had been turned down. That's one blessing. Would you like some tea?'

Joanna refused, with thanks, and then said, 'What frame of mind was your husband in when he left to go into Bath?'

'Well, glad really because he needed the job. But I knew he was being careful as he didn't trust the man.'

The woman's edginess caused Joanna to ask, 'Have you had any further damage to anything here after your pick-up was vandalized?'

'No, but . . .' The woman broke off, frowning.

'Please tell me.'

After hesitating again, Mrs Adams said, 'I don't suppose it's anything important, but a few nights ago, last week now, Bobby reckoned that someone was hanging around outside. The dog lives in the barn at night – he likes it that way; we don't chuck him out there – and he started barking. But poor old Olly can't see as well as he used to and barks at just about anything that moves. But Bobby reckoned he'd seen someone; he said something about it being a different bark to usual. I don't know, my dear – oh, I hope you didn't mind me calling you that – but when I'm in the kitchen with things bubbling away on the stove, I can't be listening out for things like that.'

No, quite.

'Anything else?' Joanna asked.

'No, not really. But you've no idea how all this is upsetting me.'

'Is there anything that I can do for you?'

'You're not allowed to give people lifts, I suppose. I really want to go to the hospital and see how Bobby is. I can get the bus back.'

Joanna said yes, of course she could. It was an unmarked police car anyway, and this lady was a sort of witness.

There was no Devon shovel in the Adams's barn – not that the pair of them could find one after a quick search, that is.

Having dropped off Mrs Adams and determined to check up on the well-being, or not, of her own husband while she was at the Royal United – having been trying to push the fact that he was unwell to the back of her mind – Joanna had a sudden ghastly thought. She knew only the main details of the Mansell murder case and that it might have connections with other serious crimes, as discussed by interested parties at the Ring o' Bells. James had spoken about it since, but he had several investigations for which he was responsible and she herself had become involved with other cases while she had been acting as driver for him and assisting Lynn Outhwaite.

The thought that had been slammed into her mind was that Robert Adams ought to have police protection. Mrs Adams had been emphatic that he hadn't had the Devon shovel with him when he went for the bus. Why should she lie? If Mansell really had had criminal connections, his mobsters might have turned on him and . . .

'Husband,' Joanna muttered as she strode into the hospital. 'Find. Now. I don't care if he's in the operating theatre.'

He was still in the A&E department. By dint of telling the medical staff that it was of vital importance she spoke to him, she found herself in a curtained-off cubicle.

'You shouldn't have come,' Carrick said. 'I'm OK.'

'Mr Adams,' Joanna snapped. 'Police protection. Please fix. Now.'

He just looked at her.

'He didn't take that shovel with him on the bus.'

'He might have left it behind at Mansell's place when he got the sack.'

'That's possible but things like that are expensive and they're as poor as church mice.'

'Jo . . .'

'*Please*, James. I brought Mrs Adams in to see him and they're both absolutely defenceless if—'

'OK. Give me my mobile. It's in the pocket of my jacket over there.'

Having given it to him, she marched off, leaving him staring after her.

Right now there was a very thin blue line.

TEN

Lynn Outhwaite, in receipt of Carrick's call, knew from his tone of voice that there was no room for her to use her own initiative in this. Despite the fact that she had just been about to get the DCI's permission to apply for a search warrant of Adams' home, she immediately gave the appropriate order and was told that armed protection would be put in place as soon as possible. Someone would have to come over from Bristol, though, and it might take as much as an hour depending on the traffic.

'That's no good,' she muttered angrily to herself after the call, angry too that, strictly speaking, the suspect's safety should have been thought of before. It had to be admitted that there were several strange aspects to the crime. On the one hand, the boss had said Adams hadn't taken the shovel on the bus with him when he went to see Mansell. But couldn't such a tool have been in a shed at the house on Brassknocker Hill? Adams would have known it was there. It had been decided that he hadn't been responsible for the damage to Mansell's car, but had lost his job anyway . . .

On the other hand . . . 'Would Mansell really climb down and offer him his job back and say he would pay him the wages he owed him?' she said to thin air. 'Who's the criminal here, the old gardener or a gang which, according to at least one train of thought and some fairly good circumstantial evidence, has connections to Mansell, robbery and at least two murders?'

She grabbed her jacket and left the room. She would need reinforcements.

In order to reach the ward to which Adams had been admitted – he was now out of intensive care – Joanna had to pass several other departments, all with rows of chairs in the vicinity for people who were waiting to be seen. She received several startled looks and one scowl, and made a point of giving that particular youth a good hard stare back. As was normal, the place was very busy, people to-ing and fro-ing everywhere, especially harassed-looking staff.

Looking for Priston Ward, she got a bit lost, asked the way and was directed down a corridor that also led to the X-ray department. It was almost blocked by patients on trolleys and in wheelchairs, and here too there were people seated on chairs in a large recess. Priston Ward was at the end of the corridor, the name displayed on a sign over the doorway.

'I'm afraid Mr Adams can only have one visitor at a time and his wife's with him,' said a nurse when Joanna asked where he was.

'I'm not visiting him, just keeping an eye on him until someone else relieves me. But I need to cast an eye over any other visitors.'

'Please don't disturb anyone, then.'

Having walked down and then back and satisfied herself that those visitors present, mostly elderly women, could be discounted, Joanna positioned herself near the doorway. She would much rather have been out of uniform as she felt too conspicuous, but at least her presence might deter anyone approaching with malice aforethought.

Fifteen minutes went by, and she began to wonder where the protection officer had got to. Stuck in traffic? A major incident somewhere else and no one could be spared? Or, horrors, James had changed his mind?

Adams was in the last but one bed on the right-hand side of the ward. His wife was still with him, and a quick glance had told Joanna as she went by – neither of them had noticed her – that not a lot was being said. Just a couple of very unhappy people. She found herself wondering what would happen to them. Did their cottage belong to them or did they rent it? Did he have other jobs? And the work that Mrs Adams must have to do in a home with very few modern conveniences was probably too much for her.

Another twelve minutes dragged by, and Joanna began to despair. Then a man wearing a white coat approached. She registered the fact that he had blond hair at about the same time that he saw her and stopped. This hair colour was the only thing she knew about the man called Georgio who was the chief suspect in the Lisette Hornby murder enquiry, never mind anything else CID thought he was enmired in.

He decided to carry on walking and came towards her with shoulders hunched, head down, so far down in fact that when she moved to stand in the middle of the entrance, he walked right into her.

'Oh, do excuse me,' he said politely.

'You're not coming in here,' she told him.

'I'm a doctor attending an emergency.'

'You're not and you're under arrest.'

'I *beg* your pardon?' he exclaimed.

'Doctors in hospitals don't wear white coats anymore. Lab technicians do, but they take them off before they leave the department.'

'Look, dear . . .'

His hair was growing out dark at the roots.

'Is your name Georgio?' she asked, still speaking quietly.

'Fuck off or I'll kill you,' he whispered.

She was expecting to be shoved out of the way and prepared to bring into play self-defence moves that she had been taught when she rejoined the police – a refresher course actually as she'd done it all before first time around. When he moved almost with the speed of a striking snake and his hands went tightly around her throat, she kneed him in the groin and then punched him in the stomach. Cold, cold tight hands . . .

Then he jerked, released her, and she staggered away, coughing and gasping for breath. When she had recovered slightly, he was running into the ward, wrenching open the bedside curtains where they were closed, peering closely at the patients in all the beds. Joanna tore after him. There seemed to be two of her, lots of footsteps anyway, but she felt a bit strange so dismissed it as an illusion. Then, the man now at the end of Mr Adams's bed, she grabbed him by the white coat, somehow found the strength to swing him round, and he crashed into a trolley of medical equipment, toppling it over. Tripping over that, he blundered into the curtains, got entangled in them, fought his way free and came at her again. Another man shouted and Mrs Adams screamed.

The other set of footsteps manifested itself as Lynn Outhwaite who chopped him across the back of the neck at about the same time that Joanna, intending to kick him in the stomach, got him on the right knee instead. He buckled and then righted himself and bolted. In the corridor leading to the ward, he ran into two uniformed constables who were coming towards him, Lynn's reinforcements, and batted them out of his way as though they were flies.

Various members of the nursing staff appeared from seemingly nowhere and hurried to attend to their alarmed charges. A real doctor ran up.

'What we really needed,' Lynn panted, 'was Patrick.'

'Did you hit him with something out in the corridor?' Joanna managed to ask.

'No, just kicked his backside.'

Gillard was driving in the direction of home as he'd had a call to make in Wellow and it was time for a well-overdue lunch. His mobile rang when he got out of the car. It was Lynn Outhwaite. As she spoke, he made his way around to the rear of the house and entered the conservatory. Ingrid was in there, supervising Vicky and Mark, the former trying to show the latter how to make tea with his new toy kitchen. All he wanted to do was bang the saucepans together and throw around just about everything else.

'Almost a disaster,' Gillard reported, seating himself. 'Joanna almost got herself strangled, they almost arrested a man – almost certainly this character Georgio – who almost attacked Mr Adams, and Carrick's in hospital feeling like death – *probably*, I've just been informed, because he's hatching a virus and suffering from exhaustion anyway. Needless to say, the attacker's disappeared.'

'Is Joanna all right?'

'A bit shaky. Lynn sent her home for the rest of the day.'

'I'll phone her.' She regarded her husband steadily. 'I take it you intend to tell Greenway you're going to carry on giving them a hand, whether the NCA likes it or not, before Lynn collapses with exhaustion too and this maniac strangles half of Bath.'

'Something like that. Is there anything to eat?'

His wife got to her feet. 'I'll find you something. Please babysit; it's Carrie's day off.'

Five minutes later, Lynn rang again and told him that, upon being questioned, hospital staff in that particular area reported noticing the same man hanging around the previous day, only without the white coat. He would have been challenged, they had said, if he'd been wearing it. Adams had been moved to a small side ward and an armed protection officer would always be on duty to watch over him. The patient had been amazed by the 'goings on' but had not suffered any kind of setback. It was believed now that he would fully recover, and professional opinion was that he would be fit to be interviewed by the police the following day. Would Patrick like to be present, Lynn went on to ask, as Adams knew him and a 'friendly face' would be no bad thing?

'I shall have to tell him that I'm a part-time cop,' Gillard pointed out, having an idea that she really wanted him along as a minder. No one could blame her for that.

'Do what you like,' the DI replied.

'Is anyone keeping an eye on Mrs Adams?'

'Her brother's gone to stay with her, and I'm not supposed to know that he's taken along his shotgun.'

Ingrid returned shortly afterwards with a doorstep-ish cold roast chicken and salad sandwich and some crisps, and he immediately had a small queue for the latter.

After he'd had lunch, minus most of the crisps, he rang Commander Greenway.

'It must be something to do with those damned hot springs under Bath,' Greenway said on being told of the latest misfortunes in the city's CID department. 'By the way, what does the water taste like?'

'Wonderful,' Gillard replied even though he thought it horrible.

'Well, your input will have to carry on being under the same arrangement as last time. Higher authority is adamant that if you're going to continue giving them a hand, they can pay you.'

'They're still thinking about last time.'

'You'd better hurry them up, then.'

Patrick worked from home, writing reports on the Hinton Charterhouse job and the latest one that morning in Wellow. Both claims had gone to appeal after being turned down by the man who owned the red sports car, Denholm Woodstock. Gillard intended to speak to him about them as they had grounds for being accepted, although the latter case would need a professional opinion about a leak from a central heating boiler. He had arranged that that would happen the following day.

After all the nine-to-five bread-and-butter stuff, it was a relief to turn his thoughts back to crime. Georgio was extremely dangerous. He hadn't just shoved Joanna out of the way at the hospital but had tried to strangle her. Someone like that should be in Broadmoor. Suddenly, he knew that it was his responsibility to put him there.

Gillard got to his feet and called to Ingrid that he would go and visit Carrick. He might show his face at the nick too; Lynn had too much responsibility right now.

'It's nothing to do with my leg, thank God,' was the first thing the DCI said to him. 'But they're doing more tests.'

'You've been far too impatient with your recovery.'

'So how long did it take you to recover from that disaster you had when you were on Special Ops?'

'The best part of a year.'

'On crutches?'

'For some of the time.'

'You've never told me what happened.'

Gillard seated himself and said, 'It was an accident. Someone, a friendly I have to say, threw a grenade and it bounced off a door frame and ended up in the bothy where my little undercover group was lurking. I wasn't really aware of the bang, just saw a flash and was then lying on the ground wondering why the sergeant who appeared to have grabbed me by the shoulders was screaming. Then I realized it was me. The army surgeon described the state my legs were in as "soup of the day".'

'But they saved them – well, almost.'

'Yes, I had several operations spread over months. The left one's almost as good as new now but, as you know, the right eventually had to come off below the knee as the pins weren't holding and I was having to take so many painkillers I was like a zombie.

Someone I was chasing down for MI5 didn't actually help by clouting me on the shins several times with a baseball bat.'

Carrick said something lurid under his breath in Gaelic.

Gillard continued, 'The other problem, one that bothered me more than anything, was that I'd suffered damage to what used to be coyly referred to as wedding tackle. I was told that even if I could ever have sex again, I'd probably be firing blanks for the rest of my life. So when I got the job with MI5 and was told to find a part-time female working partner as the job would initially be socializing and snooping on upper-class suspects, I asked Ingrid. Official thinking was that a lone bloke looked suspicious. We'd been divorced by then – rightly, she'd found me utterly insufferable – and although we'd always got on well in public, I thought that the last thing she'd want to do was sleep with me, so I wouldn't have a challenge in that direction. I hadn't gone looking for paid sex to see what happened. You don't use young women as a kind of trials ground, do you?'

Thinking that some men wouldn't have hesitated to do so and there was every chance Patrick as a young man *had* been insufferable, Carrick said, 'Your ruse obviously didn't work.'

'No. I tried to demonstrate to Ingrid that I didn't want to sleep with her but that just had the effect of turning us both on something awful. She says that the ol' magic we'd had in our early relationship worked again.'

'And you got married for the second time.'

'Yes, and have three kids. I can't believe it really, but it's all down to Ingrid. She's always rescued things – lost cats, dogs with thorns in their paws. She rescued me, picked me up, dusted me off and as good as told me to get on with life. I owe everything to her.'

Carrick was quiet for a few moments and then said, 'That bastard could have killed Joanna.'

'You have Lynn to thank – she kicked his backside and he released her.' Patrick rose and clapped the DCI on the shoulder. 'I'm going with her to talk to Mr Adams tomorrow morning. We might learn something. Get some rest; I'll keep an eye on Joanna while you're here.'

Carrick was left feeling a bit humbled.

* * *

They were told that they could only talk to Mr Adams for about ten minutes. But although his head was swathed in bandages and he had an arm in plaster, he looked bright enough – perhaps glad to be alive, Gillard thought, as they seated themselves at his bedside. The protection officer hadn't taken any chances and had carefully scrutinized their warrant cards before allowing them through.

Lynn Outhwaite introduced herself and then went on to explain that Gillard worked part-time for the National Crime Agency.

'I thought there was more to you than insurance,' said the patient in a remarkably strong voice. 'Have you come to arrest me?'

'No, but you are a suspect in a serious criminal investigation,' Lynn told him quietly.

She had said to Gillard on the way to the ward that she would defer doing anything like that until she had assessed the situation for herself.

'Well, I were there, weren't I? What else would you think?'

'Can you remember what happened?' she went on to ask.

'Some of it. But when someone set about me with what looked like a poker and then bashed me over the head with it, that was it for I don't know how long. Nothing. Then Mr Gillard here turned up – for which I shall ever be grateful, sir,' he added.

'Can you tell us about it roughly from the beginning?' Gillard asked.

The old man gathered his thoughts for a few moments. 'Did Maggie tell you that Mansell phoned me and said did I want to call as he had a mind to offer me my job back and pay me the last lot of wages he owed?'

'Yes, she did,' Gillard replied. 'Are you sure it was his voice?'

'He sounded a bit muffled like, but I never gave it a thought.'

'Did he suggest a time?' Lynn enquired.

'He said if I wanted to come over that afternoon, he'd be in. So I did.'

'Did you take anything with you?'

'No, why would I?'

'Who does the Devon shovel belong to?'

'It's mine. That was one of the reasons I went over there. I knew it was in the shed out the back. I'd used it to deal with the gravel when the drive was done. Wrong sort of gravel, mind. He didn't even ask my advice on that.'

'Are you aware that it was used as a murder weapon?'

'It wasn't. That bastard strangled him first. Then they must have bashed him around to make it look as though I'd done it. I can't be too sure of anything that happened really. I think I was on the floor then. Everything went a bit kind of fuzzy.'

'Had you fetched the shovel from the shed, though?'

'Yes, before I rang the doorbell. I left it in the porch.'

'Would there have been any mud on your boots?'

'I weren't wearing boots. Shoes. You must know that. Anyhow, the paths to the shed are good. No need to go on any open ground.'

'Mr Adams, you don't seem to be too upset by these ghastly happenings,' Lynn said.

The old man sighed. 'I can't get what happened out of my head really, but it's no good cracking up, is it? I did a stint as an ambulance driver in the sixties when I couldn't get a gardening job. That was before you did a lot more training and ended up as what I think's called a paramedic these days. When you've helped to pick up bits of folk after road accidents . . .' He shook his head sadly and then whispered, 'I'm just so glad to still be around.'

Gillard said, 'Did Mr Mansell give the impression that he was expecting you?'

'No, that's when it all started to go wrong. He wasn't and got really angry, said I was a damned nuisance – only he didn't say it that politely. We were standing in the hallway and suddenly this mob of roughs – they had hoods on – rushed in behind me and virtually carried me up the stairs. Then they started hitting me.'

'Had Mansell opened the door?'

'I suppose he must have done.'

'Did you try to fight back?'

'Too right I did! But there were four or five of them, so they'll only have a few bruises.'

'Where was Mansell while this was going on?'

'Oh, yes, that's right. He were flapping about, shouting at them. Wanting to know what the hell they were doing and why they'd barged into his house. They told him to shut up and then he tried to run from the room. They grabbed him.'

'At no time, then, because they wore hoods, did you see anything that might identify them?'

'Only that the one in charge, the one who strangled Mansell, had green eyes. A strange sort of green if you ask me, like an alien in a film. As well as being rotten to the core, I reckon he's nuts.'

Mr Adams was obviously tired now, so Lynn thanked him, told him they might need to talk to him again, and she and Patrick left.

'Is he too calm and remembers too well?' Lynn said when they were walking to where they had left their cars. 'I still have to regard him as a suspect, but there's no firm evidence to arrest him.'

'People of his generation had to work too hard for a living to be snowflakes,' Gillard pointed out.

'Well, at least he won't be going anywhere for a while and forensics might be able to tell us about any other people in that room.' She stopped in her tracks. 'I ought to go and find out how the boss is.'

'Avon Ward,' Gillard called after her hurrying figure. 'Green eyes,' he then went on to muse aloud. 'And probably hiding in plain sight.'

This was likely as, Mansell's murder apart, the force had been searching out all offenders who could possibly have a connection with the crimes under investigation and questioning them. Ben Baker and Jez Smithson – the latter discharged from hospital after being kept in for just over twenty-four hours with suspected concussion – were both questioned, by Lynn, that afternoon. They both refused to say a word other than to confirm their identities. And, of course, rules prevented Patrick Gillard from being present.

It didn't, though, prevent him from conducting his own inquisition.

Ben Baker, he of the broken nose, was, like his brother Zak, of no fixed address, the latter having been remanded in custody as he had been found to be carrying a knife. The other two involved in the assault on Gillard had been released on police bail, Smithson to go home to a basement room at the bottom of Lansdown Hill that he got rent-free in exchange for cellar work and cleaning at the pub above it. At present, Ben was staying with a slightly disabled aunt. This was a family arrangement, mostly on account of everyone being of the opinion that this demanding and bad-tempered woman was a thundering nuisance, but at least he got free board for helping her with shopping and anything else that needed doing. In reality, he helped very little other than himself from her purse when she wasn't looking. His conscience was clear on this as she was reputed to have a fortune stashed away somewhere in the house. He assiduously searched for that, also when she wasn't looking.

Released from the police station after being questioned, he headed, on foot, in the direction of his aunt's house in Twerton, not noticing the tall man slouching along, hands in the pockets of his anorak not far behind him. When he did notice him, it was too late and he found himself remorselessly steered down a side alley, around some waste bins and then parked in the lee of some larger bins outside the rear entrance to a Chinese restaurant.

'I won't punch you on the nose again as it looks quite smart in that dinky little bandage,' his new companion whispered. 'That is as long as you tell me where the bastard lives who put you up to that ambush on me the other night. And be warned, I used to be in a specialist army unit and can easily kill you with my bare hands. Starting a bit like this.'

He gave Baker a violent shake and slammed him against the wall behind him.

'It's all a bit difficult, with Georgio threatening to wring the life out of all of you if you step out of line, isn't it?' Gillard went on. 'I know that he's the man in charge and that he has killed several people. I don't like it when people add me to that kind of list.'

'*No one* knows where Georgio is for most of the time,' Ben Baker honked, this due to the state of his nose. 'No, honest,' he hooted, his voice going up an octave when Gillard tightened his grip on the front of his fleece jacket. 'Word has it that he's got another job – another life really, an ordinary one – and that's how he stays hidden.'

'Go on.'

'We all want out, but he seems to know everything that goes on. He knew where you might be the other night. Honest, that's the truth. He gives orders and we do stuff and that's it. He doesn't turn up all the time – only for important things.'

'Like strangling children, for example,' Gillard said through his teeth.

'No, that wasn't planned. The kid turned up like – looked through the window.'

'Were you there?'

'It was a meeting after we'd done a job.'

'The first jewellery shop heist?'

'Yes.'

'This was the house at the bottom of Brassknocker Hill belonging to a man by the name of Mansell.'

Baker nodded.

'And you were there.'

Baker groaned. 'I still feel bad about it.'

'And Archer?'

'He was just a pain in the backside. He had to get rid of him really.'

'Why did Georgio kill Mansell?'

'He was getting to be a pain in the backside too. Georgio thought he'd grass on us.'

Gillard loosened his grip a little. 'Don't you agree with me, then, that the sooner this man's out of circulation, the better it will be for everyone?'

'He's raving mad.' Baker bared his teeth in a crooked smile. 'You mean . . . for ever?'

'If you like.'

Gillard hadn't meant that at all, but this interpretation of what he'd said was actually rather handy.

'You said you were in a special army unit . . .' Baker said. 'Sort of . . . killing people?' He swallowed hard. This man had grimly nodded and seemed to have a permanent snarl on his face. 'How much would you want?'

'A couple of K should do it.'

'We might be able to scrape that together between us.'

'But you'd have to do a bit of work for me first – give me a rough idea of where he might be.'

'All I know is that people say he's got a posh red sports car.'

'What sort of sports car?'

'I think it's a Porsche. But he doesn't drive round in it when there's a job on; that's for when he does the other ordinary stuff.'

'D'you know the model?'

'No.'

Gillard released him. 'D'you have a mobile?'

'Yes.'

'Give me the number and I'll ring you tomorrow to see what you've turned up.'

'That doesn't give me much time.'

'You *do* want to make your court appointment for assault, don't you?'

Well, Baker supposed he did. He hadn't given a thought as to why he and the other two had been ordered to half kill this man. But Ben Baker didn't do a lot of thinking at all.

ELEVEN

The scenes-of-crime team working in Mortimer Mansell's house – a big job as there were a lot of rooms and most of them were filled with all kinds of things – had come across a locked room on the second floor. The key to this had not been found either on the murder victim, among his personal effects or in any drawer in furniture in the entire building. Finally, they had obtained permission from DI Outhwaite to get a locksmith to open it. The items revealed had resulted in another specialist being called in – an expert from one of the fine art galleries in the city. He had immediately contacted a colleague in another gallery whose particular field was stolen works of art and forgeries.

'So far three paintings found were stolen in London from the same house in Knightsbridge two years ago, another two from Kensington last year, and some of the rest of the dozen or so in the room are thought to be forgeries. But obviously investigations with regard to those are continuing and will do for some time,' Lynn reported from the crime scene in a phone call to Carrick the following morning. 'It might be that Mansell was cheated.'

'Possibly by the same dealers who bought stolen property from him here in Bath,' Carrick suggested.

'That could have happened,' Lynn agreed. 'But we'll probably never know for sure.'

The DCI was at home, fretting. His temperature had come down and he had been discharged from hospital; as one doctor had put it, 'It might be just one of those things.' He had added that, in his opinion, Carrick was exhausted and would carry on feeling unwell if he didn't rest.

Other evidence with regard to the Mansell case was slowly emerging. A fingerprint on the poker, just one clear specimen due to the blood smeared all over it, was Mansell's. Among others too smeared to be of any use, there was a thumb and forefinger print on the handle of the shovel. This was Adams's, which, of course, did not incriminate him as the shovel belonged to him. When shown photographs of Adams's head injuries, a serious injuries consultant said she had a good idea that they had been inflicted by something like a poker, but obviously she couldn't say for certain. His broken arm had probably been caused by a blow from a similar weapon.

Patrick Gillard hadn't mentioned his possible 'contract' to take out Georgio either to his wife or Carrick. He thought it highly unlikely that Ben Baker would be able to tell him anything useful, and it went without saying that he had no intention of phoning him on his personal mobile. He would use the phone issued to him by the NCA that ensured calls were untraceable. He was just about to do so when he suddenly remembered something that Baker had said: 'He knew where you might be the other night.' *How* had he known? Admittedly, Gillard thought, he had gone back to the car park by the same route he had used in the morning, although he usually went slightly different ways at random. This was force of habit from undercover days working for MI5. Was this man watching him? Had he followed him? The latter of these queries, he thought, could be discounted as, again, from habit, he was vigilant.

Two pieces of information then crashed together in his mind. A man with a red sports car who had an idea where he, Gillard, would be? Who was this character Denholm Woodstock who worked for the same insurance company as he did and who he'd never clapped eyes on?

He was in the right place to get answers, the office, and went along the corridor to the personnel department. He had a very good excuse to find out what he wanted to know as he needed to speak to him in connection with the two claims that had been turned down. Five minutes later, he had some information: Denholm Woodstock worked on a similar footing to he himself – that is, he was semi-freelance and worked quite a lot from home. His address, though, Gillard was told, was 'confidential'.

'Why?' he demanded to know.

The young clerk shook her head and said she didn't know, but rules were rules.

'Is the number of his red sports car on record?'

After half a minute or so of computer perusing, she said, 'Sorry, it doesn't appear to be.'

'How about a photo? We all have to have one taken for our security pass.'

The computer said that it was 'pending'.

'Have you any idea when he's next likely to be in the office?' he persevered.

'No, sorry. It's not really my job to know things like that.'

Exasperated, but not one to play the heavy to someone barely out of her teens, Gillard merely gave her a little wave and went to find his boss. Who, it appeared, wasn't around.

With work to do but no real reason to do it where he was, Gillard set off to go home. When he had just settled himself behind the wheel of the car, he remembered Ben Baker and rang the number he had been given. Amazingly, the man answered.

'They think it's a good idea,' Baker replied in response to the question Gillard had put to him in the alley, obviously still with his nose stuffed with cotton wool. 'But say they haven't the cash.'

'You could pay me some time later,' Gillard cajoled. 'I need this bastard out of my life, too.'

'OK, you do it and we'll give you the dosh afterwards.'

Yeah, right, Gillard thought. 'But I need to know where he *is*, or might be,' he stressed.

'OK . . . er – right. You could try the Spotted Dog in Stoke Marsh – he goes there a bit.'

'Does he have green eyes?'

'No.'

'Are you sure?'

''Course.'

Not quite grinding his teeth, and with the conviction that the man knew far more than he was admitting, Gillard rang off. He was in a real quandary now and had no intention of just dumbly hanging around near the pub in question; the man might spot and recognize him. If he went there at all, there would have to be a good reason and he would have to change his appearance. Meanwhile, he'd go and call on Carrick.

The DCI was found to be loafing around at home looking miserable, Joanna on duty.

'What d'you know about the Spotted Dog pub in Stoke Marsh?' Gillard asked him. 'Georgio is reputed to go there sometimes.'

'Hardly anything,' Carrick replied. 'It isn't a problem place as far as I know, but obviously it's not on my patch. Who mentioned it to you?'

'Ben Baker. We had a short conversation and he told me the gang all want out. He thinks it's a good idea for me to sort out the problem for them, preferably permanently.'

Carrick stared at him. 'You mean he wants you to *kill* him?'

'I did give him the impression that I was capable.'

'Well, that's no lie, but I'm hoping you did it for no other reason than to obtain information about the man.'

'Absolutely,' Patrick said with a seraphic smile.

'I take it you want me to do something.'

'I'm rather hoping that you'll contact chums in Bristol and ask them to put an undercover watch on the place.'

'It might turn up something, I suppose,' Carrick said listlessly. His mobile rang and he picked it up to answer it. He made little comment in response to the information given to him, thanked whoever it was and ended the call. 'You're not going to believe this,' he said. 'Lynn asked me for a warrant to search Adams's house and outbuildings as, rightly, she thought it ought to be done. The search team found nothing suspicious in the house, but under a pile of sacking in the barn they discovered a carrier bag containing a silver tray that, because of what's engraved on it, has to be the Atworths' property, a gold chain with a locket containing a miniature painting of a young woman, engraved on the reverse and possibly theirs as well, and a set of silver-plated fish knives and forks, which might also be the Atworths'. Mrs Adams, who simply can't believe it, is denying all knowledge of the find and said that someone was lurking around outside recently setting their dog barking.'

Gillard had been on the point of leaving but perched on the edge of a chair. 'A strange collection,' he mused aloud.

'In any special way that grabs you?'

'Yes, they're just about unsaleable. No fence would want

them – not engraved things that can be traced back to victims of crime. And who the hell wants fish knives and forks these days?'

Carrick momentarily put his head in his hands. 'I'm just not thinking, am I? But look, they could be the pay-off, or part of it, to Adams for killing Mansell. Adams despised and hated Mansell. The gang – and I wish to God we could get hold of the rest of them – might have been aware that if Mansell ranted and raved about him, he could be struggling financially, having lost the job. Adams is getting on a bit and perhaps easily influenced – not quite as astute as he used to be. He wouldn't know that what he had been given was pretty worthless as far as selling it was concerned.'

This sounded to Patrick like the case for the prosecution; then again, Carrick had had an austere, if not horrible, start in life and it affected his whole outlook. His unmarried mother had gone to live with her parents but fled with him to an aunt when her pillar-of-the-Kirk father had taken to trying to beat the 'sin' out of his little grandson as often as he felt he had an excuse. So, now, there was no point in arguing with him.

'Did you say that the man who strangled Mansell had green eyes?' Ingrid queried that evening when Patrick got home.

'A strange sort of green according to Adams,' he replied. 'And yet Ben Baker said that Georgio, whoever *he* really is, hasn't.'

'Perhaps he sometimes wears coloured contact lenses.'

'I don't think I knew there was such a thing.'

'They're used to change the appearance of actors, especially for horror and sci-fi films.'

'Adams did say that it made him look like an alien. What about the man you saw coming out of Mansell's house that time?'

'I'm sure I would have noticed if he'd had alien-looking eyes. I think they were just brown.'

He told her about the find of the suspected stolen property.

'What, hidden there to make it look as though Adams was part of the set-up? That's ridiculous!'

'You're assuming that he isn't. Carrick's toying with the theory that it was payment for killing Mansell.'

'That's ridiculous, too. They have a perfectly good in-house killer of their own.'

'But if it was on Georgio's orders because he didn't want any possible personal connection with the death . . .' Patrick threw up his hands in a gesture of despair. 'I need a tot.'

The preliminary results of the post-mortem on Mansell were received the next day. As far as causes of death were concerned, there were no surprises. In the view of the pathologist, and as Mr Adams had said, he had first been strangled, but damage to the face and neck had rendered this conclusion open to conjecture. She very much doubted that the injuries had been caused by the long-handled shovel found at the scene of the murder as it simply wasn't sharp enough. Far more likely was that an axe had been used.

'Well, we know they like axes,' Lynn Outhwaite said in a call to Carrick. 'But it doesn't necessarily let Adams off the hook as someone could have handed one to him.'

A sceptical and professional nature forced Carrick to agree with this, but it didn't represent progress in the case. Adams had told them that a group of hooded men had come in the front door behind him and bundled him up the stairs. If so, they must have been watching and waiting for him to arrive. They had known, then, that he was expected that afternoon. Adams had gone there, both he and his wife had said, following a call from Mansell, who, according to Adams, had appeared to be surprised to see him, so perhaps Georgio had made the call. There was also the matter of the footprints in the hall and part of the way up the stairs. This might be the gang's giveaway as it was obviously faked. The footprints had been confirmed by a member of the forensic team as having been made by boots – Wellingtons. No boots of that description had been found in the property and Adams had been wearing clean shoes – end of story.

Sick to death of going nowhere or merely around in small circles, the DCI phoned a contact in Bristol and did as Gillard had suggested: asked for a watch to be put on the Spotted Dog in Stoke Marsh. He then got on to higher authority and asked for urgent raids on every similar establishment and address associated with the Baker family and their hangers-on in the area where they lived. This, he hoped, would happen during the late evening or in the early hours of the next morning.

Carrick then phoned the nick and asked to speak to Sergeant Woods who was not, to his knowledge, necessarily on the end of a phone or with a work mobile. After a short wait while he was found, the DCI asked him if he knew of any meeting places, clubs, pubs and similar establishments in Bath where the gang might be furtively gathering.

Woods only knew of one place, but it was a private house – actually a bungalow in Lower Weston that had been raided more than once as it was the home of a drugs dealer. Several arrests had been made there in the past; during the most recent raid, around a year previously, nothing had been found. He gave Carrick the address but suggested caution as he'd heard a rumour that the property might now have been rented out. A subsequent 'visit' rather than a raid produced the information that it had actually been sold; the bus driver and his wife now living there had bought it cheaply as the place had been in such bad condition. No suspicious characters, they insisted, had come to call since they had moved in.

Meanwhile, letters to local papers and people phoning into radio stations were asking why no arrests had been made after several serious crimes had been committed. The cops, the *Bath Clarion* trumpeted, needed to get their act together. This culminated in an enterprising staff photographer of that paper ambushing Carrick and Joanna coming out of their local pub after a meal one evening. The accompanying article insinuated that the DCI, despite being on crutches, should have been at work.

Other than the arrests of a couple of minor criminals wanted to help with enquiries and the discovery of a small amount of drugs, the searches and raids in Bristol yielded absolutely nothing.

Patrick Gillard tackled his boss, Vernon Ellis, about Denholm Woodstock. Up until now he had got on very well with the man. There was no mystery about Woodstock, he was told – Gillard hadn't even hinted that he thought there was – but he had requested that he be able to keep a low profile as a previous client had threatened him.

'I need to speak to him about a couple of cases,' Gillard said. 'When is he next due in the office?'

'He's not on a strict timetable,' Ellis told him.

'I'd like his mobile number, then.'

The man pulled a face. 'He doesn't like that banded about.'

'Not even his company one?'

'No, sorry.'

'Look, I thought I was supposed to be some kind of trouble-shooter,' Gillard retorted. 'I can't do my job if other members of staff hide in cupboards. And if cases go to appeal I'm supposed to ask why a conclusion was reached that brought it about. I have two cases to query with him and have an idea that he was involved with the Mansell one as well.'

'Yes, I think he was,' Ellis said.

'Presumably, you know that Mansell's been murdered.'

'Has he? No, I didn't. I've been away for a few days. But I can't see what it has to do with Woodstock. And I do have to point out that he's a very valued member of this organization.'

Because he turned down most claims flat? Gillard wondered.

Minded to produce his NCA ID and slap it down on the desk, he nevertheless did not, sensing that something wasn't right. Surely someone had told him that one of their clients had come to a nasty end. Surely company departmental managers didn't need to look as worried as this man did.

He walked into the main office – all the offices were on the first floor – and gazed about as if looking for someone. 'Anyone seen Denholm?' he called into the room at large. Half a dozen employees were at their desks.

There was a muted chorus of 'No' and they got on with what they were doing.

'Where does he normally sit?' Gillard went on to ask.

'He doesn't,' someone said without looking up. 'We all tend to use any desk that's free.'

OK, perhaps they didn't feel like being helpful, possibly having the view that he was checking up on them all the time. Which wasn't true. And, of course, he had been given a small office of his own, which had rather surprised him. It came to him that as far as office politics was concerned, having been a lieutenant colonel didn't necessarily *help*.

He went back to his office, sat down and thought about it. The notion that he wasn't cut out for this sort of job had been at the back of his mind almost from day one. The minor investigations could be quite interesting, but getting involved with the tedious details of leaking central heating boilers and garden walls being undermined by a neighbour's activities in excavating a swimming pool were not quite the stuff of legend.

'You are old and going grey,' he muttered to himself. 'And responsible for five lovely young people. Get over it.'

The window overlooked a small car park at the side of the building. This was mainly for visitors and senior management, but as he stared out, unseeing, deep in thought, his gaze focused on an arriving vehicle. A red sports car. He got up and went closer to the window. There were no free spaces, and as he watched, it was parked across the back of another car, the driver got out and walked towards the rear entrance.

Time for a little chat.

As is usual in such places, there was a main entrance at the front on the ground floor where the public could speak to a receptionist and be taken, or not, to one of a series of rooms at the back to discuss insurance matters with members of staff. The interconnecting door was, as in most banks, controlled by security arrangements, code numbers having to be punched in on a metal plate to open it. Also at the rear of the building were staff toilets, a small kitchen and a sick room. The rear entrance, also security controlled, was situated between these utilities and the interview rooms. Gillard, heading in that direction and having descended the stairs as quickly as he dared without risking tripping and breaking his neck, happened upon the new arrival as he entered one of these interview rooms.

'Denholm Woodstock?' he enquired.

'Who wants me?'

Patrick told him.

'Oh, *you're* Gillard. Our pet pain in the neck.'

The man was broad-shouldered, had brown eyes and was almost as tall as Gillard, who was six foot two. His dark hair was very thin on top, the scalp visible despite careful combing.

'I need to speak to you about a couple of cases,' Gillard told him peaceably.

'Go on, then; speak.'

'In my office.'

'I don't get called to your office.'

'That's where all the info is.'

'Go and get it, then.'

'On my desktop computer.'

Not even this man could out-stare Gillard. He dropped his gaze and muttered, 'OK.'

They went upstairs and Gillard made sure that they walked side by side. He had already discovered that Woodstock wasn't more senior than any of the other staff who did this kind of work and hadn't been with the company all that long. His attitude, therefore, was odd to say the least.

'You should have a laptop,' Woodstock said when they arrived.

'I do – for my other job. It gets a bit of a bother with two. Besides, I think older people in particular can find that very impersonal when you're sitting there tapping away. I make notes and then enter it on this later.' He gestured towards the computer on his desk.

'So you moonlight, then.'

'Yes, for the National Crime Agency. Sit down.'

Woodstock quickly gazed around the room as if seeking confirmation of this. 'I don't believe you.'

'I don't care what you believe. Sit down.'

The man remained standing.

'Two cases,' Gillard continued. 'One in Wellow and another in Hinton Charterhouse. You turned down the claims and they went to appeal. There was no earthly reason why they shouldn't have been allowed.'

'Perhaps I just didn't like those people,' Woodstock drawled.

'And then there's the matter of Mortimer Mansell. You appeared to like him, all right, but it went to appeal because the person accused of doing the damage to his Jaguar, the gardener, denied it utterly. That damage wasn't done by the gardener's pick-up; Mansell did it himself. I think you knew that.'

'Go to hell.'

Vernon Ellis came through the door in a rush. Gillard wouldn't have expected him to knock and he hadn't. 'What's going on?' he demanded to know.

'I'm being accused of something or the other,' Woodstock simpered. 'Incompetence? Corruption? Bloody-mindedness? What is it, Gillard?'

'No, I think you merely need to hide your true identity behind a nine-to-five job,' Gillard replied. He was surprised by Ellis's sudden appearance – had he been watching for this man's arrival? – and decided therefore to go for the kill. 'Do you sometimes wear a blond wig that's dark at the roots to make it look authentic? Use green-tinted contact lenses?'

Ellis, who had gone very pale, inserted himself between them. 'Gillard, I suggest you've allowed working as a part-time police officer go to your head or even affect your judgement.'

'It's my job,' Gillard reminded him. 'I'm perfectly free to ask why certain decisions have been arrived at. People don't always remember to put every detail in a written report.'

'And the rest?' Ellis blared.

'That's none of your business. But as you're here, I'll tell you that I intend to arrest him.'

Before he could move, Woodstock bolted out of the room.

'Well, I'm going to call it gross professional misconduct,' Ellis shouted, moving to stand in Gillard's way should he set off in pursuit. 'Clear your desk and go!'

Patrick collected his jacket and few possessions in the room, smiled at him and went.

Unsurprisingly, Woodstock's car had gone from the car park. Gillard sat in the Range Rover and phoned Ingrid, knowing that he had completely and utterly screwed that up. To hell with talking; he should have grabbed him there and then and risked it being the wrong man. When she answered, sounding a bit out of breath as though she'd had to run to where she'd left her phone, he wasted no words, saying, 'Sorry. Not for the first time, I'm going to have to arrange a police watch on the house. I've pinpointed someone at work who I'm convinced is Georgio, and it would appear the boss might be in on it, too. But he might be being threatened. Oh, and sorry again, but I got the sack.'

There was quite a long silence and then she said, 'It's happening all over again, isn't it?'

And rang off, leaving him gazing unhappily at his phone.

Carrick, back at work and having just come from a difficult meeting concerning several cases, wasn't any more accommodating. 'You do realize that this character will now head for God knows where and that's the last we'll see of him. Why the hell did you confront him without back-up like that? And this boss, Ellis, has your address on file, doesn't he? I suppose you'll be asking me for police protection next.'

'Yes,' Gillard said humbly. 'I am.'

'Why didn't you let him brew, let him think he was safe? We could have put an undercover watch on him. And you've lost your job! What were you thinking?'

'Getting a serial killer off the streets,' Patrick replied. He took a slip of paper from his pocket and placed it on the DCI's desk. 'His name's Denholm Woodstock and that's the registration number of his car, a red Porsche. I've just checked on it. Under that name, he has two previous convictions for drink-driving and about a fortnight ago was clocked at doing sixty in a built-up area. That's still grinding through the system.'

After an awkward pause, Carrick said, 'OK, I'll arrange the protection.'

Gillard got to his feet and thanked him. Then he said, 'He will feel safe and cocky now, and that means he'll arrange another job because I think he's taken over this lot. I intend to find out what that'll be and when.'

'Patrick . . .'

But he had gone.

TWELVE

Ingrid didn't know what to think, never mind what to say to Patrick when he got home. However, common sense told her that you can't legally be given the sack for exposing another employee as a criminal, the boss of the department under threat or no. She wasn't particularly worried about the money side of it as he had his army pension now; it was just the feeling that he drew trouble to himself like a magnet without necessarily seeking it out – other than being in possession of a catlike curiosity, that is. 'Tilting at windmills' was how Richard Daws, his one-time MI5 boss, had described some of the things that had happened. But would they ever be free, as Elspeth had once put it, of 'armed police in the onion bed'?

'Crime doesn't have the upper hand,' she told herself. 'It just sometimes appears to.'

It seemed inconceivable to her that Patrick's departmental manager, Vernon Ellis, had refused to give him Denholm Woodstock's address or mobile phone number. No doubt James Carrick was aware of this, but why hadn't he sent someone along officially to demand the information? Ingrid thought she knew the answer to this but found it hard to understand; Carrick didn't believe him – Patrick, that is – that the man was probably Georgio. Was he a relation of Ellis's? *Did* he have some kind of hold over him?

She had known her husband long enough to be aware that he would feel driven to catch this man. Patrick had an over-developed sense of responsibility. This had manifested itself in his army days when he had gone out, personally, to find trainees lagging behind somewhere on an exercise on Dartmoor. He had been a major then – no need to get closely involved – but he had found and escorted the youngsters 'home', somehow turning their failure into triumph over exhaustion.

Hearing the Range Rover outside – it was early afternoon so the three eldest children were still at school – she shut down her computer and headed for the kitchen to make tea. She was seated at the kitchen table waiting for it to brew when Patrick came in, a rueful look on his face.

He sat down. 'Sorry.'

She still didn't know what to say to him.

'I think I'd rather you hurled abuse at me than remained silent,' he said.

'I'm not sulking or trying to make any kind of point here,' she protested. 'Just raking around in my head for a positive remark.'

'I'll look for another job immediately.'

'I'm not too sure that you've lost the first one. The company troubleshooter isn't going to be cast off if he's turned up a big crime set-up. Would you take them to a tribunal?'

'No, I want out.'

Having stirred the pot, Ingrid poured the tea.

'I'm a misfit,' Patrick muttered.

'Good. I like misfits,' she responded stoutly. 'Nice, tall, slim misfits with lovely grey eyes.'

They gazed at one another across the table and then both chuckled.

A short silence followed while they sipped their tea, and then Patrick said, 'There's a pub in Stoke Marsh called the Spotted Dog where Georgio is reputed to hang out sometimes. I intend to hang out there, too.'

'But he'll know you.'

'He won't. I'll take my second-best guitar.'

This author had never been slow. 'You mean you're going to *busk*!'

'I've always wanted to have a go at that.'

'I'll come along as well in my tart rig – you know, with that bra that makes you lose concentration on the job.'

He looked downright alarmed.

'Just testing,' she murmured.

Although she had done it several times in the past, Ingrid had no intention of undertaking what she had jokingly suggested: dress herself up as some of kind of sex worker and go to Stoke Marsh with him and perhaps give him some help. No, not at all. Those days were definitely over. Absolutely.

* * *

In bad moments, Joanna could still feel the man's cold, tight fingers around her throat. She was continuing to drive her husband to work and counting the days until his leg plaster was taken off. In short, he was almost impossible to live with. She was aware that he had been very angry with Patrick for not arresting the man at work whom he suspected of being Georgio. But what evidence had there been? Perhaps Patrick hadn't wanted to risk anyone in the office being hurt should the man have drawn a weapon. While it was true that Georgio was the chief suspect after the murder of Lisette Hornby, never mind other serious crimes, there was still no evidence to connect him with her death. People who habitually walked along that path early in the morning where her body had been found by the River Avon, perhaps with dogs, others jogging, had been questioned. No one, so far – this line of enquiry was continuing – had seen anything suspicious.

The only useable fingerprints on the set of tarnished coffee spoons – on the box, in fact – were those of Tony d'Artanonne, the manager of the nightclub where Lisette had worked. D'Artanonne had said at the time of his arrest, and subsequently in a statement, that they had been given to him in return for a favour by Lisette's boyfriend. This man fitted the description of Georgio, nothing more.

Right now, Joanna was still assisting Lynn during the day and, having just returned from making some enquiries on a shoplifting case, made her way to the DI's office.

'Right!' said Lynn on seeing her. 'The Atworths are back in the UK and have agreed – you'd think they were doing us a favour, wouldn't you? – to try to identify some of the stolen goods we've accumulated. This morning is convenient for them so please take the stuff over there. Constable Morris can go with you as back-up.'

'He's actually a liability,' Joanna said. And then, observing that Lynn might be about to pull rank on her, added, 'Sergeant Woods didn't seem to be too busy when I saw him just now.'

'Why is Morris a liability?'

'It's his attitude. For some reason, he gets on my nerves – he has an aloof and superior manner.'

Lynn could relate to this. Whether the thought then went

through her mind that this woman was the DCI's wife will never be known, but she agreed to the suggestion and had to admit that Woods, rather than the youthful Morris, would have a certain clout when visiting a premises that the owners imagined was a stately home. Joanna was happy: in *her* view, taking the youthful Morris along was a bit like turning up with a pet goldfish.

'Has anything useful emerged from forensic testing following that raid on the Atworths' place and the murder of the housekeeper?' Joanna asked as an afterthought.

'Only that Mrs Cawston had been strangled and the bloodstains were Steven Baker's. Otherwise, everything was inconclusive.'

The stolen property was packed singly in evidence bags and consisted of the picture frame with the photograph of the old lady, the coffee spoons – those were all in a bag together – and old jewellery found at the Baker's house, together with the small trophy and one gold cufflink. The items found in the Adams's barn – the silver tray, the gold locket and the fish knives and forks – were also there. Other recovered items had been identified by the managers of both raided jewellery shops as stolen new stock. Quite a lot of valuable objects were still missing from these, and Joanna's money was all on Mansell's gang of murderers and thieves having ferreted them away somewhere. Other than the paintings, a tiny bronze statuette of a horse and a silver bonbon dish discovered in the locked room, which were thought not to be connected with any recent robberies, none of it had been found. The two latter items had also been bagged up but it was recognized that they could have legitimately been Mansell's property.

Lord Atworth himself opened the door. On the way, Joanna had asked Sergeant Woods if he wanted to make the introductions as he was of senior rank to her and then they could both ask questions. Woods appreciated her tact, especially as she had at one time been a DS and Carrick's assistant. He had an idea that it wouldn't be all that long before she was back in that role.

The break in the South of France appeared to have only slightly improved Lord Atworth's temper – Carrick's account of his meeting with the man having been somewhat critical.

After a curt greeting, he invited them to enter and led them into the large living room to the right of the hallway. Lady Atworth laid aside the copy of *The Tatler* she had been reading and got to her feet.

'I understand you've found some of it,' she said to Woods.

'We may have, Your Ladyship,' he replied. 'But we've also recovered property stolen during other crimes.' He went on to introduce Joanna and the pair unpacked the evidence bags from a briefcase.

'Oh, that's Mummy!' Lady Atworth cried upon seeing the photo frame. 'And the little cup I won with Snuffles at the dog show. Ages ago, wasn't it, darling?'

Atworth grunted.

'But it's *dented*,' the woman wailed. 'This simply isn't good enough.'

Joanna wasn't about to tell her that this was due to a rather smelly old woman having sat on it.

'This is just junk,' Atworth said. 'And *one* of my gold cufflinks? Where's the other one, eh?' He glowered at the police officers. 'Look, a lot of valuable items were stolen that night and all you can bring us is this miserable lot.'

'Are all of these items yours?' Joanna asked stonily.

He shuffled around the bags, which had been placed on a small table, and then said. 'Yes, all of them.' He turned to his wife. 'Was that jewellery your mother's?'

'Yes, I think so,' said Lady Atworth tentatively. 'But it must have been at the back of a drawer for years.'

'And the little horse and the bonbon dish?' Joanna asked.

'Yes, mine,' Atworth said.

'They weren't on the list you gave us.'

'So I forgot about them.'

'Harold . . .' his wife ventured. 'I don't *think* I've seen them before but—'

'They're mine!' her husband interrupted. 'Kindly allow me to know my own possessions.'

'Is Philip Cawston still here?' Joanna asked.

Atworth looked at her blankly. 'Who?'

'The son of your housekeeper – who was murdered that night.'

'Oh, *him*. No, I think he stayed somewhere else for a few days and then came back to get his and his mother's stuff. I wouldn't have wanted him hanging around the place. He got on my nerves. In fact, I was thinking of getting rid of his mother, too; she wasn't really doing the job properly. I've approached an agency.'

'Do you have a forwarding address for Philip?' Woods asked, having shot a warning glance at Joanna before she exploded. 'We may need to ask him if he's remembered anything else.'

Atworth shook his head. 'No, but doesn't he work at some electrical shop in Bear Flat in the city?'

Joanna said, 'That gala dinner you went to at Bath's Assembly Rooms – did you see Mortimer Mansell there?'

'Yes, I did actually. But I ignored him. We had a meal at his restaurant once and it was pretty awful. The food was all right but we weren't allowed to have the table we wanted, the service was rather poor and the prices were through the roof. I had words with the manager about it and refused to pay the full bill.'

'Was anyone with him at the gala dinner?'

'You're asking really stupid questions,' Atworth countered.

'Please answer it.'

The man dropped into a large leather sofa. He hadn't invited them to be seated. After a moment's thought, he said, 'Yes, I think there was someone at his side for a while – a man. But this individual didn't stay long so perhaps he was an assistant.'

'Please describe him.'

'Look, there were hordes of people there.'

'It's very important, sir,' Woods interposed.

'I saw him,' Lady Atworth said. 'He sort of stuck out as he wasn't in evening dress. Yes, that's right, he barged past me and knocked my elbow, and I almost dropped my wine glass. Didn't apologize.'

'What did he look like?' Woods said, speaking just a little louder than he did normally.

'Oh, he wasn't at all remarkable. Just under six foot tall, I suppose, dark hair that was very thin on top – almost bald really. I seem to remember that his eyes were brown but I might be quite wrong. He didn't even look at me, you see, so I must be. I usually am,' she added sadly, glancing in her husband's direction.

'I hope you're going to leave all this stuff behind,' Atworth said, gesturing towards the evidence bags. 'For one thing I need to get on with the insurance claim as I'm not at all hopeful of ever getting the rest back.'

'We're not,' Joanna crisply told him. 'They're evidence and will be exhibits at a trial, or trials.' She gathered it all up, returned it to the briefcase, turned on her heel and walked out. Outside, going towards the car, she paused to wait for Woods.

'Go on, say it,' he urged. 'Try not to shout though.'

So she did.

Unsurprisingly, Philip Cawston looked unwell, dark lines under his eyes. He had been called from the back of the premises where he had apparently been unpacking newly delivered stock. The manager, upon hearing of the nature of the visit, invited those concerned to use his office.

They seated themselves, and Woods introduced the pair of them. Then he said, 'DCI Carrick's still in charge of the case. We're wondering if you've remembered any details of that night that might be of use to us.'

Cawston smiled wanly. 'Ah, yes, the fellow plaster sufferer. And that other guy he was with – I reckon he put Atworth right in the picture.' He was free of his personal encumbrance – perhaps the only thing he could be happy about right now.

'Have you found somewhere to live?' Joanna asked, having discussed the case with her husband.

'Yes, at least temporarily. A friend's letting me use his spare room and put stuff in his garage. Mum had a little money saved up, and when her will's sorted out it'll come to me. There's only me now – no other family. It might be enough for a deposit and a couple of month's rent on a flat or bedsit. Oh, yes, you want to know about that night . . . I have remembered something but I don't think it's that important. I wasn't exactly in a noticing mood at the time, you understand.'

'Of course not,' Joanna agreed.

'It was something one of those oafs said. I think I mentioned that one of them asked someone called Steve what he should do with whatever it was and was told to ask Georgio. At least, I think that was the name – can't be sure of any of it now. But I'm fairly sure that he – the first man, that is – then went on to say, "I bet hardly any of this will end up with old Podge", or something like that. Perhaps "old Podge" was the boss man.'

They stayed for a few more minutes chatting so as not to cold-bloodedly depart immediately, having been given this not very useful information, and then returned to the nick. Joanna reported to Lynn Outhwaite and wrote a short account of what had occurred. For the rest of the day, although getting on with what needed to be done, everyone seemed to sink into a state of despondency.

Constable Roderick Morris, he of 'uppity little sod' fame, was in the main office, writing a report on a case where young boys living on a housing estate had been throwing stones and other missiles, doing actual damage, at the home of an elderly woman who they insisted was a witch. Suffering from dementia, she hadn't helped her case by threatening to turn them all into toads. All Morris could have done in the circumstances was to talk to the neighbour who had witnessed what had happened and hope to identify the culprits. She had pointed out two houses nearby where she thought at least three of the children might live, and he had duly knocked at the door of the nearest. A hideous assortment of unshaven oafs, bull terriers, shrieking harpies and boys who should have been at school had been unleashed following his polite enquiries.

An only child and having had a sheltered upbringing – his father a university lecturer, his mother a music teacher at a girls' private school – Morris was still a bit naive, sometimes out of his depth in 'ordinary' company. He tried to cover that by adopting a distant manner. Although resembling nobody's pet goldfish he was slim, had a pale complexion and blue eyes. He was also clever, articulate and good at sports that required a fleetness of foot with reflexes to match. This was perhaps not the right stuff, he was beginning to think, for a cop. Perhaps he had the wrong attitude. He had always dreamed of being in the police but was finding that reality didn't match up to what he had imagined. No coward, though, he had stood his ground and waited until the first wave of aggression – he actually thought he glimpsed the flash of a knife – had abated before telling them that for the present the attacks on the old woman's house would be overlooked. Next time, however . . .

Deep down, though, he knew he should have been much more assertive. In his own eyes, he had run away and still burned at the memory of their laughter as he had left. There had been no one at home at the other house and he felt really ashamed of his sense of relief. He wasn't quite sure what to put in the report either.

'Are you busy?' said a man who had just entered.

'Not really, sir,' Morris replied glumly, having recognized the arrival as having been coming and going at the nick.

Gillard introduced himself and then said, 'There's no need to call me "sir" as I only have the nominal rank of constable to enable me to arrest people. May I?' He indicated a nearby unoccupied chair.

'Please do,' said Morris, a bit baffled.

'I work for the NCA, and if you're agreeable, I hope to ask the DCI for permission to borrow you.'

'Borrow me?' queried the even more baffled Morris.

'Yes. I take it you're familiar with this series of cases involving a man calling himself Georgio.'

'Indeed,' Morris replied. 'Not that I really get involved with CID.'

'No, but you might. I'm intending to hang out for a couple of days in the vicinity of a pub in Stoke Marsh, where this maniac is reputed to sometimes turn up. I'm going to dress rough and endeavour to blend into the scenery. I'm not quite sure yet what I'll ask you to do but I'd like you to dress casually. Don't shave for a couple of days, so you don't look too smart. Are you up for that?'

Morris slowly nodded. Word had it that this man went around armed with a Glock 17.

'What's with this, then?' Gillard went on to ask, pointing to the computer screen.

The constable explained. He was perfectly honest about what he regarded as his shortcomings in the matter.

'OK, we'll sort that out first.'

Morris thought that Gillard meant the writing of the report, but that wasn't the case. They left the building and he was requested to drive them to the addresses in question. They first went to the house where either no one had been at home or hadn't answered the door. This time a middle-aged man appeared, and having established that there were three boys under the age of eleven living there, Gillard presented him with a short but gut-wrenching directive concerning the terrorizing of elderly neighbours. This was repeated at the other house – no truants visible this time – the NCA man having upped his language a couple of notches, together with the volume of delivery.

No one laughed this time.

'Just bung in your report that you sternly warned them,' said Gillard as they got back in the car.

'You want to *borrow* him?' James Carrick exclaimed. 'But—' Words failed him.

'Does he look like a cop when he's in civvies?' Gillard asked.

'No, but . . .'

'Come on, you've worked undercover. He seems not too happy and should be given a chance to do something else. And I need someone for a short while to be on hand.'

Carrick decided to think about the 'not too happy' bit later and said, 'I'll have to square it with his boss.'

This was Jenny Anderson, the uniform inspector. They both worked in the same building but, strangely, hardly ever met, and she seemed quite glad to have a chat. Reluctant at first, she finally agreed to let Morris go but for no longer than a week, starting the day after next. She remarked that 'It'll do him good'.

The DCI fervently hoped so.

Gillard departed. He didn't go far to start with, just found Morris to give him the news and asked him to meet him that evening.

'Where?' Morris asked, still struggling not to call Gillard 'sir'.

'D'you have a car?'

Morris said that he did.

'Meet me in the Ring o' Bells in Hinton Littlemoor at six thirty.'

'I don't finish until eight.'

'No, but you'll still be on the job,' Gillard replied patiently. 'By the way, what do people call you?'

'Roddy.'

'D'you like that?'

'No, I don't.'

'Roderick, then. I'm Patrick. If you call me Paddy, I won't like it either.' He laughed as he left the room.

The knowledge that everything was going to be different for the next week and that he would need to live, think and work in a higher gear persisted as Morris walked through the main entrance of the old inn that evening. Country pubs weren't really his kind of thing; he was more at home in nightclubs and bars that had a lot of loud music. In here, the only sounds were quiet conversations, the occasional burst of laughter and the tinkle of knives and forks in the restaurant-cum-saloon bar that was beyond, through a wide archway. There seemed to be rather a lot of dogs.

He gazed around a couple of times, looking for the man he was supposed to be meeting and failed. OK, perhaps he was a bit early. He then actually felt the hairs on the back of his neck stir as he saw that he was being closely observed by a very rural-looking individual propping up the farthest end of the bar, a mostly empty pint tankard in front of him.

'Drink?' Gillard asked when Morris had gone over.

'What's that?' Morris asked, pointing to the tankard.

'Jail ale from Dartmoor. It's a bitter.'

'I prefer lager actually.'

'Then have what you want.'

'I'll get it.'

'No, it's OK.'

Gillard, having bought himself another pint as well, turned the collar of his jacket back down and led the way over to a spare table where he seated himself, combed his hair off his forehead with his fingers and sighed contentedly. Then he said, 'Right, let's get the semi-official stuff out of the way first. I can tell that you're a bit nervous of me because word has probably got round that I boil postmen for breakfast and was pretty senior in the army. Forget all that. You don't have to show me any deference at all; you can argue, disagree, tell me to sod off – I don't care. All I ask when we're actually *on the job* is that you do as I tell you. Your well-being might depend on it. If I think you're in danger because of whatever it is you're doing, I shall shout at you. To save your life, I might even give you a clout. The people we're dealing with are bloody dangerous; this Georgio is almost certainly a psychopath. Understand?'

Morris reckoned he did and nodded.

'Now then . . .'

THIRTEEN

'Courtesy of Bristol CID, we've located more Smithsons,' Carrick reported in a phone call to Gillard early the next day. 'If you remember, Jez Smithson was one of the three who attacked you in Queen Street.'

'I do remember that,' Gillard replied, hoping when he'd spoken that he hadn't sounded sarcastic.

'There are another three of them, first cousins of his – two brothers and a sister – and they all live in Latchworth. It's near Stoke Marsh. The brothers, Harry and Ken, live at home with their mother, Jadie; they're both in their early twenties. Sister Candice, mid-twenties, is living with a bloke by the name of Hibbs four doors away. I won't bore you with their criminal records as you don't have all morning either. Bristol thinks they're all involved with what was described – obscenities deleted in case Ingrid's within earshot – as "some bastard who fancies himself as a crime lord". This character is rumoured – only rumoured – to use another identity, but whether he's our man is anyone's guess.'

'There's more than a chance that he is,' Gillard agreed.

'I don't think there's much we can do with this info right now, but I'll send you some mugshots of the Smithsons.'

'What about Hibbs?'

'I'll check on him, too.'

At least, Gillard thought glumly, *he appears to have forgiven me for not arresting a man against whom I had absolutely no evidence.*

The lack of progress didn't really change when he received the mugshots. Those of the Smithsons showed a pair of dark-haired, unshaven youths with a faint resemblance to each other and a young woman who looked careworn and had unkempt hair who didn't resemble either of them. As far as Brian Hibbs was concerned, he had served two years in prison for GBH, and although there were similarities – the picture had been taken some years previously – he had doubts that this was the man they were after.

He rang Carrick.

'You're really not sure?' the DCI asked.

'You know what it's like with old mugshots,' Gillard sighed. 'It was taken at least ten years ago when he had a lot more hair. No, I'm not sure.'

'I'll get some more digging done – just in case.'

The 'digging' didn't reveal much more information, only that Hibbs hadn't been in trouble with the law since being released from prison. Carrick asked Bristol to send someone to the address to make enquiries, but no one was at home. Neighbours on one side of the terraced house said they knew nothing about the people next door, and anyway weren't in the habit of 'prying'. An elderly woman living on her own on the other side thought Hibbs – she hadn't known his name – went to work 'somewhere'. The woman he lived with – the neighbour assumed she was his wife – hadn't been seen by her in weeks.

This series of cases, of course, was only part of the DCI's workload. The aftermath of several serious crimes was under investigation, involving hundreds, if not thousands, of hours of painstaking work on forensic samples and endless checking following house-to-house enquiries. An unexplained death, a clutch of housebreakings, a hit and run . . .

Carrick spent the greater part of the morning dealing with outstanding reports, conducting a briefing and slogging through the never-diminishing pile of documents to read and make notes on in his in-tray. During that time, he also learned that Robert Adams, Mortimer Mansell's gardener, was making good progress in his recovery. In another call, he was told that the small bronze figure of a horse, Chinese apparently and extremely valuable, and the silver bon-bon dish had positively been identified as property stolen during a burglary in Bath several months previously. Photographs were available. Having had Joanna's account of her visit with Derek Woods to the Atworths, this, Carrick thought, was interesting. Perhaps he ought to ask Patrick to go along to give His Lordship the information.

Most interesting of all was that Philip Cawston had called,

extremely worried, as he had found an old and heavy silver bangle among his mother's sewing things that he knew hadn't belonged to her. He had decided to, as he put it, 'own up' as he thought the police might investigate him further, find it and think that the pair of them had somehow been complicit in the crime. He had been assured that wasn't likely and a request had been made that the bangle be brought to the police station as soon as possible, Philip to avoid handling it further.

Carrick sat at his desk and asked himself a few questions. Had the bangle been tossed aside by one of the robbers, thinking it of little or no value? Had Mrs Cawston's sewing box or bag been in the room where she was murdered and the bangle had either accidentally landed in it or been a handy place to stow it away for a little while before someone secretly made off with it? He prayed for there to be even part of a fingerprint on it that wasn't Cawston's.

Lunchtime. He got up from his desk feeling old, tired, depressed and as though he had been lugging around this bloody blue drainpipe for ever. His phone rang, again. He almost ignored it and then groaned and reseated himself. It was further news about Hibbs. The woman who lived with him had been found to be at home and had insisted that she was his wife. They both worked at a Bristol hospital, her husband as a porter.

Almost certainly the wrong man, then.

The following morning, just before first light and after a night of rain, Patrick Gillard got up early, donned old clothes kept specially for the purpose, quietly rummaged around to find the things he needed to take with him, had breakfast and went out. He exited through the conservatory, turned left as though intending to go down the drive but instead went through the little gate in the garden wall and into the churchyard. This was an old way, originally constructed, it was thought, so the incumbent and also the squire and his lady living in the neighbouring grange – there was a door in the higher wall at the end of the rectory garden – didn't have to mix with the locals in the usually muddy lane on their way to services. Thankfully, the lane was now made up.

The path in the churchyard meandered between the

gravestones – he could only just see where he was going but didn't want to use a torch – and led to a gap in the stone wall that bordered the church grounds. The public footpath it then became was little more than a narrow track across the pasture below that went downhill towards woodland. He had been this way many times before and knew all the paths and byways through and around the village, some dating back into the mists of history. But he didn't go downhill today, just turned left where there was a fork in the path and headed towards the village.

Unbeknown to him, Ingrid had got out of bed as he left and was standing at the window overlooking the drive. As she watched, the sky lightening in the east, he came into view. He had told her that there was no point in taking the Range Rover as it was too conspicuous and he would catch what Elspeth called 'the workmen's bus' that stopped outside the village stores. His guitar was slung across his back and a small rucksack was over the other shoulder. She stood watching until he had disappeared from view.

You don't own people just because you're married to them, she knew, but right now and although he had told her he wouldn't be away for long, perhaps a couple of days, she wanted to lock him in a cage to be out of danger. A gilded cage at that. And if he thought she was going to stay quietly at home, he was mistaken.

PC Roderick Morris was working on his own in Stoke Marsh. He knew he was on his own during the day because Patrick had told him so. That is, he had said he would *probably* be as Patrick had other things to do. All Morris had been asked to do this morning was to acclimatize himself with the place and discover exactly where the Spotted Dog was situated. Maps, on paper or the internet, he had been told, were OK up to a point, but there was nothing like walking the streets to discover the lie of the land and find out how the place 'ticked'. Under no circumstances was he to look like a cop. Nor was he to loiter or look like an undercover cop. He was to use his imagination.

Morris didn't think he had one.

Gillard had also stressed that should he see someone he thought might be the man they were after, he must not approach or speak to him, just find a place he could phone from. He had gone on to say it twice: be very, very careful.

There was a lot of new development in the village – actually, now a small town – and it was regarded by those who lived in more affluent surrounding areas as little more than a cheap dormitory for both Bath and Bristol workers as it was situated roughly halfway between the two. This disdain was reasonable as the place had been cobbled together over the years from three ancient hamlets and the farms located there – Marsh, Stoke Chantry and Little Hamsworth – all of which, according to local elderly people, had been extremely picturesque and mentioned in the Domesday Book.

The Spotted Dog could be described as a relic of the hamlet of Marsh as it was just about the only surviving building of any age. Morris had located it after having walked briskly around the centre of the town as though he was looking for somewhere or someone. Having done that, he leaned on the parapet wall of a bridge over a little stream nearby and was now frantically thinking what the hell to do next. As instructed, he had dressed in an old sweatshirt and jeans, had not had a shave for two mornings and spiked up his hair a bit. This, he felt, had only made him look rather trendy. He still lived with his parents, and his father had noticed.

'What the hell d'you you think you're doing?' he had demanded to know. 'You can't go on duty looking like that.'

Morris had explained that he had been seconded to CID for a while and was under orders. He wasn't sure if his father, a suspicious man, had believed him. He hadn't been at all happy about his son's choice of career; nor, come to think of it, had his mother. Something academic would have been their choice, perhaps in teaching. Only his mother had attended his passing-out parade. She loved him, he knew that, and insisted on doing his washing and ironing as well as cooking his meals. It came to Morris – he was in his mid-twenties – as he leaned on the bridge watching the little brook serenely moving beneath him, that it was high time he got a flat or bedsit of his own.

Imagination . . .

It was ten thirty and the town was quite busy. Outside the pub, a woman was putting out tables and chairs together with parasols and plant pot saucers as ashtrays. Morris wandered over.

'Is the boss around?' he asked.

She straightened from picking up a couple of bits of litter. 'You're looking at her.'

'Oh! – er, sorry . . . d'you need any help?'

She eyed him narrowly before replying. 'No, I don't think so.'

'Only I've sort of been chucked out of home – still at uni. I need to earn some money.'

'So where are you living now?'

'In my car. You can't get accommodation at short notice anywhere round here.'

'Because of the unis.'

'That's right.'

'Why aren't you at uni right now?'

'The lecturers have gone on strike.'

This was perfectly true.

Again, she studied him. 'You don't look very strong.'

'I'm wiry, not muscle-bound.'

Which was also perfectly true.

'I could do with some assistance part-time in the cellar and clearing tables in the evenings, but it'll only be for a little while. Someone's off sick.'

'That's fine. Thank you.'

She turned and went back inside, saying over her shoulder, 'You can start right now. The storeroom needs a good clear-out. You can scrub the floor in there while you're at it.'

Morris decided to make a good job of it. This wasn't difficult as he was a tidy soul by nature and couldn't bear to live in a mess. The rest of the morning passed quickly. He finished the storeroom, which was quite small, having thrown out a lot of rubbish that in his view was a fire hazard. The cellar, next door, was bigger, cold, as it should be, and contained a lot more rubbish – broken chairs and cardboard boxes with next to nothing in them. It really needed a skip, so all he could do was put what stock that remained in the boxes in the storeroom and ram the rest tightly into a corner so it took up a lot less space.

Surprised to be offered lunch, he fell on cod and chips, in the cellar, then went back to work. The pub got busy at around one thirty, so he was asked to don a rather smart brown waistcoat and matching long apron and clear the tables. All this was such a change from his normal police activities that he quite enjoyed himself. To be front of house was extremely helpful in connection with his real task as he could keep an eye on the customers. Outside, someone in the vicinity seemed to be playing the guitar, or listening to it on a radio in an adjacent house, but he couldn't see where the music was coming from.

At closing time and after steak and more chips, plus a lager, he went to where he had left his car, his wages in his pocket. The landlady, Barbara, had made him promise to return the following day. Other than Barbara – she did all the main cooking – there had been little time to speak to the other staff – three of them: the barman, an assistant cook and a waitress. He hadn't spotted anyone who remotely resembled the man they were after, either in his thinning-hair mode or wearing a blond wig. Very early days, Morris knew, but was this suspect one person or two, a criminal and another bloke who merely worked in an insurance office? There was still guitar music coming from somewhere.

Needless to say, he was being watched.

The old skittle alley across the yard at the Spotted Dog – Barbara told Morris that before that it had been the stables – had been turned into a games room, darts at one end and a small pool table at the other. Part of his duties when he wasn't changing barrels in the cellar and keeping everywhere tidy was to clear the three tables at the end of the room, along with the window ledges and floor, and deal with any orders for drinks and food. The waitress wouldn't work in there due to sexist remarks – and worse – from the male clientele, two men having been banned for that reason. She still refused to set foot in there.

Morris was happy with this arrangement as he now felt too conspicuous front of house. Did he really look like a student with his short, spiked-up hair? He had explained away Barbara's comment that he was managing to keep himself very clean and tidy considering he was living in a car by saying that now that he had a job his parents had relented and allowed him back home. It made him slightly alarmed at how easily all these lies had tripped off his tongue.

He had tried to contact Patrick Gillard while at work in the evenings – the man had asked him to keep in touch even if he had nothing to report – but the only place he felt he could talk freely was in the cellar and his mobile didn't work down there. And at home he hadn't bothered; there really wasn't anything to say, a situation that carried on for another day. The person who was off sick had, according to Barbara, 'disappeared into thin air', and was impossible to contact. Barbara had a husband, Jim, but he was in a wheelchair and confined to upstairs for most of the time, having been paralysed from the waist down in a serious car accident.

Inspector Anderson, Morris's boss, had only given permission for him to be 'borrowed' by the CID for a week. Well, at least, the young constable thought ironically, if nothing else, I now know how to change beer barrels and clean out the pipes. That might come in handy one day. He had also got quite good at quietly escorting out those who, near closing time, had had too much to drink and started to walk into things or cause trouble.

Then, the following evening, Friday, the whole place crowded, he was bringing a drinks order to the games room where there was a casual darts match in progress when he noticed that things were getting a bit heated. Someone, a man with blond hair, didn't appear to like losing.

Morris delivered his order to a group of customers by the pool table and hung around, busying himself wiping the adjacent tables where no one was sitting. Then he contrived to move a little closer, having spotted a used tankard on a window ledge. The blond man, who still had his back to him, had started shouting and had obviously had too much to drink, swaying a little on his feet. Some of the other players edged away from him.

'Can we keep things friendly, gentlemen, please,' said Morris as loudly as he thought suitable, approaching.

The blond man turned to him: young, brown-eyed and with a faint scar on the left side of his face. 'What's your problem, sonny?'

'I'm asking that you keep the atmosphere friendly, sir.'

For this he got a torrent of abuse.

One of the darts players had carried on calmly and threw. 'Cool it,' he said quietly.

It instantly became clear to Morris that here was the real cause of the blond man's anger, but there was nothing like a handy scapegoat, was there? He found himself grabbed and flung backwards by the blond man but somehow kept his feet and staggered into a woman's arms. He apologized profusely, unaware that she had deliberately run forward to catch him.

'He's as good at darts as he is with a knife,' Ingrid whispered in his ear, steadying him.

The remaining darts player, baggy old jeans, a well-worn sweatshirt with oil on it, another smear of the same on his face, bellowed, 'Cool it!' at the offender in a voice Morris recognized. When this didn't provide instant satisfaction, he grabbed him and propelled him out through the door into the yard outside. He returned and everyone got on with their evening as though nothing had happened.

Morris collected a few glasses and went back into the main building giving the ejected one, who had tripped and fallen flat, a wide berth. Patrick was *playing darts*?

Ingrid hadn't come on her own but had asked Joanna if she wanted to have a drink in Stoke Marsh with her. Joanna, off duty, had been delighted with the offer as she knew exactly what was going on. It wasn't difficult for either of them to change their appearance, very necessary in Ingrid's case. She had dug out a blonde wig she had bought at a Hinton Littlemoor jumble sale and wore tight orange leggings with a yellow top and trainers. Plus too much make-up. In deference to her husband's need for concentration, she hadn't worn the bra that did amazing things to her bust, and right now wasn't even sure he had noticed her in the throng.

He had.

Joanna had merely freed her long Titian hair from the tidy bun she imprisoned it in for work and donned casual clothes. She had been a bit scathing about Morris's recruitment to CID but had to admit that he had done a good job in getting himself into the heart of things.

They stayed almost until closing time and then moved to

leave. Georgio wasn't going to appear tonight. The darts match had fizzled out and it became clear they had been playing for money – Ingrid wondered if that was permitted – when the victor counted his winnings and shoved it back in his pocket. Then he collected his guitar from a corner where it had been leaning on the wall, gave Ingrid a particularly lascivious leer and blundered out. Blundered.

'He doesn't want to talk,' Ingrid hissed to Joanna. 'Let's go.'

'You know so?' Joanna queried.

'We have our codes.'

That is, he was annoyed with her for coming.

The codes also appeared to apply to the open air for there he was, leaning on a tree playing chords on his guitar not far from where Joanna had parked her car – they had come together as Ingrid hadn't wanted to bring the Range Rover. He ignored them.

'He's probably hanging around to make sure Morris isn't waylaid by that yob or any friends of his as he leaves work,' Ingrid whispered.

'Where's Patrick staying at night?'

'Heaven only knows.'

They left.

Almost as soon as they had gone a silver Audi drew into the car park and two men got out, one of whom was fair-haired. Gillard, still leaning on the tree, was ostensibly concentrating on a short classical piece. Without giving him a glance, the two went into the pub. After a short pause, he followed. He had to check as Morris had never seen the people they were after in the flesh.

The first thing he saw alarmed him: Morris was talking to the pair of them. The man with fair hair had his back to him, which wasn't helpful. Morris then gave them a cheesy grin and went to speak to the landlady; Gillard had a good idea she was about to call time. She looked at the clock, frowned, and nodded, heading towards the pumps. She then called for last orders. The two newcomers went to sit at a table which Morris hurriedly cleared for them and then fetched their drinks, also dealing with the payment.

'For God's sake, don't overdo it,' Gillard said under his breath and left the cover of a pillar to go back outside to his tree.

Thankfully, the car park, at the side of the buildings and surrounded by a mostly dead conifer hedge, was quite poorly lit. After a few minutes had elapsed, he heard time being called.

Eventually, people drifted out of the pub. The two men he had seen enter but had been unable to identify came out and went to the Audi. The fair-haired one wasn't Georgio. They drove away. Then, when most of the clientele had gone and the only sounds were traffic and the muted clatter of crockery as the clearing up was done somewhere in the rear, three men entered the car park on foot, one of whom was the man he had evicted. Gillard knew the body language.

The front door of the Spotted Dog had been closed and locked so he went down the sideway, sufficiently wide to permit access by delivery vehicles, and into the rear yard. Three cars were parked here, one of which was Morris's. No one was in sight, but light beamed from an open doorway and from several windows. Otherwise, it was gloomy; these people didn't seem to go in for lights. A woman came out of the doorway and moved as if to cross the yard to what had been the skittle alley.

'Who are you?' she called.

'Patrick, a chum of Roderick's,' Gillard answered. 'I'm worried that some friends of the troublemaker have come to settle a score.'

'What troublemaker?'

'Didn't he tell you? No matter, it wasn't that serious.'

'I'll tell him, then.'

'Please also tell him to stay right where he is.'

'I need to lock up.'

'This won't take long.'

Gillard had only just spoken when four men, *four*, walked around the corner, fronted by a Steven Baker lookalike. Another eighteen-stone hulk, then. To his left and slightly behind him was the evicted one, on his right a man who he was fairly sure was Jez Smithson and, right at the back, trying to make himself look small, difficult, another big-built man who was either seriously stooped or would be of interest to an anthropologist as his hands were roughly on a level with his knees.

The fair-haired man pointed and said, 'Him', and then called, 'Where's sonny boy, then?'

'Here,' Morris said, emerging from within the main building. 'Leave.'

'Get back!' Gillard ordered him. 'Keep out of sight!'

The hulk rushed at him. He wasn't at all sober and a flying uppercut sent him staggering away but not down, and he came back at the same time that they all laid into their target. Having had a couple of blows land on him, Gillard lost his temper. It didn't happen very often these days, but when it did, he wasn't quite sane. But while he fought them off, using tactics that had even made James Carrick wince, he became aware they were thinning out with more rapidity that he would have expected. Then, in receipt of something that made him momentarily black out, he found himself on the ground, the hulk standing over him. A whirlwind of feet and fists tore into the man and he went over backwards on to the ground like a felled bullock and stayed there. When Gillard sat up and looked around, he saw that the others seemed to have gone, except for one who was throwing up into a drain.

Panting, Morris held out a hand and helped Gillard to his feet. 'Are you OK?' he gasped.

Gillard clasped him on the shoulder with his other hand, partly to steady himself. 'You hadn't mentioned kickboxing,' he also gasped.

'Just a pastime really.' He added in a whisper, 'Do we arrest them?'

'Yes, but I think we torture this one a bit first,' Gillard replied, indicating the big man who was trying to sit up. He went over and pushed him back down, hard, with a foot, then fought to get his temper back under control or he'd end up killing him.

What happened next was filed by Morris in that part of his brain that stored Things That Never Actually Happened. This private library, to be browsed through sometimes at leisure, would eventually be joined by other happenings in the future while working for CID if Patrick Gillard was involved. Before that, though, he was asked to inform Barbara, the landlady, busy dealing with the day's takings and completely oblivious to what had been going on outside, that everything had been 'sorted'.

After he'd done that, and in a corner of the main car park,

the big man, who told them that his name was Pete Baker, half-brother of Steven, went on to say quite a lot more. This was not wrung out of him using a method that Gillard had used on 'suspects' in the past, which had been invented by the ancient Japanese and caused horrible agony. No, all that was applied was terror and the sight of an Italian silver-hafted throwing knife that felt distinctly sharp against the skin of his throat. No doubt the distinct inability to walk in a straight line afterwards and the feeling of being weak and wobbly was down to the six pints of beer and couple of whiskies he had drunk that evening. After initial hesitation and prompted by questions, he gave the information willingly and actually said that he saw it as a get-out as he was sick to death of the madman who was ruling his life. Georgio. Now, though, he was told he would be arrested and charged with assault and kept in custody for his own safety.

'So that's it, then,' Morris said sadly when the man had been taken away in an area car. The one being ill had also quietly disappeared.

'Regrets?' Gillard queried.

'In a way. And I disobeyed your order to stay out of sight.'

'I'm rather glad you did.'

'Was it Georgio?'

'Neither of the blond blokes was. But the one I'd chucked out and who came back may well have been part of his rat-pack. Can you remember everything that Pete Baker said?'

'I think so.'

'Write a report when you get home – don't leave it until the morning. Are you on duty tomorrow?'

'Yes, I am.'

'When you get to work give the report to the DI – I happen to know that she's in, too – and await further orders. What Baker said will have to be acted upon immediately, but don't worry, I'll speak to the DCI.'

'OK.' Morris gazed around. 'I shall have to hand in my notice here.' For some reason, he felt a bit sad.

'I expect the landlady's still around.'

'There's no need for you to stay.'

'Right now there is. I'll hang on here until you're safely off the premises.'

'Thanks. Where's your car?'

'I didn't bring it – came by bus. I haven't missed the last one if you get a shift on.'

'So you're going home?'

'For tonight, yes.'

'I'll give you a lift.'

They left after Morris had spoken to Barbara and, as had Carrick recently, Gillard felt a bit humbled.

FOURTEEN

'What this man said, if true, will have to be acted upon immediately,' James Carrick said. 'But *was* he speaking the truth?'

'I think so,' Patrick Gillard replied. 'Morris thought so, too.'

It was Saturday and they were holding a briefing in the old rectory kitchen at Hinton Littlemoor.

'Before we talk about this, how did you get on with Morris?' Carrick asked.

'In my opinion, he has the makings of a good CID officer. Not to mention the kickboxing. He floored Baker with a fast series of moves that made me feel old and decrepit.'

'I'm gobsmacked,' Carrick said.

Gillard still felt a bit decrepit this morning, but nothing would have made him admit it. Worse, even though he'd been aware that Ingrid had been looking at him with a little smile in a way that he couldn't fail to recognize, he had crashed off to sleep like a beached flounder. He didn't want her to think it had been some kind of revenge for her turning up at the Spotted Dog, but so far this morning there had been no chance to speak privately.

Joanna, who had parked the car at the rectory but walked back to the village to buy stamps at the shop-cum-post office, now came into the room, followed by Ingrid who set about brewing coffee.

'Council of war?' the latter enquired.

For some reason, this made the DCI immediately assume the role of chairman. 'Just to recap, then,' he began, 'Pete Baker, half-brother of Steven, gave Patrick the information that Georgio is planning a raid on a private art collection here in Bath. Apparently, Mansell had mentioned to Georgio that it was his next intended target as he had foreign buyers for some of the paintings and artefacts in the collection. Georgio, it would seem, knows who these dealers are because Mansell had decided to put him in charge of the gang and shared the details with him. That was Mansell's fatal mistake – Georgio no longer needed him, and after the abuse he gave them following the botched second jewellery raid, together with his refusal to pay them, there was open mutiny.'

Gillard said, 'You must appreciate that this is a translation into everyday English from a diatribe of expletives, broken sentences, grunts and glottal stops.'

Carrick gave him a look and carried on. 'The raid is due to be carried out in five days' time – four now – and involves one of the large terraced houses in Great Pulteney Street. The collection belongs to a man who, Baker said – and how true this is, is anyone's guess – has bought stuff from Mansell in the past. In other words, unless he did it in good faith, he's dodgy. Baker didn't know his name.'

'Did he say anything else of interest?' Ingrid asked.

'Yes, it's something Georgio said to them, and I tend to believe it. He said that he hoped the man's new girlfriend would be at home.'

'To kill her?' she said in hushed tones.

'Looks like it. Pete reckons he's impotent but gets turned on by the prospect of murder.'

There was a short reflective silence while everyone digested this.

'Like just about all the others we've grabbed in the gang, Pete wants out,' Gillard said.

'Do we know exactly which house in Great Pulteney Street it is?' Joanna asked.

'Baker said he didn't. But it shouldn't be too difficult to find out. There can't be too many folk with large and valuable private art collections in that area.'

Ingrid shook her head but made no comment.

'But if he is dodgy, discovering who he is *will* be difficult,' Joanna pointed out, putting Ingrid's reservations into words. 'And one can hardly go knocking on doors.'

Ingrid said, 'But it's worth asking the art experts who looked at what Mansell had in his locked room. They must have their grapevines and know what's going on in the city and who has what.'

They discussed it a little longer, drank their coffee and then the DCI said, 'Right. Morris can go and see the experts and find out if they have anything to say.' He turned to Patrick. 'Do you have his mobile number handy?'

Morris, loping through the city a little later that morning, was still enjoying the anonymity of not being in uniform. People now ignored him in the same way they did when he was off duty. He could surreptitiously watch them. He had decided to have a shave this morning, though, as he was no longer working undercover, and his father had approved of this. His mother was upset that he was no longer in blue as she seemed to be under the impression that it was some kind of demotion. Morris had told her that the situation was only temporary but found himself hoping that it wasn't. He rather felt that remaining living at home was temporary, too.

The advantage of coming from what might be described as a 'good' family background and having been taken during his childhood to all kinds of art galleries and museums including some in London – excursions that he hadn't necessarily enjoyed at the time – meant that he did not feel at all intimidated by his brief. Just under two hours later, having spoken to three people owning art galleries, commercial and otherwise, and one other, the three having already helped the police with the case, he had gathered quite a lot of information. Returning to the nick, he hammered it all into a computer and printed it off in case someone wanted a hard copy.

Lynn Outhwaite didn't quite know what to do with the report and had her hands more than full already. She got on the phone.

'The DCI's working from home,' she reported after the call. 'But right now he's having what was described to me as a late working lunch following an early working breakfast at the Gillards' place and wants you to take it over. D'you know where that is?'

'Yes, but I can email it to him,' Morris said.

'I think he wants you to take it personally.'

Morris left his car in a parking space outside the church at Hinton Littlemoor and went the rest of the way on foot. He was quite surprised to see a police presence at the gateway to the rectory and was stopped and asked his business. As he walked down the drive, he saw an elderly lady supervising a couple of young children playing in the garden. She waved to him and he waved back. Patrick's mother?

Joanna, who was nearest and at Ingrid's request, answered his ring at the front door. 'Oh, hello,' she said.

'Some information for the DCI,' Morris said holding out the envelope containing the hard copy of his report. There was every chance that if Gillard had not come into the hallway just then, she would have taken it, thanked him and shut the door in his face.

'Come in, Roderick,' he said. 'We're in the conservatory.'

Morris gave Joanna a big smile and went in. *Just because you're the DCI's wife*, the smile said, *it doesn't mean I have to be treated like the dog's dinner.*

A dark-haired woman who was probably Patrick's wife called to him as he went past the kitchen door. 'Hello, I'm Ingrid. Have you had lunch?'

Morris said that he hadn't.

'Go in, take a seat and I'll bring you something.' Moments later, as he was going away, 'You're not a vegan or anything, are you?'

'Never,' Morris replied.

The conservatory was large and a bit like a jungle, Carrick and Gillard, a slightly daunting pair, sitting to one side of it, virtually underneath the foliage of a tall palm. Morris flippantly told himself that no, they weren't man-eaters. On a bad day though . . .

'Well, Morris, what do you have?' the DCI asked.

Diffidently, Morris handed over his envelope and sat down on one of the cushioned cane chairs.

Carrick extracted the printed sheets and read. Once or twice as he did so, he looked up and stared at the constable in amazement. Then he whispered, 'Bloody hell,' and carried on reading.

'Obviously interesting,' Gillard commented dryly, needing to know some details.

'It's dynamite!' Carrick said, coming to the end.

Morris, who had had a ham sandwich presented to him

partway through the reading, avoided Joanna's gaze and carried on eating.

'This,' Carrick continued, giving the report to Gillard, 'if correct,' he added cautiously, 'means that we can catch not only this madman calling himself Georgio but a man by the name of Rufus Barnfather – which I happen to know is one of several aliases he uses – who is on the Most Wanted list of several European police forces. He specializes in handling stolen art of all kinds and has been behind thefts from galleries and private collections, in the course of which several people – guards, witnesses – have been murdered. Barnfather had disappeared, but according to this is now living in Bath, in Great Pulteney Street. Whether Mansell knew about this character and that he was now living here, having somehow got himself out of Europe, is open to conjecture – they appear to have the same interests, after all – but the man may well have bought stuff from him, personally or through an agent.'

'And made low offers perhaps,' Ingrid suggested. She turned to Morris. 'Please tell us about the person who gave you this information.'

Morris cleared his throat. 'I spoke to four people, three of whom are the ones who helped us before in identifying stuff in Mansell's collection in the locked room. We have their names and addresses on record, which made them easy to find as they have galleries in the same area of the city. The fourth, the person who told me about Barnfather, wishes to remain anonymous and said she wouldn't say a word to me if I demanded to know personal details.'

'Any guesses as to why this woman has an axe to grind with regard to Barnfather?' Gillard asked.

'No, but she seemed to be very angry with him about something and glad for the opportunity to drop him right in it. Given this man's history, she might be frightened for her own safety as well. She's an associate of one of the others I spoke to – possibly in a relationship with him and he pointed me in her direction. But she is an art expert in her own right.'

'Did you go to her home?'

'Yes, an apartment, but it was only just around the corner in Queen's Square. He rang her first. He told her, winking at me, that I was house-trained.'

'I'd have been livid about that,' Joanna muttered.

'I've found it sometimes pays to have a sense of humour,' Morris said to her.

Ouch, Ingrid thought and repressed a smile, with difficulty.

'There's even the address of this man in Great Pulteney Street,' Carrick went on, glancing through the printed sheets. 'D'you reckon any of the people you spoke to were aware of Barnfather's criminal activities?'

'They might have been, sir, but were cagey, so I didn't like to probe too much, thinking they might clam up as their professional reputations were at stake. The woman seems to know all about him, though – it was she who gave me his address.'

'This will have to be handled very, very carefully, but what we need to do first is reconnoitre the place.'

'I'll do it,' Morris offered.

'You won't,' Carrick told him. 'Your face has been seen by quite a few folk in connection with this, and as we have no idea whether this character has any minders or hangers-on lurking about it's too great a risk. Stay away from those areas of the city until the case has been resolved, even when you're back in uniform. I'll mention it to the DI.'

'Yes, sir,' Morris muttered.

'Is Monday your last day with us?'

'I think Tuesday is.'

'Right, see you on Monday morning, then. And good work.'

Gillard escorted him to the door. 'Just go with the flow,' he said quietly. 'And please remember that orders from the DCI are mine too. It's for your own safety.'

Morris went back to the nick and spent the afternoon doing small jobs, interviewing witnesses in other cases for Lynn Outhwaite. Surely, he thought, if he wore a hooded top and sort of slouched along, it wouldn't matter if he just walked past the house in question in his free time this evening . . .

At almost all times of the year, the streets and arcades of Bath are busy during the day with tourists and visitors from all over the world. Tour buses jam the narrow roads to the extent of concealing the sights that people have actually come to see. But at night, when they are in their hotels or have gone elsewhere, the old parts of the city look quite different. Those exploring on foot and in possession of an imagination can almost see the men who once tottered along between the shafts of sedan chairs, and hear the sharp and fast clatter of shod hooves on stone as the wealthy were whisked in their phaetons to their evening entertainment. In the unfashionable, darker areas, people used to watch where they trod, the narrow ways fetid with animal dung and the run-off from small slaughterhouses.

Great Pulteney Street has never had the misfortune of being anything but the refuge of the wealthy. At over a thousand feet long and a hundred feet wide, it is the grandest thoroughfare in the city. The man at present calling himself Rufus Barnfather lived at the end of the street farthest from Pulteney Bridge, and Roderick Morris already knew what the house looked like as there is a lot of information on the internet for students of architecture and curious cops. All he was going to do, he told himself, not for the first time, was walk by, cross the road and return on the other side. Then he would go and have a drink in a wine bar before he found something to eat. He had told his mother he was going out for the evening, and she had looked upset but said nothing. No doubt when he returned home, his father would have something to say about it. He had had something to say about the kickboxing ('yobs' sport'), the way a swear word sometimes slipped out, the girlfriend who had dyed her hair bright orange for a dare and whom he had been stupid enough to take home ('I don't want that kind of person in my house').

It came to him that the man's attitude was barely believable in the twenty-first century and the situation would have to stop. He would find himself a flat, a bedsit or a large cupboard and be independent.

Morris had walked from home – taking a car into the city centre is a bad idea as there's hardly anywhere to park – and had got as far as Grand Parade where he paused to lean on the balustrade to look over at the river. Below him was the horseshoe-shaped weir; to his right, Parade Gardens. Pulteney Bridge, illuminated after dark, the light not penetrating into its darkly grim three arches, was on his left. When he crossed it in a couple of minutes' time, he would be in Argyle Street which led to Laura Place with its fountain. If he paused when he reached there, he would be able to see down the whole length of Great Pulteney Street.

For some reason, he then had a sudden and unwelcome memory of the recent occasion he had gone into the Ring o' Bells in Hinton Littlemoor and failed to see Patrick Gillard until he had almost felt that keen gaze on him. Morris knew now that he had been doing that deliberately, demonstrating how to disappear. Had he since been watching him from somewhere in the vicinity of the Spotted Dog? Was it Patrick who had been playing the guitar? Was he, in fact, watching him *now*?

And here I am, he thought, *disobeying orders. Again.* His skin crawled.

Abruptly, he did an about-turn and quick-marched away, only pausing a couple of minutes later outside the Old Apple Tree pub. He had never been inside the place and, curious, he went in. It was quaint, sufficiently quaint to stop him in his tracks. There was a fireplace with a good hot log fire in it – the nights were still unseasonably chilly – and the pub's wood-panelled interior reminded him of an old railway carriage. The few people in there didn't give him a second look.

'Yes, sir,' called the barman with a smile.

His nerves still jangling, Morris carefully scanned the customers – no Patrick – and then the beer pumps. It didn't seem to be the sort of place that served lager willingly. He settled for a half of Gem, a local beer, found a corner table and sat down for a think. He couldn't remember the last time he'd had a real think, but had only got halfway through his beer and as far as deciding to go and have a meal when the door opened and in walked someone he preferred not to meet just then.

Patrick Gillard looked around as though expecting to see him and then came over. 'May I join you?'

'Of course.'

Gillard made himself as comfortable as possible on the hard settle.

'Can I get you a drink?' Morris went on to ask coolly.

'Not just now, thank you. Afterwards.' He lowered his voice and said, 'I can't say that I didn't expect to see you somewhere around here tonight – that would be a lie – but do want you to know that I'm not lurking in this area in order to spy on you. I came into the city tonight to do a little quiet surveillance on the house belonging to this Barnfather character and was crossing the road in the Orange Grove when I spotted you coming this way.'

'I was going to walk by the house,' Morris confessed. 'But changed my mind.'

'Good, because if I'd come upon you near the bridge I'd have had a very strong inclination to chuck you in the river.'

Morris didn't smile. 'I'm a pretty good swimmer,' he retorted.

'Make up your mind, Roderick, and realize that with a lot of careers people have to start at the bottom. If you're in the police or armed services that means obeying orders and not thinking that you know better.'

Initially having had a strong inclination of his own to punch this man on the nose, Morris kept quiet. Honesty told him that there was nothing to get angry about as everything Gillard had said slotted neatly into his own perception of himself. Perhaps also he had unconsciously developed his father's superior attitude to cover up the fact that he wasn't very sure of himself.

'Right now, though, do you want to come and do a bit of snooping with me?' Gillard continued.

Morris nodded. Then he said, 'The DCI said I wasn't to go anywhere near the place.'

'So he did. I'll take the flak.'

'OK then.'

'Sure?'

'I might get in the way.'

'Hardly.'

They left the pub and went across the bridge, which is unusual in that it has shops on either side. The night continued to be cool, a strong breeze in their faces as they walked on the right-hand side of the road, and Morris noticed in a detached kind of way that there was the merest halt to the other man's gait. Traffic was quiet and they were too; there was no need to say anything. Morris tried to remember all the details of the house in question; although the facades appear to be almost identical, he had learned, again on the internet, the same couldn't be said of the interiors and the structures to the rear. It was here, Morris guessed, that they would do their 'bit of snooping', perhaps having gone down a sideway.

The front of the house was as imposing as the others with black-painted iron railings and a shiny front door to match. Box plants clipped into spirals in lead containers stood like sentries on either side of it. Other than a light in a first-floor room – blinds or curtains hadn't been drawn – the house was in darkness.

Gillard, who had also researched his subject on the internet, only on restricted police websites, muttered, 'Change of plan' and, to Morris's great surprise, went up the short flight of steps and rang the doorbell. After a short wait a young woman wearing a long black dress opened the door. She didn't look too pleased to have visitors.

'Yes?'

Gillard produced his warrant card and introduced the pair of them. 'We'd like to speak to Mr Barnfather.'

'I'm afraid he's busy.'

'So are we and it's very important.'

'Wait here.'

And shut the door.

'One out of ten for lousy manners,' Gillard commented.

Morris reckoned she'd heard that.

They waited.

Finally, the door was opened again.

'He can spare you five minutes.'

'It'll take longer than that,' Gillard told her.

She shrugged in uninterested fashion and led the way across a large hall with a deep-red carpet and up a flight of stairs. At the top she turned left along a passageway then went through an open doorway, again on the left. Leaving them she shut the door as she went out.

Well, he's the right colour for a Rufus, Morris thought, as a large man with red hair rose from a sofa to stare at them. He was actually bald on top, his remaining hair long and tied back in a ponytail. His clothes, a blue velvet suit worn with a matching silk shirt and black leather slip-ons, were expensive and looked remarkably dirty.

'What's the problem?' he demanded to know.

They both produced their warrant cards and Gillard introduced them for the second time. Then he said, 'Although my colleague is with the CID here in the city, I work for the National Crime Agency. I'm here on behalf of Detective Chief Inspector Carrick and we're hoping for your cooperation.'

Morris wondered if the boss actually knew anything at all about this.

For a moment or two, the man carried on staring at them and then laughed. 'Is this some kind of joke?'

'It isn't,' Gillard said. 'May we sit down?'

Barnfather vaguely gestured to a couple of armchairs and they seated themselves.

'I know all about you,' Gillard quietly went on to say. 'No, don't interrupt,' he said as the man began to bluster. 'This is very important. As I've just said, I know everything about you. Under several aliases, you're on the Most Wanted list of several European police forces on account of handling stolen art from museums and art galleries. These raids have resulted in the deaths of security guards and witnesses, which makes you an accessory to murder too.'

'I deny all that.'

'Denying won't save you.'

'Who the hell are you – *really*?' Barnfather asked furiously.

'I have a lot more clout than you think as I also undertake a few jobs for one of the security services. There's strong evidence that you also dabble in selling industrial secrets to a country that's no friend of the UK. All of what I've said is fact, and now the NCA's involved because you disappeared and have resurfaced here in the UK. So I'm minded to tackle the fact that you're a fence with blood on your hands *first*. Does the name Mortimer Mansell mean anything to you?'

'No, not a thing.'

'I'm pretty sure you're lying. He was murdered recently, although not a lot about it appeared in the media. He was up to the same thing as you, only he organized the raids personally. Perhaps you did too, perhaps you didn't – I don't care. He was butchered with an axe – and I mean butchered – when his gang mutinied because he'd refused to pay them after a job had gone severely wrong. A man I'll describe as his second-in-command has taken over. He's a psychopath and gets a kick out of strangling people.'

'How does this affect me?' Barnfather asked grimly.

'We've received a tip-off that you're at the top of his list of places to raid next. Your girlfriend, who might be the young lady who answered the door, is in line to be strangled. As I've just said, he enjoys strangling people – preferably women.'

'This is all nonsense.'

'It would appear that it was Mansell's idea originally and he told the other man about you. To get even for some reason? You tell me.'

'And when is this supposed to happen?' Barnfather sneered.

'It's all a bit vague but perhaps the day after tomorrow or the one after that.'

The man looked distinctly taken aback and said, 'I'll expect police protection.'

'You won't get it.'

Morris felt that they were now trotting briskly into Things That Never Actually Happened territory.

'Why not?'

'As I said, it's all a bit vague,' Gillard drawled. 'Can the word of an informer be trusted? And, don't forget, police resources are very expensive.'

Barnfather glowered at the ceiling and then said, 'What do you want from me?'

'For a start, the truth. I have an idea that you bought stuff from Mansell, and because you knew he wanted shot of it quickly, you gave him very little for it. No doubt he resented that. Did you go to his house?'

There was a pause and then Barnfather said, 'Oh, all right. Yes. Once.'

'Once?'

'No, it was twice, come to think of it.'

'Was a man by the name of Georgio there on either occasion?'

'I wasn't given any names.'

'He's quite tall, has broad shoulders, is probably in his

mid-forties and has blond hair growing out dark at the roots, although we think it might be a wig.'

'Someone answering that description opened the front door on the second occasion. Look, does my giving you this information mean the police won't arrest me?'

'No, we have every intention of arresting you.'

'That's not good enough!'

'What it does mean is that you'll probably stay alive. On a previous raid the owners of the country mansion targeted were out for the evening but their housekeeper was murdered. She didn't confront them but ran off to hide in a back room. Georgio found her and strangled her.'

Barnfather remained silent.

'Where is the rest of your gang?' Morris asked, thinking it about time he said something.

'I don't have a gang!'

'OK, I'll call them your criminal assistants.'

There was a long pause and then the man replied, 'In France and Germany.'

The door opened and the young woman re-entered. She was carrying a small sub-machine gun of some kind and approached them all with a little smirk on her face.

'Thanks, Dana,' Barnfather said. He turned to his two visitors. 'Now, gentlemen, breathe a word of your visit here and you're as good as dead. But right now, your visiting time is up.'

Gillard and Morris got to their feet. Morris didn't even think about it: he carried on smoothly moving and kicked her, hard, on the wrist. She shrieked and the weapon fell from her hands. It was swiftly retrieved by Gillard who then sat down again with it on his lap.

'Er – no,' he said. 'And you can stay right where you are!' he told Dana. To Barnfather, he continued, 'I'm not really interested in an art thief and fence who fancies himself as some kind of Mr Big. I have an idea Mansell was like that too, but at least he didn't arm airheads with automatic weapons to look after him.'

'I'm not an airhead,' Dana whinnied.

'Shuddup!' Gillard bellowed at her. He resumed, 'My interest is this man calling himself Georgio. Is there anyone else in this house?'

Morris prayed that if there were, they weren't along the lines of Odd Job; truly, this whole episode was turning into a Bond film.

'No, not at this time of day,' Barnfather muttered. 'I have cleaners in during the mornings and a gardening contractor some afternoons.'

Dana had subsided on to a sofa and was holding her wrist while darting poisonous glances at Morris.

'You and Mansell were both in the crime business,' Gillard went on, sliding the weapon beneath his chair. 'And I have an idea it was a case of I'll scratch your back if you scratch mine. But you got greedy and decided to screw him into the floor when it came to prices. But he needed money as his bunch of morons kept messing up the jobs he gave them. People were murdered and that kept Georgio happy, but the wherewithal to pay them dried up. Indirectly, then, you're responsible for his death, too.'

'You are just guessing.'

'Yes, but constructively. I'm also guessing that for some reason or other you hated him. Too many pike in the same pond? I want you to tell me more about Georgio because I reckon you know him rather well. Did you recommend him to Mansell? He might not have come back from London with him.'

The other man frowned and then said, 'I know for a fact that he didn't come back from London with him, and no, I didn't recommend him to Mansell.'

'Have you upset him, and to get some kind of revenge he's going to raid this place and wring your neck? Be quite sure of this: he's extremely dangerous. Worse, he seems to be living a double life and has what I'll describe as a normal job.'

Barnfather thought about it for about a minute and then said, 'I'm warming to the idea of saving my own skin here. That's if what you're saying is true.'

'As I told you, the news of the raid is from an informer. Most of the rest is police evidence. And Georgio?' Gillard went on to prompt.

Barnfather lit a cigarette without offering one to anyone else. Then he said, 'I don't mind dropping him in it. He does lead a double life. One of the names he uses is Denholm Woodley or Woodstock – not sure which. His uncle – haven't the first clue who he is – was pressured to get him a job in the insurance company where he works.'

'Was the man threatened?'

'Probably.'

'Have you been threatened?'

'Obliquely. I haven't upset him. I think I've only seen him just that once at Mansell's place, but he might want to take over my business too if, as you say, he has Mansell's. I have an idea he's not quite sane.'

'People who strangle others are usually like that,' Gillard said. 'What did you mean by "obliquely"?'

'Mansell told me once that he expected those he did deals with not to do the dirty on him – as he put it. The man was insufferable really. Preening – seemed to think that he was perfect. Perfect! And if this Georgio character was some kind of jobsworth of his and . . .'

He stopped speaking as three masked men armed with hand weapons came into the room. 'Where the bloody hell have you been?' he roared. 'I've been chatting away wondering where you'd got to!'

'Don't shoot me!' Morris shrilly wailed. 'Please don't shoot me!'

Everyone in the room but Gillard gawped at him, time enough for Gillard to draw his Glock and shoot the weapon from the hand of the man standing slightly in front of the other two. Morris flung himself down behind his armchair with the wisdom of a man unarmed and stayed put as several more shots were fired.

'Roderick!' Gillard shouted. 'Out! Get out!'

Morris got out, dashed from the room, down the stairs, wrenched open the front door, leapt down the steps on to the pavement and tore along the street. He pelted along for around a hundred yards before slithering to a standstill to find his phone to call for assistance.

Then he went back.

FIFTEEN

The front door was still open. Morris paused, not quite sure what to do. It was all very well, he thought, calling up help, but by the time anyone arrived Barnfather and his mobsters might have got away. He was trying not to think of what might have happened to Patrick. Struggling to concentrate, he crept into the hall and immediately encountered Dana who looked as though she might have been coming to shut the door.

'One squeak and I'll get you again,' Morris hissed. 'Right on the end of your stupid little snub nose.'

She opened her mouth and shut it again.

He swiftly grabbed her and bundled her into a side room. 'Stay there,' he whispered in her ear. 'Or you might get shot as well.'

This seemed a ridiculously flimsy threat to him and not the sort of thing he ought to say at all, but to hell with that. Moving as silently as possible, he shifted a heavy antique chair to wedge the back of it against the door handle. Praying that the stairs didn't creak, he went up.

He was halfway up when he heard muted voices.

'Is your colleague always such a coward?' Barnfather's voice said.

'Absolutely,' Gillard replied, his voice sounding slightly muffled.

'He'll have gone to get help, though.'

'No idea.'

'Well, you're our insurance to get away safely.'

Bent low, Morris went up the remaining stairs like a ferret up a drainpipe and dived into a room next to the one he had just left. It was in darkness and he had no intention of putting a light on. Leaving the door open just a crack, he peered out. He could hear movement and, almost immediately, a man appeared and went in the direction of the stairs. His right hand was hanging limply by his side.

'What about Jed?' someone still in the room asked.

'Leave him,' Barnfather answered abruptly. 'Get the car. Bring it round to the front.'

'Bastard!' another voice shouted, probably Jed.

A threesome came into Morris's limited view. Gillard was in the centre, hopping on one leg, his other hanging as limply as had the other man's hand. On his right, and having to support him, was another walking wounded, his right arm dripping blood. Barnfather was on the other side, carrying a Glock pistol as though he didn't quite know what to do with it.

As the three reached the top of the stairs, Barnfather laughed and said, 'Go on, chuck him down.' Whereupon Gillard collapsed on to the floor, forcing his supporter to release his arm or be dragged down with him. The man was then perfectly positioned for Morris to run up behind him and adminster a savage kick to the small of the back, sending him plummeting down the stairs. He cannoned into the first man, who was still halfway down and the two rolled to the bottom. Barnfather let out a squawk of alarm but then followed his henchman as Gillard, flat on his back on the carpet, lashed out at him with his good foot and got him behind a knee.

Morris reached down a couple of stairs to retrieve the dropped Glock.

Matter of factly, Gillard said, 'I'm really glad to see you. Did you phone?' He eyed the three who were in a heap down in the hall.

'Of course. How badly are you hurt?'

'Not at all. I have a tin leg and something broke in the ankle joint. Good acting, by the way.'

Something similar had happened to him twice before, shots smashing the articulated ankle joint that now replaced the one with which he had been born. He had an idea the whole thing would have to be sent to the manufacturer in the States. While that happened, he would have to rely on crutches.

Right now, though, and in receipt of his Glock, he went on to whisper, 'Go on down and arrest them, Constable Morris.'

'I don't know what to say to you,' James Carrick admitted late the next morning, shaking his head.

The quandary behind his remark was sitting opposite and surveying him gravely.

Carrick then discovered that he knew precisely what to say. 'I hope you realize that any hope of catching Georgio, or whatever the hell this maniac's name is, has flown out the window. By now, what happened in Great Pulteney Street will be all over every grapevine, law-abiding or not. They'll abandon the raid.'

Gillard said, 'You obviously haven't yet had a chance to read the report I wrote on Ingrid's computer and emailed to you just before I came out. Barnfather, hoping to save his skin, told us that Georgio's name *is* Denholm Woodstock – or at least that's the one he's using at the moment – and he works for the same insurance company I do. Incidentally, I'm not crowing. My boss, Vernon Ellis, is his uncle. It looks as though Ellis was forced to push for his nephew to be employed and gives every impression of a man under serious pressure. I have to admit that I hadn't expected Barnfather to have a resident private army, although when they were unmasked and asked nicely for their names and addresses, it was obvious that they were little more than yobs – drug addicts probably – plucked off the streets.'

'One of whom is injured.'

'Yes, being on the floor, I missed the weapon he was holding and hit him in the leg.'

'Barnfather and the other two had to be taken to A and E, Barnfather with a twisted shoulder, the others with fairly minor hand injuries.'

'That's what happens when a weapon is shot from your hand. You know that, James. Barnfather was holding my Glock, so I assisted him down the stairs. It's all in the report.'

They were talking in Carrick's office, the DCI having wanted to receive information first-hand. Needless to say, he wasn't happy. Again, this wasn't the way he wanted things done.

'Your job now,' Gillard went on with a smile, 'is to carry on the good work.'

'I don't need you to tell me my job,' the DCI said through his teeth.

'Sorry, I put that very badly. All I'm saying is that I'm not going to take over your case.'

There was a little silence during which Gillard decided that he was fed up with tiptoeing around this man, and then Carrick thawed.

'And Morris?' he asked.

Gillard chuckled. 'He's rapidly turning into my minder.'

'Surely not!'

'I'll give it to you in a large nutshell. We met in a pub. He'd been planning to walk past the house to take a look but changed his mind, probably because it would have meant disobeying orders. By asking him if he wanted to accompany me for a recce, I realized that I was encouraging him to disobey your order. I regret that. Anyway, when I told him I'd square it with you, he agreed. But then I changed *my* mind and rang the doorbell. A young woman let us in and took us to the room where Barnfather was seated. After he gave us some info, the woman came back carrying a Scorpion sub-machine gun. Morris kicked her on the wrist and she dropped it. Then Barnfather was encouraged to talk a bit more before the three aforementioned yobs burst in, all armed. Morris played the stupid ninny, begging them not to shoot him, and when all their attention was on him, I shot the weapon from the hand of one of the blokes. Someone fired back wildly, but I'd already thrown myself down, busting my fake ankle as I did so. The remaining two were slow, so I still succeeded in disarming them before they jumped me. I yelled to Morris to get out and he did. He called up assistance from somewhere out in the street and then came back just before Barnfather and co were about to toss me down the stairs. By then, he was to our rear, and between us we sent *them* down the stairs.' He finished by saying, with just a trace of sarcasm, 'As is usual, my report is couched in police-speak leaving out all unnecessary details.'

'Like what, for instance?' Carrick demanded to know.

'The detail that the pair of us got a real buzz from booting the bastards down the stairs.'

There was a longer silence this time, and then Carrick's gaze fell on the second pair of crutches in the room. A little smile twitched at the corners of his mouth. Then he grinned widely.

'Something sheered off in the ankle joint but there's a company in London licensed to undertake repairs, so with a bit of luck I might be fully mobile before you are,' Gillard said. Then he also smiled and went on to say, 'Vernon Ellis is at work today, but Woodstock isn't. I checked.'

'Pick Ellis up?'

'Your case, chum.'

It was obvious that Vernon Ellis was a frightened man. Lynn Outhwaite had taken Sergeant Woods to the insurance office with her. At first, she had invited Ellis to be merely formally interviewed about his nephew, but he had furiously refused, giving her no choice but to arrest him. The man had then become beside himself, shouting, 'This is all Gillard's doing!' He was still shouting when he was taken to an interview room and refused to answer any questions. Lynn asked Constable Morris, who happened to be the first person she caught sight of, to stay with Ellis and went to refer the matter to her boss.

'Right!' Carrick said a few minutes later, seating himself in the chair recently used by the DI. He introduced himself, told Morris he could stay where he was for a few minutes and then said, 'Mr Ellis, I would like you to tell me, when you haven't been charged with any crime, why you're behaving like this.'

'Because it's outrageous!' Ellis shouted. 'That man, by his digging into my family's affairs, has caused me to be treated like a common criminal. I gave him the sack and he's getting some kind of twisted revenge on me.'

'Please calm down.'

'I refuse to calm down. I demand to see and confront him.'

'You're wasting my time and that wouldn't be at all appropriate. We have strong evidence that your nephew, Denholm Woodstock, is a criminal, and no shouting and time-wasting on your part is going to help anyone.'

'That's utter rubbish!'

'It's obvious to anyone observing you that you're under extreme pressure.'

Ellis folded his arms. 'I'm saying nothing. Take me back to work.'

Carrick rose. 'You're not going anywhere. I'll get you some coffee.'

'I don't want any coffee.'

The DCI left the room, for coffee and to decide what the hell to do with him. But first of all, he went into the room next door where he could watch and overhear what was being said.

Morris studied the man seated facing him. Knowing the calibre of the killer they were after, he felt a certain sympathy.

'You can't charge me with anything,' Ellis suddenly said.

'We can,' Morris told him. 'Assisting an offender.'

'But no one's been found guilty of anything.'

'No, but intelligence and witness statements point to the identity of a man who tried to strangle a woman constable in a hospital. She was guarding an elderly man whom the same suspect had also endeavoured to murder. You're here to try to prevent anyone else from being killed. Likes axes, does he, your nephew?'

'What a strange question.'

'Another of his victims was running the gang he worked for. He was strangled and then his face was hacked off with an axe. The suspect does seem to prefer to just strangle people, though – especially women. Someone said it's revenge because he's impotent but is turned on by murder.'

'Oh, God,' Ellis muttered.

Morris fleetingly wondered if Ellis was talking to him because of his comparative youth and therefore thought him 'harmless'. He said, 'Tell me what he's threatened you with.'

'Nothing.'

'Or your wife, your children?'

For a heart-stopping moment, Morris thought the man was about to tell all. But he clamped shut his mouth and, when Carrick returned, lapsed into stubborn silence.

Ingrid was trying to write but failing miserably. She was haunted, taunted really, by the fact that if she hadn't called on Mortimer Mansell, thus showing her face to the man who opened the door and who was almost certainly Georgio, then Patrick wouldn't have ended up recruiting Morris. She had absolutely nothing against the young constable – quite liked him, in fact and could hardly fault the way he had seen his mentor home. But if she herself had been present, with the Smith and Wesson, Patrick might not have ended up with a damaged ankle.

Having had to stay for quite a long time at Barnfather's house to give accounts of what had occurred to the attending police, the pair had taken a taxi to a late-closing Chinese restaurant where they had had a much-needed meal. Then another taxi had been called to take them to where Patrick had parked the Range Rover. Fortunately, he had been able to stand, after a fashion, but not walk without assistance, and could certainly drive as the vehicle was automatic and had a hand throttle. He had dropped Morris outside his house and then come home. She hadn't really minded him phoning her from the rectory's drive at just before one in the morning with the request to take him the pair of crutches that were always kept, just in case, in a cupboard.

Then there was the matter of MI5. She knew that Patrick was still involved with the security service and occasionally was asked for information relating to cases he had worked on during his time with D12. It was amazing the way that certain people, released from prison, kept coming back like bad drains, intent seemingly on reacquainting themselves with old contacts, old haunts and criminal connections in order to make money by carrying on doing harm to the security of the UK. But the MI5 person likely to contact Patrick, James Dixon, the man with the whispery voice, had been quiet of late.

Her mobile rang and it was James Carrick wondering if she would help him out and talk to someone. He emphasized that she would be in no danger as, so far, the man in question hadn't been charged with anything and the interview would be conducted at the nick. Trying not to sound too happy at thus being released from writer's block, she agreed.

Carrick gave her the details on the way to the interview room. Ellis, meanwhile, had grudgingly drunk his coffee and been put in a cell for a while. When he was brought back for further questioning, he was calmer but otherwise still as obdurate. Ingrid had aired reservations at talking to Ellis on the grounds that, through her husband, she could be said to have an interest. Carrick had smiled and told her that his hearing wasn't too good this morning.

Morris had been ordered to resume his seat to keep an eye on the proceedings and operate the video recorder. He gave Ingrid a little smile when she entered and seated herself.

'Good morning, Mr Ellis,' she began breezily. 'My name is Ingrid Langley, and to put my cards on the table straight away, I shall tell you that Patrick Gillard is my husband and I also work part-time for the National Crime Agency. He's not permitted to question you because you know one another. I'll also tell you that when the DCI went to get your coffee, he left the recorder running. What happens in here can be monitored in the next room, so he heard the recording and Constable Morris asking you the nature of the threats against you.'

'There are no threats against me!' Ellis grated.

'Then why are you behaving like a complete idiot?'

Ellis, who had given every impression of being surprised by the nature of his new questioner, remained silent.

'Is your nephew Denholm Woodstock?'

He nodded reluctantly.

'He appears to be very bad at his job.'

Silence.

'Which you gave him, or at least recommended him for.'

Another nod.

'Under duress, because, as the saying goes, he's mad, bad and dangerous.'

Ellis said, 'I got him the job because he needed one badly.'

'As cover for his criminal activities.'

He just shook his head.

'Mr Ellis, where is this man?'

A shrug.

'Who will suffer if the police go anywhere near him?' When he still remained silent, Ingrid raged at him, 'How many more people will have to be murdered before you help us to get him behind bars? You'll get armed police protection until he is. *Who* is in danger?'

The silence was so protracted this time that Morris thought this stunningly attractive lady had failed, but finally Ellis whispered, 'I'm so ashamed.'

'Please tell me,' Ingrid begged quietly. 'Who?'

'Me.'

'You? How?'

Ellis took a deep breath. 'He's living in my house, sleeps in my bed, eats my food, drinks my wine and laughs in my face.'

'So where are you living?'

'At night, I'm in the shed.' After a pause, he added, 'Locked in. Every night. And now I won't even be there – I'll be dead.'

'As I've just said, you'll get police protection.'

'How can I expect you to understand?' Ellis agonized. 'He told me that if he couldn't get to me personally, he has contacts all over the world. Someone will come after me even if he's in prison – or dead.'

'I don't believe he has contacts anywhere. He's deluded.'

'And he killed my lovely little dog in front of me . . . with his bare hands . . . just to show me how strong he is. Then he threw her body at me.'

'I'm really, really sorry about that,' Ingrid said softly. Her writer's imagination had presented her with every ghastly detail. Those strangling hands . . .

Ellis covered his face with his hands and wept, just managing to say, 'I really loved her.'

'Bloody hell,' Morris said under his breath.

'Please go and get him some tea,' Ingrid requested. 'And biscuits.'

Outside in the corridor, he almost collided with the DCI who appeared to have been hovering. He explained his mission.

'OK, I'll sit in. Bring me some, too. Problem?' he went on to enquire when Morris still stood there.

'No, sir. It's just . . .'

'What?'

'The bastard killed his dog.'

'Has he said where he is right now?'

'No, not yet. Sir . . .'

'*What*, Morris?'

'I think it might be better if you stay away and just monitor what's going on. Miss Langley seems to have a certain rapport with him.'

Carrick wasn't used to constables who used words like 'rapport' but nevertheless went in the next room.

Patrick Gillard had gone home after speaking to Carrick. There wasn't a lot he could do until he was fully mobile again. There had been a small family crisis since his replacement ankle had been damaged. Vicky, who, it seemed, hadn't remembered ever seeing her father wearing shorts, which he did during hot weather, had been devastated, thinking him terribly hurt as nearly half his leg wasn't there anymore. Explaining to a four-year-old had been difficult. Not easy either was accepting that whereas he might have normally taken a stroll around the garden right now, being at a loose end, it really was too much of a bother. Perhaps, he told himself, he should have been a bit more understanding of Carrick's irascibility.

His mobile rang and it was Ingrid. Due to some kind of communications failure, he hadn't been told that she was at the nick. Noticing that his mother's car was missing from outside the house, he had assumed the ladies had gone out together for shopping or a coffee somewhere.

'James asked me to question Ellis,' she continued. 'Didn't he tell you?'

'No,' Gillard replied. 'But go on.'

'Woodstock is living in his house like a parasite and banishing him to the garden shed at night. He killed his little dog, and that seems to be the significant factor in Ellis's behaviour. The shock of having it killed right in front of his eyes has affected him dreadfully – emotionally and mentally. He doesn't know where the man goes for the rest of the time when he isn't at the office, but he's usually at Ellis's place during the night hours. James is arranging an early-hours raid.'

'Woodstock might have already left if he finds out that Ellis has spoken to the police – or even if he's not at home when, or if, he himself gets there.'

'That's what I said, but it's the only lead that James has to go on at the moment.'

'And Ellis?'

'He's been taken to a safe house. See you in a bit.'

Aware that, temporarily, he might not be pulling his weight with regard to helping in the home, Gillard turned some bread rolls, cold meat and salad into lunch so it was ready when Ingrid got back. There was also the prospect that his wife would not be at all pleased when she knew what he was going to do.

'But you can't!' she exclaimed after he'd waited until they'd eaten.

'I intend merely to go along as an observer,' Gillard countered.

'Patrick, you simply aren't sufficiently mobile at the moment. It's crazy.' Then, when all visible evidence indicated that she was arguing in vain – that is, the stubborn look on his face – she said, 'Then I'm coming, too.'

'You can't.'

'I am.'

The house was like hundreds of thousands of others in cities across the country, semi-detached and set in a quiet suburban road lined with trees, in this case ones that had been ferociously pollarded. Ingrid noticed this detail in passing – she hated seeing trees thus mutilated. She had driven past the property, slowly, turned and parked about ten yards away from being directly opposite but on the other side of the road. They had borrowed Elspeth's car as their target might recognize the Range Rover. It was almost one in the morning, or 'thirteen hundred hours' as Patrick would prefer to call it, fifteen minutes before the raid was timed to take place.

She turned off the headlights and sat quietly. She wasn't sure what Patrick intended to do, if anything, and wasn't about to badger him with questions. Quite often previously, when he, or the pair of them, had gone along on similar occasions as 'observers', they had ended up in the thick of what could have been described as small wars. Not this time, she told herself hopefully, even though she had been surprised how mobile he was with elbow crutches. Plenty of practice in the past, perhaps.

There had been no vehicles parked in the short driveway in front of the garage and no visible lights in the house itself. She had opened her window to listen for any suspicious sounds but the whole road was quiet. Almost too quiet. She instantly scolded herself for allowing her imagination to interfere, as it often did, but the feeling persisted.

'What are your cat's whiskers doing?' Patrick asked after a pause.

'They're off the scale,' she told him.

'Any particular reason?'

'They haven't explained yet.'

They sat in silence for a little longer.

Then, 'If he has got wind of Ellis being picked up,' Ingrid said, 'and/or, as you said, arrived here earlier, and Ellis wasn't around as he normally would have been, then he could well have suspected that something was going on.'

'What d'you reckon he'd do?'

'I'm working on it.'

There was another silence.

'If he's got to the stage where he's desperate, and there's no way of knowing whether he is or not,' Ingrid went on, speaking slowly, 'he might stage something like an ambush, try to kill as many people, police, as possible before making his escape. Get away in what he would regard as a blaze of glory.'

'But where would he stage an ambush from?' Patrick murmured, looking around, now an ex-soldier talking to himself.

'Your turn. Where?' Ingrid prompted after a few moments.

'From one of the neighbouring houses – ideally, the one directly opposite.'

Which was probably a matter of two houses from where they were parked.

'Shall I stroll by to have a look?' Ingrid queried, hand on the door.

'For God's sake, *don't*.'

A couple of minutes later, with the time for the raid less than five away, a car drew up outside the house to the right of Ellis's and a couple of men got out. Through trees in the front garden, it was just possible to see that a light was on in the downstairs front room of the house. The men went through the gate and presumably indoors – the door was out of sight. Seconds later, there was a sudden commotion within and a woman started screaming. Then she came into view and ran into the road, crying for help. Immediately, she was swooped on from the rear by at least three individuals and dragged back, still yelling. There was the sound of what might have been a blow and she went quiet.

'A cool head is required right now,' Patrick muttered and grabbed his mobile.

He rang his emergency NCA number, gave his ID, precise location, the perceived degree of seriousness – the highest in this case – relayed further concise information, and waited. Ingrid didn't put her thoughts into words: that whereas at one time they might have conducted their own raid, now they could do nothing.

Nothing.

They sat and waited while absolutely nothing carried on happening and a little eternity went by. Then several unmarked vehicles arrived at speed and personnel from an armed police unit silently poured from them and took up positions in the lee of the cars.

'I think we ought to do the same,' Patrick whispered. 'I have no desire to be killed in cross-fire.'

'D'you want a hand out?' Ingrid offered. In the Range Rover, he could have almost literally fallen out and landed in a standing position, but not a conventional saloon car.

'Please.'

It was comparatively dark where they were parked, between street lights and beneath a large evergreen oak in a front garden.

Another police vehicle arrived and a group got out and hurried into the front garden of Ellis's house. Moments later, the door was battered in followed by shouts of 'Police!'

'They're doing the right things,' Patrick said under his breath as sounds of banging and trampling boots came to their ears.

Ingrid, who couldn't see what was going on, glanced in his direction and saw that he was sitting on the pavement peering round the front of the car. She crawled along so she could do the same at the rear. There wasn't a good view so she went down the kerb, bashing her shins as she did so and then lay flat in the road so she could see without being seen.

A sudden crash of gunfire broke the comparative stillness and she reversed at speed until she was back on the pavement. The firing continued: bullets hitting metal, smashing windows and windscreens. A man screamed, followed by a splintering noise.

'A couple of them were up a tree in the neighbouring garden,' Patrick reported quietly when Ingrid got closer to him. 'One's been hit and fell out, the other's gone quiet. I think I can get him from here.'

But he stayed where he was when a small group emerged

from the house. A figure, a man, leading the way, was holding someone in an arm lock around the throat in front of him – difficult to see who, but it was probably the woman who had tried to escape. A handgun was being held to her head. She started to struggle but he kicked her legs to make her keep walking. Another two men were doing their best to hide behind them.

'You raided the wrong house!' a man's voice jeered. 'And this is Karen,' he went on. 'Her husband, mother and two children are inside with guns to their heads. We're leaving and they only stay alive if we do.'

'It's Woodstock,' Patrick said in a whisper. 'The stupid bastard's like something out of an old American cop show.'

'Armed police!' the officer in charge of the police team shouted. 'Stay still! Lay that weapon down! Do you want to go down for murder too?' He obviously had not been told how many people this man had killed already.

Woodstock laughed and the little group began to edge slowly away. Then the two at the rear broke away and ran. The police dared not fire for fear of hitting the woman.

'Help me up,' Patrick requested. Having shifted himself just a few inches, he then silently laid his crutches on the ground and, holding on to the car with his left hand, drew his Glock. 'Please steady me,' he went on to whisper.

Although it was deep shade where they were, they were in full view of those across the road, who were sideways on to them, but each group's attention was fixed on the other.

Arms around his waist, her forehead between his shoulder blades for added support, Ingrid braced herself. She felt him breathe slowly and deeply twice as he took aim. Then he fired. Once.

When Karen screamed and sank to her knees, Ingrid immediately thought she had been hit. Not so. Woodstock was flat on his back on the tarmac, dead. A shot at such close range had ensured that some of his head was now missing and it looked to be a few feet away on the road. But it was just the tattered remnants of a blood-and-brains-splattered blond wig.

SIXTEEN

There was a meeting in Carrick's office that same morning, but in order for the Gillards to get some sleep, it had been timed for eleven thirty. They were on time. Notwithstanding the fact that they were good friends – for most of the time anyway – the DCI had thought it only fair to include Ingrid and was determined to keep everything on a professional basis. His smile, therefore, when they entered and he returned their greetings, was restrained even though he was delighted by what had happened. He was also totally flabbergasted and wanted to give them both a hug.

The two seated themselves on chairs at the side of the room and there was a little silence that Carrick broke by saying, 'As you might now know, we collared the lot, the two who ran plus another three indoors who were still holding hostage the husband of the woman, who has been treated for minor injuries, their two children who they'd dragged out of bed, and her mother. The three threw down their weapons when the armed support group burst in. The family are being supported. Oh, and there was no one at all at Vernon Ellis's place.'

Gillard said, 'They were still looking for the first two when we were allowed to leave and had called up a chopper and a dog handler.'

'The armed support group could easily have opened fire on you.'

'I hope not; when I called in, I reported our position and gave them the car's registration number.'

This man, Carrick had to keep reminding himself, had fired a handgun with staggering accuracy in poor light while, in effect, standing on one leg.

'We'll never know all the ins and outs of this case,' Carrick continued. 'That info died with Mansell and Woodstock.'

'How's Ellis?' Ingrid asked.

'He's receiving support, too. Apparently, his wife died last year. Patrick . . .' He really didn't know what to say this time.

'No, I don't know how I did it,' Gillard said. 'I haven't been for weapons' practice in months.' He went quiet for a few moments and then quietly added, 'Please don't think that I'm pleased with myself. By doing what I did, though, I might have saved a few other lives.'

'A search team is still at Ellis's house,' Carrick said. 'They've found a cache of silverware in a pillowcase at the bottom of an airing cupboard, and the last I heard they were heading for the loft.'

Where, an hour later, he received the news that a hoard of stolen property had been found, most of it, at a guess, items that hadn't been handed over to Mansell after the first jewellery raid, together with quite a lot of things that might have been at his house. But there was no one to identify them. The key to the locked room was never found.

Three weeks later, a celebratory meal took place at the rectory, both Gillard and Carrick now fully mobile. There was minimum discussion of the Mansell case, or cases, as there had already been numerous debriefings and meetings in the aftermath of the final arrests. All that had been said in various reports was that a 'police marksman' had shot Woodstock in order to save the hostages' lives when he had refused to surrender. Some criticism about 'heavy-handed' police action had appeared to peter out when the nation had discovered that the man had killed his uncle's dog.

One positive result was that Joanna had been to see Mr and Mrs Adams – he was now at home – to find out whether he would consider helping with their garden when he was fully recovered. He had said he would be pleased to.

Ingrid was pensive, glad that it was all over but still sad that she was involved with the NCA no longer. Morris couldn't be drafted in if Patrick was needed to help with an MI5 case, could he?

It turned out that he could.